WALLFLOWER

a Redemption novel

JESSICA PRINCE

Copyright © 2021 by Jessica Prince
www.authorjessicaprince.com

Published by Jessica Prince Books LLC

All rights reserved.
No part of this book may be reproduced in any form or by any electronic or mechanical means, including information storage and retrieval systems, without written permission from the author, except for the use of brief quotations in a book review.

A Note from the Author

Hey, guys!

As some of you may have noticed, the name of Pope's MC changed. When I first started writing the Redemption series, they were known as the Iron Riders.

Well, I've made a decision recently that those badass dudes will be getting stories in one form or another . . . and because of that, the club name has changed to Iron Wraiths.

I'm sorry for any confusion! But trust me, no matter what their name is, you're going to want what I have up my sleeve. ;)

Happy reading!
Love, Jess.

Discover Other Books by Jessica

WHISKEY DOLLS SERIES

Bombshell

HOPE VALLEY SERIES:

Out of My League

Come Back Home Again

The Best of Me

Wrong Side of the Tracks

Stay With Me

Out of the Darkness

The Second Time Around

Waiting for Forever

Love to Hate You

Playing for Keeps

REDEMPTION SERIES

Bad Alibi

Crazy Beautiful

Bittersweet

Guilty Pleasure

Wallflower

THE PICKING UP THE PIECES SERIES:

Picking up the Pieces

Rising from the Ashes

Pushing the Boundaries

Worth the Wait

THE COLORS NOVELS:

Scattered Colors

Shrinking Violet

Love Hate Relationship

Wildflower

THE LOCKLAINE BOYS (a LOVE HATE RELATIONSHIP spinoff):

Fire & Ice

Opposites Attract

Almost Perfect

The Locklaine Boys: The Complete Series Boxset

THE PEMBROOKE SERIES (a WILDFLOWER spinoff):

Sweet Sunshine

Coming Full Circle

A Broken Soul

Welcome to Pembrooke: The Complete Pembrooke Series

CIVIL CORRUPTION SERIES

Corrupt

Defile

Consume

Ravage

GIRL TALK SERIES:

Seducing Lola

Tempting Sophia

Enticing Daphne

Charming Fiona

STANDALONE TITLES:

One Knight Stand

Chance Encounters

Nightmares from Within

DEADLY LOVE SERIES:

Destructive

Addictive

Chapter One

WILLOW

"Come on, come on. We can do this. Nice and easy," I coaxed. I twisted the key in the ignition, hoping that terrible whining noise I'd been hearing for the past few minutes would actually lead to the engine turning over this time.

It didn't.

"You've got to be kidding me!" I shouted, giving the steering wheel a couple smacks for good measure before trying the key again. "Come on you stupid piece of crap!"

As if giving me the metaphorical finger, the car let out a frightening wheeze before a plume of smoke coughed up from the tailpipe. Then . . . nothing.

This wasn't happening. It could *not* be happening.

The frustration that had been beating behind my ribs all morning finally broke free, and the noise that came from deep within my chest sounded like something a wild, wounded animal might make.

Gripping the steering wheel so tight my knuckles turned

white and the worn leather creaked beneath my grasp, I lowered my forehead against it and worked to calm my breathing. My father had always told me that nothing good ever came from losing your cool, and I'd taken those words to heart. No matter how many times I wanted to scream at the top of my lungs. And that happened *a lot*, especially lately.

Once the unforgiving squeeze around my lungs finally loosened so I could breathe again, I lifted my head and grabbed my cellphone from its resting place in the cup holder. It wasn't all that surprising that neither of my sisters had bothered to answer my calls for help. There had been a shift between us in recent months, and it was feeling more and more like, unless they needed or wanted something, they couldn't be bothered with me.

With no other choice, I hung up midway through my oldest sister's voicemail greeting and called for a tow.

Fifteen minutes later, the tow truck with the familiar Banks Body and Auto Repair decal on the side pulled up. My shoulders slumped in short-lived relief when the driver's side door flung open and the only man who had the ability to scare the hell out of me and make me feel completely alive at the same time climbed out of the cab.

Gavin "Stone" Hendrix.

The very man I had a wildly imaginative crush on since the first moment I laid eyes on him.

He wasn't the type I usually—more like *ever*—went for. The few guys I'd dated and been intimate with had all been safe and unassuming. To put it plainly, they were boring and, well, let's just say extremely average in the looks department. In other words, they were on my level. Men like Stone usually sent me skittering in the other direction, but there was just something about him. An invisible lure that kept pulling and pulling at me, and for the first time in my life, I actually wanted someone to see me. I wanted *him* to see me. I didn't want to be a wallflower where he was concerned. I wanted to be a woman on Stone Hendrix's level.

The way he moved around the hood of the truck reminded me of a jungle cat. Power radiated from his entire body. Standing close to six and a half feet tall, there wasn't a single inch of his impressively large frame that wasn't roped with thick muscle. Yet, despite his size, he moved with a commanding grace, almost like he was prowling.

Tattoos spanned his arms from the backs of his hands, all the way up, some of them even peeking out of the collar of his shirt and up the side of his neck, making me wonder how much of the skin beneath his clothing was also inked. His body was a literal work of art that was always wrapped in faded jeans, worn, threadbare tees, and motorcycle boots. And he *always* looked incredible. I'd fantasized too many times to count about being close enough to him to inspect all that ink, maybe even trace it with my fingers—or, you know, my tongue.

I'd heard it said a million times by women in town that there must have been something magical in Redemption's water supply, and I had to agree. Even though this was a small town, it wasn't lacking when it came to attractive men. And in my humble opinion, Stone was the most attractive of them all.

I saw him for the first time when he came into my workplace to see my boss, Jensen Rose, and my crush had formed right then and there. Sadly, if it hadn't been for the fact he had to go through me to get to Jensen whenever he came to visit, I didn't think he'd know I even existed, which made my crush borderline pathetic, really. He'd never in a million years give me a second glance. As a matter of fact, every time I spotted him around town, I was pretty certain he'd looked right through me without even realizing we kind-of-sort-of knew each other. Not that it was a surprise. Men like him didn't go for women like me.

He was big and bold; I was small and timid.

He was sex on thick, athletic legs and I was the very definition of Plain Jane.

He rode a motorcycle and I could barely keep my balance on a bicycle.

I'd seen the types of women he'd been drawn to. In a town like ours, it was impossible to miss them. They were all long-legged, curvy knockouts with big hair. They all dressed in tight clothes that showed a ton of skin, and their heels were sky-high and pencil-thin.

I didn't have the confidence to be like any of those women, so there wasn't a chance in hell I'd ever find the courage to make a move on the man heading my way right that second.

If I were being honest, he'd kind of frightened me at first. He was just so . . . *big*, so intimidating. And it didn't help matters that he walked around with a scowl on his face most of the time. The man really came by his nickname honestly, because if you didn't know him, you'd think he was hard as stone in pretty much every way. It was the vibe he put off. He wasn't mean—at least that was what I surmised, based on what very little I knew of him, most of that intel gathered while I secretly watched him across rooms and streets like a creeper—he just held everything close to the vest.

I'd caught him smiling and laughing a few times now, and each time I did, my heart rate amped up and my skin began to tingle. Those smiles took him from rough and angry looking—in a very hot way—to downright gorgeous.

"You call for a tow?"

"Uh . . ." My brain short-circuited just like it did every time I saw him, and I struggled to form even the most basic sentence. "Y-yeah. Yes. That was me. I don't know what happened. It let out this sound, kind of like a cat that got its tail caught in a fan, then just . . . wheezed to death."

The dark slashes of his brows lifted high on his forehead. I thought I caught the corner of his mouth quirk up, but I wasn't certain. The same was the case with his seductive light brown gaze. It looked an awful lot like humor was dancing in those melted honey eyes I fantasized about regularly, but that couldn't be right. "That's a pretty colorful description."

I shrugged and lowered my head, looking up at him from beneath the fan of my lashes. My cheeks began to heat from the inside, and I knew my pale skin was quickly turning pink. God, I hated that blush, and I *hated* that I had absolutely no control over it when it came to him.

"All right. Let me get this hooked up and I'll give you a lift to work on my way back to the garage."

"Oh, um . . ." That heat in my face turned into a

straight-up burn as I bugged my eyes out. "You-you don't have to do that."

His forehead pinched in a frown. "So you *don't* want me to take your car in?"

"No. I mean yes!" I gave my head a shake in the hopes of clearing my jumbled thoughts. "Yes to the car, that is. I was just saying that I don't expect you to give me a ride, is all."

Oh God. I couldn't have possibly screwed this up any worse if I were actively trying to. Why the hell couldn't I just be normal?

It was times like this that I wished I could be more like my older sisters. Crissy and Elaina had always been so . . . *normal*. They never struggled with the things I did. My sisters were outgoing and social. They had tons of friends all through school. They'd actually thrived on being the center of attention.

They always knew what to say or how to act. Meanwhile, I tended to turn into a bumbling idiot in any type of social setting. It had been easier for me if people didn't even realize I was in the room. I'd gotten really good at blending into the wallpaper, only now, standing here with Stone, I would have given anything for just a smidge of their confidence.

He arched a single eyebrow, managing to look bored and curious all at the same time. It was a look I'd never have been able to pull off, even if I wasn't a shy, awkward wallflower. "You got another ride into work already?"

"Uh . . ." My gaze darted around, like an alternative would suddenly appear out of thin air. "Well, no."

"Didn't think so. Hop in the truck, Willow. And don't worry, I'm not gonna bite."

I wasn't worried about him biting. I actually got a little tingly at the thought of him doing just that. What I was really worried about was making an even bigger fool of myself in front of him, something I seemed to excel at.

Instead of attempting seduction and teasing that there was nothing wrong with a little harmless biting, I silently made my way to the tow truck and climbed inside while he went about hooking my car to the back.

The inside of the cab smelled like a forest. Inhaling deeply, I pulled the scent of cedar and musk with a small underlying note of motor oil into my lungs. It might not have seemed like the most appealing combination, but to me, it was euphoric. It was distinctly Stone, and I couldn't get enough.

My anxiety spiked when Stone's door opened a few minutes later and he climbed behind the wheel. Just like that, the cab felt like it had shrunk. He was so damn big, it felt like he took up all available space. Even the air felt like it was thinner, but that was probably due more to me not remembering how to breathe than anything else.

His long, tattooed fingers wrapped around the gearshift, but instead of shifting out of park, he looked at me, his brow furrowed. "You okay over there?"

"Yeah, of course," I chirped with *way* too much enthusiasm. "Why do you ask?"

"'Cause it kind of sounds like you're hyperventilating."

Oh God. I was starting to sweat behind my knees. Who knew a person could sweat *behind their knees*? So gross! "Nope.

All good here." My giggle was awkward and uncomfortable and ended on an unfortunate snort. "I'm just a little hot." I lifted a hand and began fanning my face. "Is it hot in here to you?"

He gave me a look like he wasn't sure what to think of me before reaching over and cranking up the air conditioner.

Thankfully, my phone chose that moment to ring, giving me an excuse to divert my attention from the man currently taking up all the oxygen.

I gave Stone an apologetic smiley grimace and reached into my purse for my cell, seeing my sister Crissy's name on the screen.

I answered quickly. "Hey. Thanks for calling me back."

"Sure thing. So what's up?"

"My car kind of broke down this morning," I started to explain, but before I could get much further, she cut me off.

"I've been telling you forever now that you need to get a new car, sis. That thing's a piece of crap."

I stomped down my frustration at her words. She might have been on me for a while now to get a new car, but she seemed to forget that I didn't have the funds for something like that, considering what money I had left after paying my bills usually went toward taking care of *our* father.

"That's beside the point. Is there any way you could pick me up from work on your way to Dad's this evening?"

"No can do, babe. That's actually why I called you back." My stomach sank like a rock. "I totally forgot there's a parent/teacher conference at school this evening, so I need you to handle Dad tonight. Sorry."

Twisting toward the passenger side window, I leaned down and lowered my voice, like that would give me any kind of privacy in the small cab. "Crissy, come on. That's three weeks in a row you've bailed and I've had to step in for you." And that wasn't even counting the times I'd had to take over for my oldest sister, Elaina, because she was always too busy.

Crissy huffed through the line. "It's not even that big a deal. All you're doing is making him dinner and keeping him company for a bit. It's not like you have a life or anything. Elaina and I have husbands and kids. We can't just drop everything at a moment's notice."

"It's not a moment's notice," I continued to argue quietly. "We worked this schedule out weeks ago. And maybe I'd actually have time for a life if you guys weren't bailing all the damn time."

Crissy let out a snort that made my blood boil. "Come on, Will. You know as well as I do that all you plan to do tonight is sit at home in front of the TV." I pushed down the pain my sister's words tried forcing to the surface. It was bad enough *I* knew I was lame but hearing it from Crissy's mouth felt like a million papercuts across my heart. "Why are you giving me such a hard time?"

"Because he needs *all* of us," I hissed angrily. Our father's illness had been a big blow to us all, but while I'd faced the reality of it, my sisters continued to bury their heads in the sand and act like nothing had changed. At least that was what I hoped, because the alternative meant they just didn't care. Sure, they could be cruel assholes, but they weren't *completely* heartless.

Silence carried through the line for several seconds before Crissy finally breathed out heavily. "You're right; I'm sorry. I've dropped the ball. I know that, and I'll do better. Can you please just help me out this one last time?"

I was a sucker for sisterly guilt. I knew that. I told myself over and over I was going to stop falling for it, only to succumb the next time they pulled it from their arsenal.

"Fine," I relented with a defeated sigh. "But you have to promise to do better."

"I promise," she said quickly. "Cross my heart. You're the best, babe. Thanks!" With that, she hung up.

Of course.

She'd gotten what she wanted, so there was no point in dealing with tedious things such as saying *goodbye* or *love you*.

"Love you too," I grumbled, staring down at the screen that had already gone black.

Chapter Two

WILLOW

"Everything square?"

I'd gotten so wrapped up in my conversation with Crissy that I'd temporarily forgotten where I was and who I was with until Stone's gruff voice gave me a jolt and yanked me back into the present.

"Sorry, what?"

"That call sounded kind of intense. You all right, mouse?"

My head jerked around in his direction. "Mouse?"

I caught one corner of his mouth hiking up infinitesimally in a smirk that made my heart palpitate. "Yeah," he said on a shrug. "You're quiet and shy. Like a cute little mouse."

He looked over and winked right then, setting a whole mess of butterflies flapping up a hurricane in my belly.

A voice that sounded an awful lot like it belonged to a teenaged girl popped into my head, squealing, *"He gave us a nickname!"*

"Oh." I ducked my head, hiding behind the curtain of my plain brown hair so he couldn't see the battle I was waging to keep from smiling like a ridiculous schoolgirl.

"You didn't answer my question."

I tried to remember anything he'd said before revealing his nickname for me and the reason behind it but came up blank. "Uh . . . what was the question?"

That curve in the corner of his lips tipped up a little bit more as he tapped his long, inked fingers against the steering wheel. "You good after that call?"

"Oh. No. I mean, yeah! I'm good. Just . . . sister stuff, you know?"

He let out a deep, gravelly chuckle, the sound making my heart flip flop like a gold medal gymnast. "Yeah. I get that. I love Shane, but she can be a serious pain in the ass when she wants to be, and it feels like she wants to be more often than not."

I tried not to let the fact that these meager few sentences were the most we'd ever shared turn me into a flustered idiot. I desperately wanted to keep the conversation going; the only problem was I couldn't think of a damn thing to say. It was as if my brain had decided to power down like a laptop that had just run out of juice.

The silence that enveloped us was tense and awkward—at least for me. My skin started to feel tight and tingly. However, Stone was the epitome of calm, cool, and collected. I tried not to stare, but my eyes refused to follow my command and kept drifting to the side to take him in.

He had one hand braced on top of the steering wheel while his other was wrapped around the top of the stick shift that came out of the floor between us. My gaze flitted between that hand and his powerful thighs as the muscles bunched and flexed beneath the denim every time he let off the gas and pushed in the clutch. It was like watching an orchestra perform; I was transfixed.

By the time my brain came back online, and I was prepared to say *anything* in an attempt to initiate a conversation, the truck jerked to a stop.

"All right. Here you go."

Momentarily confused, I looked out my window to see we were parked outside the old brick building that was used to move moonshine during prohibition, but now housed Elite Security, the company I worked for.

My shoulders sank and my expression drooped before I got control of my physical reaction. I pasted a stiff smile on my face and turned to look at him.

"Thank you for the ride," I said as I reached for the door handle.

"Hold on. Let me come around and help you out."

The name of the game was escape. Any longer in Stone's presence and I was bound to say or do something so humiliating I couldn't come back from it. "Oh, no. That's not necessary. You've already been a huge help."

"Really. It's kind of a long drop down—"

I pushed the door open, prepared to climb out. "No worries. I got it." Only I didn't have it. Far from it, actually. I didn't realize until it was too late, but apparently holding one's body stiff as a board for more than a handful of minutes cuts the blood supply off to a person's legs and causes them to fall asleep, something I didn't know until I'd swung myself out of the tow truck. My ankles gave out, my knees buckled, and before I could stop it, the pavement came at me with lightning speed.

"Oh, merciful hell!" I yelled as I went down like a Jenga tower some idiot had just taken a side piece from, my arms flailing in the air like Kermit the Frog.

I landed against the unforgiving concrete with all the grace of a donkey trying to do ballet.

I bounced off the rough surface like a deflated basketball—knees, hip, wrists—before finally coming to a stop once I was flat on the ground.

"Oh, shit," I heard Stone grunt, followed by the slam of his door. As if him seeing me swan dive onto the sidewalk wasn't bad enough, the door to my building opened, accompanied by the sound of my boss's voice.

"Jesus, Willow, are you okay? That looked bad."

I rolled to my back with a groan, looking up at the blue sky dappled with fluffy white clouds, and prayed for the ground to open up and swallow me whole. "Ouch," I wheezed once the air returned to my lungs.

Multiple faces came into view, blocking the cheerful sun.

"Willow, are you all right?" Lark, the office admin asked, her glossy dark blonde hair shimmering in the sunlight. "Are you hurt?"

Just my pride, I thought to myself. *And there's no chance in hell of it healing.*

"I'm okay," I groaned as I tried to push to sitting.

"Don't move," my boss, Jensen, ordered, placing his hand on my shoulders. "Did you hit your head? Christ, you slammed into the ground like a sack of bricks."

Adding to my shame, Jensen's partners, the other men that made up Elite Security, came rushing out to see what was going on. Just like Jensen, Gage Langdon and Laeth Harker were insanely good-looking. Not as hot as Stone, mind you, but enough so that I had to keep eye contact to a minimum, something that made working as their receptionist all the more difficult.

Fortunately, they seemed to be used to my . . . quirky nature and just let me be. However, being the center of attention for four gorgeous men made me all kinds of itchy. If I'd been a turtle, I would have ducked back into my shell forever ago.

"Maybe we should call an ambulance," Jensen said, worry etching lines into his forehead.

Oh God, no.

Images of me in a C-collar, strapped to a backboard, and being loaded into an ambulance by paramedics while Stone watched filtered through my head. I couldn't imagine that would be a good look for me, *at all*.

"I'm fine, seriously."

Stone's chiseled face was marred with concern. "You sure?"

"Yeah, totally." I was sure my smile came out as more of a grimace, but it was the best I could muster given that my whole body was throbbing like one giant bruise. I bit the inside of my cheek until I tasted blood to keep from wincing as Stone and Jensen helped me up off the sidewalk. "See?" I took a step, pain like the fires of Hell shooting through my hip. "Everything's perfectly fine."

"You sure you don't need an ambulance?" Stone asked dubiously.

"Nope. I'll just head into the ladies' room and clean up a bit, then I'll be good as new." *All lies.*

"All right," he said hesitantly. "If you're sure."

"Yep. Totally sure. Sure as sure can be. Never been surer of anything in my life. Is surer even a word, or is it supposed to be more sure?"

"I think it's surer," Lark answered with a grin.

"Okay, then that. I'm that. The most surest." *For the love of all the bacon in the world, Willow, stop talking!*

"Okay, then I'll just"—Stone hooked his thumb over his shoulder—"get your car down to the garage so I can take a look at it. I'll let you know what I find."

"Okay, thanks."

I didn't dare move a muscle as I waited for him to round the hood of the tow truck and climb in. Once he pulled away from the curb and started down the street I let out a sigh of relief and oh-so-carefully started for the building.

"You sure you're good, Willow?" Gage asked, looking me up and down from head to toe, assessing the damage.

"Yep. You guys can head back inside."

"I got her. Go on in," Lark ordered, coming to my side and taking hold of my arm.

The three men wavered for a second before finally turning and disappearing back into the building.

Once they were gone, I felt Lark look toward me, her eyes on the side of my face. "You need my help or do you have this?"

For some reason, I felt I could be honest with her. Lark

and I weren't necessarily friends, more like friend*ly*, but since she started at Elite a few months ago, she'd gone out of her way to be nice to me, and the more I got to know her, the more I liked her.

"Please don't let go of me," I begged, clinging to her arm with a death grip. "If you do, I'm eating gravel for the second time in five minutes."

She tried and failed to muffle her laugh as she guided me toward the building. "No problem, babe. I've got you."

I did my best to walk normally as I asked from the corner of my mouth, "You think they're still watching?"

"Nah. I'm sure they're back in their offices."

"Oh, thank God." With the coast clear, I allowed my body to slump over and I finished the trek inside shuffling like a little old lady who needed both hips replaced.

She helped me toward the restroom and propped me up against the counter while she ran out to grab the first aid kit.

"On a scale from one to ten, how bad was that little scene out there?" I asked once she returned, placing the kit on the counter and flipping it open.

"Um . . ."

"That bad, huh?"

"It's nothing you can't come back from," she assured me before waggling her eyebrows. "I mean, if you're worried about how you looked in front of a certain hot, tatted mechanic."

I let out a pained groan and covered my face with my hands. "Am I that obvious?"

"Stop that," she said with a light giggle. Man, I wished I could giggle all cute and tinkling like her. Every time I laughed, I ended up snorting like a bull with a sinus infection. "It's not as bad as you're thinking. I only noticed because I've happened to be at your desk a few times when he's come in."

A sense of worry washed over me. "Do-do you think he's noticed?"

She blew out a little raspberry as she worked on preparing everything she needed to fix the damage I'd done to myself. "Doubt it. Men can be pretty oblivious. All right, let's see what we're working with." She took stock, starting with my lower half, spotting the holes in both knees of my slacks. "I hope you didn't like those pants, because I think it's safe to say they're ruined." Her top lip curled up in a grimace. "Although, maybe that's a good thing."

I looked down at the front of my slacks before returning my questioning gaze to her. "You don't like my pants?"

"I'm sure they'd have been fine . . . if they weren't two sizes too big." She gave me a dry look. "You have the cutest little figure. I can't understand why you hide it behind plain, ill-fitting clothes."

I bit down on my lower lip, dragging my teeth over it as my mind began to race.

I was only a few weeks from my thirtieth birthday, a milestone, and what did I have to show for it? I was single and desperately lacking a social life. The few times I ventured out, I'd done it by myself because I didn't have any girlfriends to call. The closest relationship I had was with my DVR. Hell, I was so pathetic that when I hit up the makeup counter at Sephora a few months ago—buying a ton of makeup I'd still yet to use—my bank had called to make sure my card hadn't been stolen.

It was time for me to actually start *living*.

"I've never been really good when it comes to fashion," I admitted quietly.

Lark looked up from dabbing the scrapes on my left knee with a peroxide-soaked cotton ball.

"To be honest, I'm not good with hair or makeup either. I've kind of failed at all that girly stuff."

"Well, it's not like you really need all that stuff anyway. You've got natural beauty."

I let out a laugh that ended on an obnoxious sort. "Yeah, right," I said with a roll of my eyes.

"I'm serious!" she insisted vehemently. "You're adorable as hell. You just need a little confidence boost is all." She waggled her eyebrows at me. "It's amazing what a bit of makeup and some lacy undies can do to make a woman feel good in her own skin."

"Do you think you could help me?"

Her head shot back, her eyes inquisitive as she looked up at me. "Help you to be more confident?"

"Well, I was thinking like a little makeover or something, nothing too drastic. I just need some help because I don't know what the hell I'm doing."

She stood up, letting out a squeal of delight. "Really? Oh my God, absolutely! This is gonna be so much fun! I'll have to call Aurora. She'll definitely want in on this. She's kind of a genius when it comes to all things girly."

I'd met Lark's best friend, Aurora, a couple of times when she swung by to get Lark for lunch. The woman was more than a little intimidating. Not only was she gorgeous like Lark, but she was also loud and had no problem telling you what she was thinking—whether or not those thoughts should be voiced for the general public.

But now wasn't the time for me to tuck back into my shell. Standing there in the middle of the ladies' room with scraped palms and knees and a throbbing hip, I made myself a promise.

Thirty was going to be the year for me. No more hiding, no more being a wallflower. I was going to get that life my sisters thought I was incapable of having . . . no matter how uncomfortable it may be.

"Sounds great. How about we start this weekend?"

Chapter Three

STONE

Cannon Banks came out of the first bay closest to the office, wiping his grease-stained hands on a rag as I finished backing the tow truck into the empty bay next to him and killed the engine.

When I first returned to Redemption, Tennessee several months back, the plan had been to stay only as long as it took to run my sister's no-good, piece-of-shit ex off and make sure she was good before heading back to the home I'd made for myself in San Francisco.

I'd taken off when I was still pretty much a kid, barely old enough to drink, leaving my old life behind. It hadn't been easy, especially in the beginning, but I'd shucked off the unhappy memories and started over somewhere new, somewhere where I wasn't Carley Hendrix's bastard son. Where I wasn't known as the kid who used to get the shit beat out of him by his miserable drunk of a father before the prick finally did us all a favor and disappeared. I was sick and fucking tired of being looked at as Uncle Scooter and

Aunt Caroline's charity case: the poor kid who'd had to be taken in when his piece-of-trash mom finally bailed for good with some shithead she'd hooked up with in some dive bar.

San Francisco had been my home for years. I'd put down roots. I'd had friends I looked at as family and a garage that was all my own.

I was content with the life I'd built there. Then I came back for Shane and her son and had my eyes opened to some pretty ugly truths.

Specifically, that I'd been a pretty shitty big brother and uncle. When I skipped town, I'd left my little sister behind. She never said anything about me staying gone for as long as I had, and I'd made the mistake of thinking it was because she didn't care.

That had been a lie I told myself in order to feel better. The truth had been that Shane was such a kind person with such a tremendous heart that she didn't want to pressure me about coming back, even though she and her son Brantley both needed me.

I had some serious amends to make, not only with Shane and Brantley, but with my aunt and uncle who'd gone out of their way to make me feel wanted, only for me to turn around and take off. I still had a long way to go, but I'd taken the first step by making the choice to stay put this time around.

For the second time, I'd packed up my entire life, only this time, instead of running, I'd returned to where it all started. I'd had no plan, no home, and no job.

That was, until Cliff Banks decided to retire from Banks Body and Auto Repair, leaving the thriving garage to his only son. As soon as everything was handed over to him, Cannon came to me, offering to take me on as a full partner if I could buy my way in.

I hadn't hesitated to fork over the cash if it meant I got to team up with a man I respected the hell out of *and* continue being my own boss.

"What've we got?"

"Willow Thorne called this mornin' in a panic," I answered as I lowered the Honda Civic that was at least two decades old to the ground. "Car's completely dead. Didn't get a chance to really look it over when I got there, just enough to know it wasn't the battery. Had to give her a ride to work before heading over here."

His face broke out into a shit-eating grin. "Bet that was one of the most awkward car rides of your life. That girl's so damn shy it's a wonder she can even function."

"She's not so bad," I defended in a low, brusque tone.

I thought back to the tumble she'd taken out of the truck and winced, feeling bad for her all over again. She tried to play it off, but the woman had zero poker face. It was obvious she was trying to put a brave face on while in serious pain.

Sure, she was shy and awkward almost to the point of painful, and while I didn't know her well, it was so bad that it brought out some sort of protective instinct in me, and I felt my muscles clenching tight at Cannon poking fun at her, even though I knew he most likely didn't mean anything by it.

"Come on man." He moved toward me and clapped me

on the shoulder. "You know I'm just kidding. Nothing against her. I think she's a sweet girl."

My mind flashed back to the conversation I'd overheard earlier. I'd only gotten Willow's side of the exchange, but it was more than enough to figure out something was going on.

My curiosity got the better of me, and before I could stop the words from coming out, I found myself asking, "She's got a sister, doesn't she?"

"Two, actually."

I turned my head to look at him. "You know anything about them?"

He didn't bother to hide his shit-eating grin at my out-of-character questions before grinning and teasing, "Why the sudden interest? You looking to be set up or something?"

The answer to that wasn't just no, it was a hard as granite, hell to the fucking no. To say I wasn't a fan of dating would have been like calling the Pacific Ocean a kiddie pool —a serious goddamn understatement.

Growing up with my mom was like a lesson in what *not* to do: namely, tie myself to one person for any longer than it took for me to get her off, blow my own load, then get the hell out of there.

From the time I was old enough to develop memories, she'd had a revolving door of shitty relationships, each one lasting only as long as it took for the asshole she was with to take off. And there hadn't been a single goddamn winner in the whole bunch.

Losers, drunks, druggies, abusive pricks, unemployed wastes of flesh and bone. You name it, she screwed it. She had no standards whatsoever. There was even that one bastard who lasted six months, all while having a wife and two kids at home.

I wish I could say my mom didn't know about that, but it would have been a lie. She knew, and she hadn't hesitated to out the guy to his wife when he tried ending it with her. She'd driven to his house in the middle of the night and thrown a bomb on his marriage, causing a scene so loud everyone on their street heard all the intimate details. The cops were eventually called and Mom was locked up for the night, leaving me with the responsibility of taking care of my infant sister. I didn't have a goddamn clue how to take care of a baby, but had my mom given a damn about that? Had she stopped to consider us before acting like a psychotic bitch? Hell no.

That was her MO. She expected me to take care of her shit every time she got in a jam. That was why it was so easy for her to bail on Shane and me when I was nineteen. She knew I'd do what I had to in order to take care of my sister, whether I wanted the responsibility or not.

I was done being depended on. I'd had more than my fair share. There was only one creature on the planet I was willing to make an exception for, and that was only because he was low maintenance. All I had to do was dump kibble in his bowl once a day, make sure he had water, and open the door so he could go outside to take a shit. That was all it took for him to love me unconditionally.

I scoffed as I unhooked the car from the tow truck. "Not a chance. You know my rule, brother."

"Yeah, yeah. I know. You don't do monogamy. You're a lone wolf, or some shit like that."

My chuckle rattled around in my chest and throat. "Yeah, something like that."

"But you know she's into you, right?"

I let out a sigh as I wiped my forehead with the back of my arm. "Yeah, man. I know."

I wasn't blind or stupid. At nearly forty, I'd been around the block enough times to know when a woman was into me, even one as awkward and nervous as Willow.

It wasn't just about the fact she was so far from my type it wasn't even funny. It was also that I didn't want the responsibility of caring for another human being. That was the reason Willow Thorne sat in the top spot on my Not a Chance in Hell list, her name written in thick, bold black letters.

Beneath all that anxiousness was a sweetness that called to certain kinds of men, men who wanted to save and protect, to play the white knight to the damsel in distress.

Whether she knew she was putting that out in the world intentionally or not, everything about her screamed damsel in a shit-ton of distress. A woman like her needed to be taken care of and protected from all the ugliness that infected this world, and I wasn't the white knight type. I was too fucking hard and jaded for that.

I looked to Cannon, my expression carved with seriousness. "But you know it's never gonna happen."

"Yeah, man. I know. Even if you were down for the old ball and chain, I've seen your type, and skittish librarian it is not."

"Exactly."

"Anyway, since you asked, I don't know the Thorne girls well. Never really ran in the same crowds, you know? But from what I can tell from what I've heard people sayin', the older sisters are known for having sticks up their asses."

"How do you mean?"

"Well, when their mom died about six years ago, their dad struggled for a while and Willow took the brunt of helping him pull through. Word is, Jon got sick recently. Don't know any of the details or what with, but apparently, those two can't be bothered to help; so again, the responsibility falls on Willow's shoulders."

"So, what you're sayin' is her sisters are bitches."

"Yup. And stuck up too. But that's always been the case with those two. Don't know how someone like Willow can share blood with two chicks so totally different than her in every way." He paused, arching an eyebrow, too damn smug for his own good. "But that's not your problem, right? Because you don't do relationships."

"Yeah," I grunted. "That's right."

"All right, bro." He clapped me on the back again. "Then I'll let you get to it."

I did just that, going about my job like it was any other day.

The whole time trying to convince myself that Willow Thorne and her avalanche of problems were none of my damn business.

Problem was, I knew I was full of shit.

Chapter Four

WILLOW

I limped up the walkway and stuck my key in the lock, only to discover the door was already unlocked. I told him all the time to be sure to lock his doors, even when he was home. Most of the time he forgot, other times he just couldn't be bothered. Letting out a sigh, I pushed the door open and stepped inside the house, calling out, "Hey, Dad. It's me."

I kicked off my shoes and lined them up inside the door out of habit. Back when she was alive, my mother had been a bit of an obsessive cleaner, always dusting and mopping and vacuuming no matter how clean the house already was. She'd been a stickler when it came to wearing shoes in the house, and although my dad didn't have an issue with shoes on the carpet, it had been ingrained in me from an early age to take them off any time I came to visit.

"Dad?" I called again when he didn't answer. I made my way deeper into the house, fear clutching my chest when I heard nothing back from him. Used to be I wouldn't think twice about it, but lately I tended to fear the worst.

Turning into the kitchen, I spotted an un-manned saucepan sitting on a front burner of the gas stovetop, the dial turned up as high as it could go, spitting bright orange flames along the sides of the small pot. Whatever was inside was burnt and boiling over, making the flames hiss and spark angrily.

I rushed over and shut off the gas, pulling the pan off the stove and carrying it to the sink to dump the contents and run it under the water.

"Dad!" I called a little more frantically. "Where are you?"

I heard his loud, booming voice coming from upstairs. "Colleen, honey, get up here! We've been robbed!"

After the day I had, I'd really hoped I could come here and relax with my father, enjoy dinner, and watch some television with him. My whole body hurt from that humiliating tumble I took out of the tow truck earlier that morning. I'd done my best to play it off in front of the guys, refusing to limp or show pain, but I was pretty sure my hip was double the size it was supposed to be, and I had a feeling that when I took off my clothes, my body would look like a Jackson Pollock painting of black and blue bruises.

Then there was the conversation I'd had with my oldest sister, Elaina, when I called her on my lunch break to ask for a ride home after work.

As soon as the call connected, her voice came through the line with an air of annoyance that was becoming commonplace whenever I called her.

"Hey, Willow. Listen, now's not really a good time."

It seemed like, more and more lately, it was never a good time to talk to my oldest sister.

"I know. I'm sorry, but I'm in a bind. My car completely died on me this morning when I was leaving for work. I got a ride in earlier, but I don't have any way home. Would you mind coming to get me this evening?"

She let out a harried sigh. "I can't, Willow. I've already had a busy day and I still need to hit the grocery store and dry cleaner before my Pilates class. I don't have time."

"Couldn't you skip Pilates just this once? I could really use your help."

"Sorry, but I can't. With it being so last minute, they'd still charge me, and I can't just flush money down the drain like that."

That tightness I'd felt in my chest this morning when everything started to snowball into an avalanche of crap had returned. Squeezing my eyes closed, I filled my lungs slowly, swallowing down the knot of emotion that was suddenly causing my throat to swell up. My morning had been bad enough, the last thing I needed was to start bawling like a baby in the middle of the office for everyone to see.

"Elaina—"

"Look, I have to go. I'm in the middle of the cereal aisle right now and can't talk. Just call an Uber or something." With a rapid-fire, "loveyoubye," she disconnected the call, leaving me flustered, irritated, and dangerously close to tears.

The saving grace had come when Lark came out of her office to invite me to lunch a few minutes later and saw the red splotches on my face that always came when I was close to crying. I was a seriously ugly crier. She hadn't let up until I told her what was wrong, then, after calling my sister a few choice words—I hadn't minded, she'd pissed me off—she informed me she'd give me a ride home.

It had definitely been the worst day in a years-long streak of underwhelming days, and as I took the stairs up to my dad's bedroom, the anxiety clutching at me grew worse with each step.

When he'd been diagnosed with Alzheimer's a few months ago, it felt like the rug had been pulled out from under me. I'd been a daddy's girl all my life. Growing up, he'd been the only one in my family who'd gotten me. He'd accepted me for exactly who I was and never once made me feel lacking or tried to get me to change or to be something I wasn't.

My mom, God rest her soul, hadn't been able to understand why I was the way I was. She'd tried to "coax me out of my shell" on multiple occasions, all but forcing me to be social with other kids I barely knew. It had blown up in her face every time, until finally, Dad put his foot down and demanded she just let me be me.

There was one particular conversation I'd overheard back when I was in high school that stuck with me to this day.

I'd woken up late one night to go to the bathroom and heard their low voices creeping through the crack in their partially closed bedroom door. I'd been prepared to backtrack and return to bed until I heard my mom say my name.

"I just don't understand it, Jon. Why can't she be more like Elaina and Crissy?"

"Because she's not Elaina or Crissy, Colleen," my father had clipped in irritation. "She's our Willow, and just because she's different doesn't make her any less special."

"I'm not saying that. I know she's special."

My dad's voice came out in a low, menacing growl I'd never heard from him before. Dad was always the soft-spoken, reasonable one in our family, hardly getting angry. Hearing that tone coming from him made my skin erupt with goosebumps. "Then maybe you should start treating her like it instead of constantly acting like you're ashamed of her for being different."

My chest suddenly felt uncomfortably tight, like someone had reached inside and was squeezing and twisting, stretching my organs like they were made of Silly Putty. What he was saying was the very thing I'd been feeling for as long as I could remember, and hearing my parents fight about it was like being sucker-punched in the gut.

"I'm not ashamed of her!" my mom exclaimed. "I could never be ashamed of her. I love her to death. I just wish . . . I don't know. Doesn't she want to make friends? She has to be lonely."

When my father spoke again a few seconds later, his voice was calmer. "She'll find her people, Coll, you have to trust that. You have to let her be her own person, and in the meantime, I'm done standing idly by while you do and say things to make her get down on herself."

"Jon, I'm not—"

"No. I don't want to hear anything but that you get me.

Willow is Willow and you'll take her as she comes. Am I clear?"

My mom hesitated for a beat and I could picture the scrunched look she got on her face whenever she and Dad entered into one of their rare but ridiculous standoffs. That hardly ever happened, but when it did, it was over the silliest things and always ended with Dad tickling Mom until she started giggling like crazy. Then all was better.

My parents had been crazy in love for as long as I could remember, and after that late-night conversation years ago, my mom had turned a corner. She'd done exactly as my dad told her and accepted me for me. From that moment on, our relationship blossomed. I'd always been so grateful to him for doing that for me.

When she'd lost her battle with breast cancer six years earlier, we'd all been crushed, but my father had been devastated. I'd stuck by his side through it all, doing everything I could to be the rock for him, the shoulder he could always lean on, but trying to help someone past losing the love of their life was practically impossible. Still, I'd done my best, and it had only cemented our relationship that much more, bringing us even closer together. If that was possible.

The fact that the man who'd carried me on his shoulders when I was a little girl as he ran through the sprinklers during the summers didn't even remember who I was some of the time broke my heart and hurt in a way I wouldn't wish on my worst enemy.

I found Dad in his bedroom, yanking open drawers frantically. "Colleen—" he started to yell but stopped when he spun around and spotted me in the doorway. "There you are. I've been yelling and yelling. We've been robbed, Colleen. But it's the weirdest thing. They only took your stuff. But they took all of it. Your clothes, your jewelry. It's all gone. All of it!"

"No. Dad, it's me. Willow. Your daughter."

His frenzied gaze darted around the room and the panic and confusion on his face tore at my insides. My heart was breaking in half as I stood, waiting for him to recognize me.

I took a step closer, crossing the threshold hesitantly as I worked to keep the tears at bay. "Daddy?"

I could see the shift coming over his face. He blinked and it was like a fog had cleared and the present came back into focus for him. "Willow?"

I gave him a small smile and closed the rest of the distance between us. "Yeah, Dad. It's me. You okay?"

"I don't . . . ." He shook his head like he was trying to clear the cobwebs left behind from his most recent episode before his eyes went wide. "Oh hell. I was going to cook dinner—"

"It's okay. I took care of it. The stove's turned off but, unfortunately, whatever you'd put in that pot was beyond saving."

The grin he gave me was full of sadness. He hated losing time just as much as I hated it on his behalf. "Probably for the best. I never really was any good in the kitchen, was I? That was your mom's domain."

"Very true. But that's why I'm here. Lucky for you, Mom taught me all she knew. Come on, you can keep me company while I make dinner. Sound good?"

"My precious Willow girl. Always taking care of me,"

Dad murmured lovingly as he hooked his arm around my shoulders and led us out of the room.

"Always, Daddy. Never ever doubt that."

I closed my eyes for a brief second as he leaned in and pressed a kiss to my temple, the familiar scent of the same aftershave he'd used for as long as I could remember filling my senses and coating me in a nice, warm bubble of familiarity.

It was moments like this, when he was lucid, when he was his usual affectionate self, that I held tightly to, knowing it was only a matter of time before these moments were fewer and farther between. They'd eventually be gone for good. As it was, they were coming faster than they had just a few weeks ago, and I didn't want to think about what that meant.

I managed to push down the melancholy and sadness as I prepared dinner. We ate and talked and laughed like it was any other day, and afterward, not ready to leave him just yet, I hung with him so we could watch mindless TV together.

It was only when he started to doze off in his recliner that I decided it was time to leave. I got him up to his room, making sure he took all his pills before he climbed into bed. I made sure everything was turned off and locked his house up tight before heading for my own home only a block away.

It wasn't until I got inside and locked the door behind me that I gave in to the tears that had been pricking at the backs of my eyes all evening and cried for the father who wasn't gone yet, but who I was losing faster than I was ready for.

Chapter Five

WILLOW

By the time I reached Elite Security the following morning my clothes were sticking to me in the most uncomfortable places. My face was glowing bright, so damn red it felt hot to the touch, and I was wheezing so badly I sounded like an eighty-year-old, life-long smoker desperately trying to get oxygen into her lungs.

In my infinite wisdom, I'd decided it would be smart to save my money by walking to work instead of calling for an Uber, knowing that whatever was wrong with my car would more than likely be a significant hit to my bank account.

Every little bit counted, and I figured a few miles wouldn't kill me.

I'd been very wrong.

Thanks to the genes on my mom's side of the family, I'd come by my lithe frame naturally. Which had been a blessing since I hated all things exercise.

The first half-mile of my walk to work hadn't been so bad. Sure, the heat had made sweat pebble across my hairline, but that was no big deal since I wore my hair in a low ponytail most days anyway.

It was after the one-mile mark that things started to go downhill fast. That thin sheen of sweat had turned into a torrent that felt like it was coming out of every single pore. And it only got worse the farther I went. It ran down the back of my neck like an open spigot, traveling down my spine to my butt crack. I was sweating in places I didn't know could even sweat. I mean, who sweats in the bends of their elbows? And I didn't know you could develop a stitch in your side simply by walking at a leisurely pace. I thought that only happened to runners.

Cardio was for the birds. It could go straight to hell.

If the reception area had been empty when I got to work, I gladly would have collapsed face down on the cold tile floor while I waited for my heart to stop trying to *Shawshank* its way through my ribcage.

Unfortunately, that wasn't in the cards. As soon as I walked through the doors, four sets of eyes shot in my direction.

"Hey," I panted, swiping at my forehead where my hair had stuck to the perspiration. "Hi. Good morning."

"Holy God," Laeth muttered. "What happened to you?"

I wiped beneath my eyes, hoping my mascara—the only makeup I wore—hadn't melted down my face, but I wasn't going to hold my breath. "What do you mean?" *That's right, Willow. Play it off.*

"Did you walk to work?" Lark asked, her eyes wide.

"Jesus, Will," Jensen started. "It's the middle of summer. The heat index is already close to ninety."

"Well, I don't have my car back yet, and I figured a little cardio wouldn't kill me. I don't live that far. It's no big deal."

Gage looked me up and down skeptically. "Really? Because you look like you're about to keel over from heat exhaustion."

I waved his comment off, refusing to let my humiliation show. "I just need some water and I'll be right as rain." I cleared my throat and batted at the bead of sweat that was trailing down my cheek from my temple. "Now, if you'll excuse me, I'm going to get a drink then get to work."

Ignoring the way their eyes followed me, I headed straight for the breakroom, but instead of getting a glass of water, I moved to the refrigerator and yanked both doors open, sticking my head in the freezer and letting out a sigh of relief as the cold penetrated my overheated skin.

My whole body sagged closer to the open doors as the cool air inside helped to temper my flush and make it so I didn't feel like I was two seconds from melting right into a puddle of Willow goo in the middle of the floor.

"You okay?"

Any other time I might have shrieked at being caught in such a strange position, but honestly, at that moment I was just grateful to feel my body temperature lower to normal. I was convinced I'd been dangerously close to cooking my insides.

I turned to find Lark standing in the doorway with a sly grin on her face.

I reached into the freezer and grabbed an ice cube. With no shame whatsoever—you couldn't be embarrassed when you were as close to boiling to death as I was—I pulled my shirt away from my body and dropped it right down the front. "Better now," I answered as the ice cube began to melt against my skin.

"Yeah. I can see that." She stepped into the breakroom, moving casually toward the coffeemaker, and started to prepare a cup for herself. "Babe, why don't you get a rental car so you don't have to subject yourself to"—she circled her hand in front of my body—"all of this."

I let out a sigh as I closed the refrigerator doors and headed for the water cooler in the back corner. "I looked into it," I told her. "But my insurance won't cover the cost of one, and I don't have the money to pay that out of pocket right now."

Her brow furrowed with worry, and a pang of discomfort slammed dead center into my chest. If there was anything I hated more than being so damn awkward around pretty much everyone, it was the pity I saw in people's eyes when they looked at me. I'd been getting that look all my life just because I was different, so I'd become accustomed to dreading it, even if I received it for different reasons.

"Willow, honey, are you having money problems? Because I'd be more than happy to help—"

I cut her off with a raised hand. "No. It's not like that." I pulled in a deep breath before giving her the truth I'd been keeping to myself for so long. "My dad got sick a while back," I admitted, saying those words out loud to someone other than my sisters for the very first time. Until that moment, I hadn't talked about it to anyone. As illogical as it was, I was afraid that putting those words out into the world would give them some sort of power. Make them real. So I'd kept the truth tucked deep inside where it had begun to fester.

"Oh, sweetie. I'm so sorry."

"It is what it is," I said with a shrug. "I had a nice little nest egg saved to start remodeling my house, but then . . . things changed. My father's retirement and social security only go so far. His medical bills were steep after his diagnosis, and I'm helping him out on top of all my own stuff, so my monthly expenses have gone up a bit. Things are just a little tight, so I want to save where I can, you know?"

"God, Willow . . . I don't know what to say."

"There's nothing to say, really. It's just the way things are."

And wasn't that the truth. It was the very reason I'd cried myself to sleep alone in my bed the night before.

Lark stepped closer and reached out to take my hand, doing her best to offer comfort. I appreciated it more than she could possibly imagine. "Have you told the guys?"

"You're actually the first person I've told," I confessed. "It feels kind of nice to talk about it. Like a weight has been lifted."

She smiled, her fingers tightening around my hand. "I'm honored you picked me to talk to. And just so you know, if you ever need to talk more, or vent or yell or cry, I'm here. You know that, right?"

Honestly, I didn't. Not until that very moment. Truth was, I'd never really had any friends. The few I'd managed to make through school either got tired of trying to pull me out of my shell, accusing me of being boring and weird, or they'd grown up and started their own lives, causing us to drift apart.

Lark was the first person to ever make any kind of real effort, and she was so damn kindhearted that it was impossible not to let her in.

"Thank you," I whispered, feeling a lump form in my throat. "I—just . . . thank you."

"That's what friends do, right?"

"Yes," I answered with a smile, because that sounded a lot better than admitting I didn't really know because I'd never had a real friend before.

"Now I'm even more excited about this weekend than I already was," she said, her tone holding a hint of giddiness. "You need a break from life for a bit. Rora and I are going to treat you to lunch, then we're going to give you the best girls' day you've ever had. It's going to be so fun."

Until that moment, I'd completely forgotten I'd recruited Lark the day before to help make me over. But the more she talked about it, the more her excitement grew until it began to rub off on me.

"Can't wait," I said with a sincere smile.

She headed out of the breakroom a second later, and I chugged my glass of water in an effort to replenish the fluids my body had practically cried out during my walk to work.

I really hoped Stone finished my car soon, because I worried that if I had to keep up with this whole cardio thing, I'd risk drying up and looking like a piece of fruit that had been in the dehydrator too long. And I couldn't imagine that was a good look on anyone.

LATER THAT MORNING, after three more glasses of water and a long trip to the restroom to repair the damage that walk had done to my appearance, I was finally feeling well enough to switch to a much-needed cup of coffee.

I was returning to my desk with a fresh, steaming cup of caffeinated goodness when my cell phone rang inside my purse. My phone hardly ever rang, and with how the past several months had been, I automatically jumped to thinking every call was to tell me something had happened to my dad.

I scrambled quickly around the desk, spilling the piping hot liquid over the edge of the mug and onto my skin. "Ouch! Son of hellfire!" I hissed, plopping down in my chair and placing the coffee mug on my desk so I didn't cause any further damage. I shook out my stinging hand while I rummaged through my purse with the other one.

The number flashing across the screen wasn't one I was familiar with, so I quickly swiped to answer before it rolled over to voicemail. "Hello? Hi, hey. I'm here. Hello?"

"Willow?" the gruff, raspy voice on the other end of the call asked, sending goosebumps cascading across my skin. "Hey, it's Stone."

My back shot straight in my chair. "Hi. Hey. Yes, it's you. And I'm . . . me."

For the love of God! Squeezing my eyes closed, I smacked myself in the forehead with my injured hand and let out a string of mumbled curses.

"Everything okay?"

"Yeah!" I chirped, infusing way too much cheer into my tone. "Yes. Everything's good. How—" I cleared my throat and tried to calm my frazzled nerves. "How are you?"

When he spoke next it almost sounded like I could hear a smile in his voice, but without seeing him, I couldn't be sure. "I'm good. I'm calling about your car."

"Oh! Yeah, my car! Right. Of course. Is everything okay with it?"

"Well, not really," he answered, deflating my hope. "Your alternator's fucked and the ignition switch needs to be replaced."

"Oh. Uh, okay. That sounds . . . expensive?"

"It's not too bad. Problem is, the garage is really backed up at the moment and we don't have all the parts I need on hand, so you're lookin' at about a week, maybe two, before I can get it back to you."

"Oh," I repeated, slumping in my chair. "Okay."

"Is that all right?" he asked, like he could hear the disappointment loud and clear in those two words.

"Yeah. No, it's fine." I waved my hand even though he couldn't see me. "Nothing you can really do if you don't have the parts or time, right?" I tried to laugh casually and ended up snorting. *Eff my life so freaking bad!*

"I gotta be honest, mouse," he continued, giving me a little thrill with the use of that nickname. "Even with those parts replaced, the car's still a piece of shit. You really should look into getting something more dependable."

"Yeah, maybe you're right," I offered in a placating tone, even though I had no intention of buying a new car.

"Well, thanks for calling to let me know. I guess I should let you get back to work."

"Yeah. And I'll let you know when the parts come in."

"Thanks, Stone. I appreciate that. Have a good day."

The call ended, and I stuffed the phone back into my purse with a sigh as I slumped in my chair.

Another week—at least—of walking to and from work. If this morning was anything to go by, I wasn't totally confident I could survive it.

I was going to have to invest in some athletic wear, because there was no way in hell my work clothes could survive that much sweat.

Chapter Six

STONE

Summer was in full effect and the temps outside were steadily climbing. It wasn't even nine in the morning, and the thermostat had already slipped past eighty. It wasn't often that I thought about my old life in San Francisco, but on days like this, when the heat felt like it was slapping you in the face, I missed the cooler temperature.

Standing out on my back deck, I took in the view of the bright green trees that surrounded me as far as the eye could see. I'd bought this place once I decided to stay because of the solitude it provided, something the city had been sorely lacking.

Out here, there wasn't any of that obnoxious traffic. There were no honking horns, no people rushing around in a hurry to get nowhere special. The pace in Redemption was chill. The people were content to just be. I could get down with that.

My place sat on ten acres of wooded land tucked in the foothills of the Smoky Mountains just outside of town. The house itself was bigger than a single guy like me needed, but the selling point was the building that sat about a hundred yards away from the house.

It hadn't been much to look at when I first got here, but it was big enough to convert into my own personal garage with two bays so I could work on my own restoration projects during my downtime.

For space where I could focus on the one thing that kept my mind at ease, I'd have gladly paid more than the asking price, but most people buying a house in the woods didn't want an eyesore of an outbuilding just outside their back door, so the previous owners were geared up to tear it down until I swooped in with a generous offer.

I'd fixed the building so it didn't look like a rusted-out wreck, and now my passion projects sat in the closed bays, waiting for me to find the time to spend with them.

Sucking down the last of my coffee, I moved back inside and dropped the empty mug into the sink before bending down to give Chief's head a rub. I'd had the old boy for years now, finding him out in the alley behind my old garage in San Francisco. He'd been rummaging around in the trash, looking for something to eat.

The grey pit bull had been dangerously emaciated, so skinny I could count each of his ribs from a distance. His back leg was in bad shape, and his fur had started falling out.

At first I thought he was a random stray until I spotted his collar. Some asshole had decided that a big dog like him wasn't for them and had abandoned him, leaving him to die on the streets.

It hadn't been easy getting him to trust me. It had been obvious he'd been on his own for a while, and he was leerier of me and the rest of my guys from the shop than we were of him. But with enough coaxing, I'd managed to earn his trust, and eventually, the dog that had wanted nothing to do with humans—and rightfully so—became mine. I nursed him back to health, and it had been just the two of us ever since.

"Keep an eye on the place while I'm gone, will you?" I asked as he looked up at me, his tongue lolling out the side of his mouth as he panted happily and thumped his tail against the floor. "I'll take that as a yes."

With one last pat, I headed out the door and hopped on my bike. I took the ride down the mountain faster than most people might, the thrill of the wind across my face was a rush of adrenaline filling my veins. It made me feel alive. It was the closest to pure joy I assumed I'd ever feel.

I hugged the curves as endorphins flooded my bloodstream. I was a bit of an adrenaline junky. Always had been. But after losing my best friend in a car crash a few years back, the carelessness that used to fuel my adrenaline high was no longer there. It was no longer about seeing how far I could push my luck. That drive disappeared when Will died after some asshole decided he had the right to get plastered and climb behind the wheel of his car, putting everyone else on the road in danger. I wouldn't do something like that. Now it was just about that temporary feeling of freedom.

I let up as soon as I hit the town limits where the traffic picked up a bit more. I was maybe ten minutes from the garage when I spotted a lone figure walking along the side of the road. The woman's brown hair was pulled into a ponytail that sat high on the back of her head, the long strands hanging down to her shoulders and swaying in the hot breeze.

She was dressed in a bright-colored tank that fit her torso like a second skin, dipping in at her trim waist. The cropped yoga pants showcased her long legs and, I noticed the closer I got, a *really* nice, round ass.

For some strange reason, she was carrying a small duffle bag hooked across her body, the bag bulging at her waist and bumping against her hip.

The closer I got, the stronger the feeling of recognition grew, but that didn't make sense, because I was sure I'd never seen this woman before. With a body like that, I *definitely* would have noticed her before now.

The roar of my bike's engine drew her attention when I was only a few yards away, and when she turned to look over her shoulder, I damn near swallowed my tongue. My grip on the handlebars fumbled, and I had to jerk them straight to keep from going ass over elbow.

I pulled past her and nosed up to the curb before killing the engine and pulling my helmet off. "Willow?" I asked, my eyes doing a slow, bewildered trek down her lithe frame. Never in a million years would I have guessed what this woman was hiding beneath all those plain baggy clothes she seemed to favor. I looked back, noticing the flush on her heart-shaped face and a dewiness to her skin that I could only assume was due to the heat, but for some reason, it looked really good on her makeup-free face.

Her baby blue eyes went wide as she gave me the same

attention I'd just given her, looking from my booted foot resting on the concrete, all the way up to my face. "Stone," she said with a slight pant. "Hey. Hello. Um, h-how are you?"

Christ, why did I think the fact she got so damn awkward around me was cute? This was *not* the type of woman I should find cute. Add to the fact that I now knew she was hiding a rocking body behind all those frumpy-as-fuck clothes, and it was a *big* problem. But just like every time I encountered her, that unsettling protective urge I desperately tried to ignore came rushing to the surface.

"What the hell are you doin' out here, mouse?"

Her tongue came out to swipe across her bee-stung lips as her gaze darted around behind her, like she expected me to be talking to someone else. When she faced me again, the skin between her brows was adorably crinkled in a confused frown. "Uh, walking?"

I looked down at the duffle bag she was toting and arched a brow. "With luggage?"

She glanced down at the bag at her hip. "Oh. Those are my work clothes. I learned a few days ago that it was best to carry them with me and change at the office instead of wearing them on my walk to work." Her nose scrunched up. "It was *not* a fun lesson. Trust me."

"Jesus, Willow. It's a million fuckin' degrees outside. What the hell are you doing walking to work when you live at least five miles away?"

"Well, uh . . ." She lifted he arms out to her sides and shrugged. "I don't have a car. It's either this or burn my

PTO until my car is fixed, and I can't really afford to do that."

Not your problem, Stone, I silently berated myself. *Don't get involved.*

But damn if I could help myself.

"Why the hell didn't you get a rental?"

She pulled her bottom lip between her straight white teeth and bit down, anxiety crawling across her features. She hesitated for a few seconds, and I could see that what she was about to say was weighing heavily on her. "My insurance wouldn't cover it, and I couldn't afford the cost out of pocket."

Son of a bitch. "Hop on. I'll take you the rest of the way."

Her sky-colored eyes bugged out comically wide, and it took everything I had to keep from grinning outright. I'd never met someone so socially awkward in my life, but somehow, Willow Thorne made it adorable as hell.

"Hop on what? Your *motorcycle*?" she asked in a tone that made it sound like I'd just asked her to go on a killing spree.

There was no controlling the grin this time. One corner of my mouth hooked up slightly as I answered, "Yeah, mouse. On my motorcycle. Just step on that peg there"—I pointed down to the foothold—"and swing your other leg over."

She shifted her weight from foot to foot. "You know, I'm really okay with walking. It's only another"—she looked down at the Apple watch on her wrist where she was obviously keeping track of the distance, and let out a pained groan—"two and a half miles," she finished on a whine. "Oh, God. Why does it have to be so damn hot?"

"Welcome to summer, babe." I grabbed the helmet I'd been wearing earlier and extended it to her. "Now put this on and climb on."

Willow took the helmet and looked down at it like she was waiting for it to sprout wings and fly away before turning her attention back to me. "If I'm wearing this, what'll you wear?"

"I'll be fine."

Her trepidation grew as she clutched the helmet in a white-knuckled grip. "I don't know. Aren't those things really dangerous?"

"Only if the person driving it is a careless jackass. I know what I'm doing, Willow. You'll be safe with me, I swear."

She looked back out at the distance, as if mentally calculating how many more steps she had to go to get to work. With a deep inhale that strained her tight top and made her round, perky tits pop out, she nodded like she'd been having a silent conversation with herself and pulled her ponytail out so she could put the helmet on. I helped her adjust the chin strap so it stayed snug to her head and started the bike back up while I waited the ten seconds it took her to find the nerve to climb on behind me.

She sat with a good-sized gap between our bodies and rested her hands on my shoulders. "Okay!" she called over the rumble of the engine. "I'm ready!"

Reaching back, I hooked my hands under her knees and yanked her closer so her chest was flush with my back and my hips were cradled tight by her thighs.

For fuck's sake, Stone. Do NOT get hard. This chick isn't even your type, I scolded when I felt my cock stir behind my fly.

I barely heard her cute little "Oh" of surprise when I took her hands off my shoulders and wrapped them around my waist.

"Hold tight, just like this," I instructed. Her fingers gripped the material of my T-shirt like she was holding on for dear life. "You ready?" I asked, looking over my shoulder.

Those soft blues were wide as dinner plates and the flush on her high cheeks had bleached with fear. But instead of letting that get the better of her, she nodded with determination, setting the helmet that was about two sizes too big bobbling all over the place. I had to respect the hell out of her for doing something that scared her instead of chickening out.

As I promised her, I was careful, going slightly below the speed limit so she wouldn't freak out. By the time we hit downtown, her hold on my shirt had loosened, and I felt her sit up a little straighter. She'd occasionally let out a little squeal or a peel of laughter, letting me know she was finally beginning to enjoy the ride. I kept my focus on the road, but there was no stopping the smile that pulled at my lips and stretched my cheeks.

Chapter Seven

STONE

I pulled to a stop outside Elite Security a few minutes later, and Willow didn't waste a beat climbing off and stepping in front of the bike. Her face glowed with excitement as she bounced up and down on her toes, exclaiming, "Oh wow! That was so cool!"

"Glad you enjoyed it, mouse." A chuckle worked up my throat as I watched her unclip the strap from under her chin and pull the helmet off. It had been a huge fucking mistake to stare, because now I couldn't miss the fact that this was the first time I'd ever really noticed Willow with her hair down, and she had *great* hair. The sun shined down on the chocolate brown locks, revealing natural streaks of blonde and auburn peppered in the long strands.

This woman had a gift for hiding, I could say that for damn certain. With the clothes and her hair usually tied back in a plain style, she tended to blend in to her surroundings, going unnoticed. But like this . . . well, that would-be wallflower would definitely stand out in a crowd.

"I really did. It was so much better than walking to work, and not just because I hate doing that because cardio sucks, but because it was such a *huge* rush!"

I wasn't sure I'd ever heard her talk so much without peppering her sentences with um's and uh's. This had to have been some sort of record for the longest conversation without her going all skittish, and something in me was stoked she'd loosened up enough to look me in the eye for more than a handful of seconds at a time.

"And look!" She held her arms out at her sides. "Only minimal sweat. This will be the first time in days I'm not totally gross for work, so yay!"

My head fell back on a loud, booming laugh that rumbled from the pit of my stomach all the way up my throat.

When I was finally finished, I straightened my neck and found Willow staring at me with a look that could only be described as having hearts in her pale eyes. I needed to shut this shit down fast.

"I should get going," I said, throwing my thumb over my shoulder at nothing in particular. "Busy day and all that."

"Yeah, I should go too." She lifted the duffle bag and gave me a wonky smile. "Gotta change into something more professional."

"Okay, well, have a good day."

I pushed down the uncomfortable ball that had formed in my stomach at the sight of her smile dying slowly. "You too, Stone. And thanks again for the ride. It was a lot of fun."

I began backing my bike away from the curb, needing to

get the hell out of there. "Yeah, sure. Not a problem. See you around."

With that, I took off, refusing to let myself look back to see if she was still standing there.

A few minutes later I turned into the lot for the garage, driving past the open chain link fence and parking my bike off to the side of the forecourt, away from the clients' cars. It wasn't until I'd killed the engine and swung off, planting both thick-soled boots on the ground, that I realized I'd completely forgotten about my helmet in my rush to put some distance between Willow and me.

"Good morning, Stone," our assistant, Gloria, greeted as I stepped into the office.

"Mornin' gorgeous," I returned, shooting her a wink as I headed for the coffee machine over by the waiting area. "You wised up and left that old man of yours yet so I can have my shot?"

At sixty-five, Gloria pretty much ran our garage, and she did it with an iron fist. She'd been recommended by Cannon's mom, Bev, when his old man decided to retire and I came on as a partner. Apparently the ladies were book club buds. I'd been hesitant in hiring someone so close to the previous owners, but it turned out that concern was all for nothing. Gloria had to be, hands down, the best assistant I'd ever had. She didn't take any of our shit, she rocked the administrative side of the business, and the woman *loved* to bring in the leftovers from whatever dinner she made the night before for all of us.

And *damn*, the woman could cook.

"Not on your life," she said with a snort. "I learned in

my youth never to trust a man as sly and good-looking as you. That's why I married Arnie. The man might have a horse face, but he'd walk across broken glass for me."

I placed my hand over my heart. "You wound me, Glo. Seriously. What I feel for you is very real."

"*Pfft*. What you feel for me is directly tied to your empty stomach." She pointed to the credenza behind her desk. "But if it'll make you feel better, I did stop off and pick up some donuts on the way in. Got the first batch that had just come out of the fryer."

"Have I told you lately that you're the best thing that's ever happened to me?" I flirted as I headed toward the closed box.

I could still feel the heat coming off the box, telling me they were nice and fresh. I bit the first donut clean in half and let out a grateful moan just as the door that led out into the garage opened and Cannon stepped into the office, wiping the sweat off his forehead with a clean shop towel.

"Christ. It's hotter than Satan's asshole out there."

"Language," Gloria admonished with a scowl.

Cannon gave her a flat look before looking to me and asking, "Remind me again why we thought it was a good idea to hire my mom's best friend to run the office?"

I stuffed the last bite of the first donut into my mouth and snagged a second, holding it in the air as I garbled through a full mouth, "Because she feeds us."

"Farah feeds us too," he said, speaking of his wife.

"No offense, my man. You know I got nothing but love for your woman, but she can't cook for shit. The guys we got out there to do the grunt work won't touch her stuff, even though she's the boss's wife. That's gotta tell you something."

He opened his mouth to defend her, but quickly snapped it closed, knowing I was right. "Whatever," he eventually grumbled as he headed for the mini-fridge we kept stocked with cold beverages. He grabbed a bottle of water and twisted the cap off. "She's getting a little better."

"Uh huh." I smirked. "Keep telling yourself that."

"Stone," Gloria spoke, pulling my focus from ragging on Cannon. "The parts you ordered for that '01 Honda Civic should be in later today. You want me to call the owner and let her know her car should be ready in a day or two?"

I thought back to seeing Willow in those goddamn leggings, showcasing a body I hadn't even known existed. "Nah. Hold off on that for now." Even after installing those new parts, that car was still a piece of shit, no two ways about it, and for some reason, thinking about putting Willow back into it rubbed me the wrong way.

"You sure?"

"Yeah. I'll give her a heads up myself. Don't worry about it."

I shifted my focus to Cannon who'd just finished draining his water and was wiping his mouth with the back of his hand. "We got any loaners we can put Willow in until I get her car squared away?"

Instead of answering, he stared at me in silence, blinking slowly. I let out a frustrated sigh, knowing exactly what he was thinking. "Whatever's goin' on in that head of yours, just stop."

He held up his hands in surrender. "I didn't say anything."

I crossed my arms over my chest, feeling my biceps strain with added tension. "You didn't have to. It's written all over your face. She's just a client, that's it."

"Uh huh," he mumbled skeptically. "Sure it is."

"I'm serious," I grunted. "Whether we have the parts or not, it's still gonna take me a few days to get to her car, and I just caught her this morning walking to work. Apparently she's been doing it for days."

His chin jerked back. "In this heat?"

"Exactly. Look, you said it yourself, her sisters are bitches. Doubt they're gonna help her out now that she's without a ride. She needs a way to get around. Besides, didn't you say her dad was sick or something? That's all I'm concerned about."

I could tell he desperately wanted to give me shit, but fortunately let it drop. "Wish I could help you, man, I really do. But all our loaners have been lent out."

"Shit."

"*But . . .*" he dragged out, a shit-eating grin stretching across his face, "Big Red's still out there in the lot. You know, if you're willin' to part with her for little while, that is."

He was talking about the '66 Chevy C10 Fleetside I'd restored years ago. That pickup had been one of my first restorations, which kind of made it my baby. I'd gone out of my way to keep everything as authentic as possible, right down to the paint job. The body was a sleek, shiny red with a white roof and stripe down the side. It was a sweet-as-hell ride, and I'd never been a fan of letting anyone else get behind the wheel of her.

Without saying a word, I stuffed the last of my third donut in my mouth and started for the garage.

"You're gonna let her drive it, aren't you? I knew it!"

I lifted my hand, holding my middle finger in the air as I walked off. There was nothing left to say, really, because I *was* going to let Willow drive Big Red. I was going to loan her my baby just so she didn't have to walk in the heat anymore.

"Tell her I said hey when you drop it off," he called after me before the door to the office closed on his obnoxious voice.

There wasn't a doubt in my mind I was in for endless harassment from my partner over this. And that was the last thing I needed.

Son of a bitch.

Chapter Eight

WILLOW

I sat at my desk in the quiet reception area, chewing on my thumbnail as I stared at the helmet resting on the ledge.

When Stone had taken off earlier, neither of us had noticed I'd still been clutching the only thing that would come between his head and the unforgiving road if the worst came to pass and he were to crash.

He needed that helmet back fast.

Problem was, after the endorphin high from my ride on the back of his bike had finally worn off, reality set in and I burrowed deep in my own head, replaying everything I'd said and cringing at the case of verbal diarrhea I'd come down with.

My whole morning had been spent trying to decide if I should call, text, or if it would be better for me to go right to the garage so there wasn't a delay.

After way too much time and contemplation, my anxiety finally got the better of me, and I decided to go the text route. Unfortunately, that meant overthinking what I was going to text. I'd drafted and deleted about a million messages.

Me: *Hey, Stone. It's Willow.*
"No." *Delete*
Me: *Wassup!*
"Oh God." *Delete.*
Me: *To whom it may concern . . .*
"What the hell is wrong with me?" *Delete.*
"Hey Willow. Whatcha doing?"

"Gah!" I threw my hand out in a karate chops motion and I whipped around in my chair so fast I spun two full rotations before smacking my hands on my desk to bring me to a stop.

"I'm so sorry. I didn't mean to scare you. I thought you heard me come in." Shane, my boss's wife—but more importantly, Stone's sister—was standing in front of my desk. Her lips were curled between her teeth to suppress her smile.

"No, it's fine. Sorry. I wasn't paying attention."

She waved me off. "It's cool. Sweet karate chop, by the way. You aim that at a person's throat, they'll go down for sure."

My whole face flushed a hot, dark crimson. "Oh, uh . . ."

"Don't be embarrassed," she said. "Honestly, you looked really cute doing it."

I felt the corner of my lips tick up in a grin. Like Lark, Shane had never been anything but nice to me, always stopping at my desk to chat for a bit before moving to the back to visit her husband. I really liked her. "Thanks."

She giggled happily. "No problem, babe." She leaned her elbows on the ledge of my desk. "So how are things? What's new with you?"

It was the same question she asked every time she came in, and I gave her the same answer I always did. "Nothing new with me," I admitted, wishing I actually had something to share. "Same old, same old."

She poked her bottom lip out in a pout. "Seriously? No new man we can dish about?"

I felt that blush return and lowered my head a bit. "No man," I said quietly, all the while thinking to myself, *unless you count my pathetic crush on your older brother.*

"You know, one of these days, I'm gonna come in here, and you'll be singing a different tune." She shot up straight with an enthusiastic, "Ooh!" like she's just been hit with a brilliant idea. "What if I set you up with someone? I know a lot of great guys who'd gladly trample over each other for a chance to take you out."

"Oh, uh . . . I don't know. I've never been very good at dating." I wasn't sure there'd ever been a bigger understatement in the history of the world. To be honest, it was sheer luck and blind determination that I hadn't ended up a sad twenty-nine-year-old virgin.

She opened her mouth to say something, only to cut herself off when her eyes shifted across my desk, landing on the helmet. "Is that Stone's helmet?" she asked, pointing to where it sat.

My back shot straight and my skin began to tingle

uncomfortably. "Y-yeah. He forgot it after he gave me a ride this morning."

Her eyes widened for a split second before returning to their normal size, and I got the distinct impression that she was attempting to school her features into a neutral look for some reason. "He gave you a ride this morning? Like, on his bike?"

"Um . . . yes?"

"Interesting," she muttered so quietly it was almost like she'd been talking to herself.

My head tipped to the side in confusion. "What's interesting?"

She blinked, as if coming out of a daze, and shook her head. "Oh, nothing. Nothing at all. Don't mind me. I'm just gonna—" She pointed toward the back where Jensen's office was.

"Oh, yeah. Sure."

"Talk to you real soon, babe."

For some strange reason, the way she said that made it sound like a promise.

THE SHOW I'd turned on played at a reasonable volume, but as my focus drifted once more to the helmet resting on my coffee table, it turned into background noise, like voices muffled by running water.

As hard as I tried to keep my mind from drifting, I just couldn't seem to help myself. It seemed like every minute my thoughts traveled back to this morning when I'd been on the back of Stone's motorcycle.

At first, the fear of crashing had kept me from focusing on anything else, but eventually, I realized that Stone had told the truth. He really did know how to handle himself on that bike, and as the seconds ticked by that fear faded. Surprisingly, I really did feel safe with him, and once I'd loosened up a bit, I was able to enjoy myself.

With that came the realization that I was pressed against the man I'd been thinking about for months so tight not even light could get through. Being that close to him had been a particular fantasy of mine for longer than I cared to admit, and thinking back to that morning made my skin feel fevered and tight. When I remembered how the muscles in his stomach had flexed and rippled against my palms through the thin material of his T-shirt, a dull, persistent throb took up residence between my legs.

He was just so damn big, and being wrapped around him like a koala had been out of this world. I wasn't ashamed to admit there were a few—dozen—times during the short ride that I'd burrowed my nose in the back of his shirt and inhaled deeply. His usual motor oil and woods scent smelled fresher, like the wind that had been whipping around us had made it crisper somehow.

If I thought I'd been addicted to his scent before, it was so much worse now that I'd been up close and personal with it.

I was pulled out of my daydream by the rumble of a loud engine coming down the road. Determined to put Stone out of my head and focus on the show I'd been attempting to watch, I snuggled deeper into my cushy sofa and forced my eyes to stay the hell away from that helmet.

Instead of passing by, that engine grew louder and louder until it sounded like it was coming from right outside. I hopped up and moved to the front door, swinging it open, and quickly discovered it was because the truck making that noise was currently parked in my driveway.

The bright cherry red gleamed in the late evening twilight, and the white roof was shiny and clean. It was, without a doubt, an awesome truck. But I didn't understand what the hell it was doing in my driveway.

The rumble cut off just as I crossed my arms over my chest and stepped out onto the front porch. A second later, the sound of the driver-side door opening broke through the quiet of my peaceful little street, and Stone came sauntering around the hood, all graceful and predatory as usual.

His dark hair, cut short on the sides but kept longer up top, flopped over his forehead, and when he lifted a hand to push it back, his muscles flexed beneath all that tantalizing ink.

It was as if my overactive imagination had conjured him up out of thin air. Either that or I was living my very own *Sixteen Candles* moment and my own personal Jake Ryan had just shown up outside my door.

Get it together, Willow. This is real life, for crying out loud. Not some 80's teen romantic comedy.

"Hey," I said in greeting.

He lifted his head, those whiskey-brown eyes hitting me full on with all the strength of a sledgehammer. That ever-present blush I suffered whenever he was near flamed to life on my cheeks and neck. "Hey, mouse. Hope it's okay I swung by unannounced."

He could swing by unannounced any time he wanted, in the dead of night or at the butt crack of dawn for all I cared. Instead of saying that, I nodded and replied. "Uh . . ." I cleared my throat, determined to play it cool and not make a fool out of myself like I *always* did. "Y-yeah. Totally. It's totally fine. I wasn't doing anything. I swear."

So much for cool. *Damn it.*

One side of his mouth quirked up in a grin that made my nipples stiffen beneath my bra.

That's okay, you can still salvage this. Crossing my arms over my chest to hide my body's natural reaction to Gavin "Stone" Hendrix, I summoned up my nerve and attempted small talk that would contain no mention of sweat. "So, um, nice truck. That yours?"

He looked toward the vehicle while scratching at the few days' worth of stubble coating his jaw.

I wonder how that scruff might feel between my thighs.

"I guess technically it's yours. For right now at least."

That statement pulled me out of my erotic thoughts and back to the present. "I'm sorry. What?"

He moved to the base of the porch steps, resting one foot on the bottom stair and extended his arm to brace his hand on the banister. The veins in his forearm throbbed and bulged. It was arm porn at its absolute finest. "It's your loaner."

A sense of dread washed over me. I couldn't imagine that a classic truck like that would be cheap.

As if sensing my rising panic, he spoke again before I

could get a word out. "It's from the garage, not through a rental company," he said quickly. "There's no cost to you at all. The truck's yours for as long as you need it."

My mouth opened and closed several times as I gaped at him like a fish out of water. "You mean like, for *free*?"

"Yeah, mouse," he said on a chuckle. "For free."

That sounded way too good to be true. "Stone, I can't—"

"We do this all the time, Will," he interrupted. "It's just a loaner. It's not a big deal. You needed a ride. Well"—he flung his arm out at the truck—"now you have a ride."

I caught my bottom lip between my teeth and bit down as I studied the truck sitting in my driveway.

It really was fine as hell.

"Just one thing," he said, pulling my attention back to him. "You can drive a stick, right?"

Chapter Nine

STONE

I'D BEEN GRITTING MY TEETH SO HARD IT WAS A WONDER my molars hadn't turned to dust. Each time she shifted gears and the truck made that godawful grinding noise, I could feel my balls burrow up into my stomach a little more.

I'd silently apologized to my baby more times than I could count for what she'd been going through the past ten minutes.

When I'd asked Willow if she could drive a stick, she'd assured me that her father had taught her when she was younger, but that it had been a long time since she'd driven one, so I'd offered to take her out for a refresher.

And now I was living my nightmare. By the time I got Big Red back, I'd probably have to replace the entire fucking transmission.

"Sorry!" Willow called loudly over the grinding gears as she attempted to shift from second to third. "I swear I've done this before. I just need to get back into the rhythm of it."

I unclenched my jaw, swallowing the blood inside my mouth from biting the inside of my cheek. "It's cool." I offered her a grin that I hoped didn't look as forced as it felt. "You're doing great."

Lying wasn't wrong if you were doing it to make the other person feel better, right?

Willow cringed as she shifted again. She was sitting so close to the wheel it was nearly fused to her chest, like the closer she was to the pedals, the better she'd be able to drive.

She shifted into neutral as we closed in on a stop sign, pressing down on the brake until we came to a stop. "I don't know if I should do this."

"You got this," I reassured her, wanting, for some reason I couldn't fathom, to make her believe in herself. Awkwardly shy was one thing, but I had a feeling she tended to get down on herself, and I hated the thought of that. "You just need to relax."

"I am relaxed," she gritted as she white-knuckled the steering wheel and pulled herself even closer to the dash.

"Uh huh. Sure you are, babe. I want you to do something for me, yeah?"

She nodded at the windshield, refusing to take her eyes off the road even though we were at a full stop. "Okay. Sure. Yeah. Because everything so far's been a piece of cake," she snapped.

My chin jerked back and a stunned chuckle bubbled from my throat. "Damn, was that just sarcasm from Willow Thorne?"

Her head jerked around, her eyes wide with shock. "Oh my God. I'm so sorry. That was really rude."

Fuck me, but I liked that attitude on her. "Don't you dare apologize. It's nice to see you have some claws. Seriously."

Her blush returned, and I felt my dick stir. Goddamn it, being around this woman was becoming a serious test of willpower. It didn't make a damn bit of sense why I'd feel drawn to her, but apparently my dick was a fan of bashful and unassuming. After damn near two decades of having particular tastes that ran more in the direction of biker bar babe, who knew I'd be capable of change. Problem was, Willow was most definitely *not* a one and done kind of chick. And I wasn't a long-term dude.

The best I could give her was friendship. That was, if she was willing to accept it.

"All right, so what do you want me to do?" she asked, yanking my mind out of the gutter.

"First off, how about you start by not choking the steering wheel to death?" I teased. She pulled her hands back like she'd just touched a hot pan, causing me to laugh. "Just hold it like normal, mouse."

"Okay. I can do that." She took the wheel again, this time holding it like a normal person would.

"Now scoot back in the seat. No need to be right up on the pedals. Stop thinking about *what* you're driving, and just drive like you always have. You know how to do this." I pointed at the stop sign through the windshield. "Now go."

She blew out a breath and nodded resolutely. Easing her foot off the brake, we started to roll, and she smoothly shifted into first gear, then into second, and so on until we were moving smoothly.

"I'm doing it!" she squealed delightedly, hopping a bit on the bench seat. "I've totally got this!"

"Yeah, you do, babe." I sat back with a grin, my balls dropping back down to where they belonged now that my baby was no longer at risk.

Willow

"WILLOW MATILDA THORNE, you sexy little land mermaid." Aurora planted her hands on her hips and gave me a shit-eating grin as I stood before her and Lark inside the first store we'd hit at the mall in Richmond. Just like Lark, she was sweet and kindhearted, but in her own loud, peculiar way. I'd laughed more in the past hour in her company than the whole last week combined. "Who knew you were hiding that perfect rack behind all those baggy clothes! You sneaky, adorable minx!"

Lark looked at her best friend like she should be locked in a padded cell. "Land mermaid? You mean human being?"

Aurora rolled her eyes dramatically. "Well, yes. But my description is a whole lot more fun and makes her sound exotic."

I lifted my hand in the air like I was in a classroom waiting for the teacher to pick me to answer a question. "Uh . . . I'd just like to add that my middle name isn't Matilda. It's Lee."

"Oh my God. Whatever," she groaned dramatically. "I felt like middle naming you, and I didn't know what it was, so I took a leap. Personally, I think Matilda is better than Lee." She crossed her arms and studied me seriously. "How tied to that name are you and would you be willing to change it?"

"Well, it was my grandmother's maiden name, so . . ." I let the rest of the sentence hang, assuming she'd get the gist of it.

"So that's a no then?"

"Yes, weirdo," Lark inserted. "It's a no."

She released a put-out sigh that made me giggle. "Fine. Enough about the middle name then. Let's talk about the fact that you are rockin' the *hell* out of that dress, baby doll."

Lark nodded in agreement. "She does not lie, honey. You look fabulous."

I trailed my hands down the soft jersey knit material. I was really far out of my comfort zone in something so fitted. There was something different between regular clothes being tight and workout clothes, but Lark and Aurora's insistence that I looked good had done wonders in bolstering my confidence.

"That dress is a winner. You're getting it," Aurora decreed. "Now let's get that fine ass of yours into some jeans, shall we?"

I tried on more clothes over the next few hours than I'd probably worn in the past six months total. Any time I blanched at a price tag or argued that it was too much, Aurora stormed up to the register, pulled out a credit card, and ordered the clerk to swipe away.

"Just let her do this for you," Lark had whispered after that very thing happened in the third store. "She's loaded, but it isn't about that. This is her way of showing you that you're one of her people. She's got a big heart and wants to do for her friends. It makes her feel good, so just let it happen."

As difficult as it was, I swallowed down any more arguments and thanked my new friend profusely for spoiling me.

"It's what I do, my angelic little starfish. And it's totally my pleasure if you wear this stuff out in public so the world can see how flipping gorgeous you really are when you aren't hiding."

Once I had a new wardrobe well in hand, we stopped for a quick lunch at this adorable little bistro before they surprised me with a trip to a salon and spa in the city where they treated me to a new hairstyle and a mani-pedi.

"So where to now?" Lark asked after sucking back the last of the champagne the spa offered while we were getting pampered. "I'm thinking we go to Sephora for makeovers."

"I actually did that a while back. I spent a small fortune on a bunch of makeup I've never worn because I'm not totally sure how to use it."

Lark let out a giddy squeak and bounced up and down. "Then I say we take this party back to Willow's for makeup lessons."

Aurora's hand went up in the air so fast it was a blur. "I second that motion."

I followed Aurora's example and finished off my champagne. "All right. Let's do this. I've got plenty of wine at the house anyway."

"Yes!" Aurora cheered, hooking her arm over my shoulders and leading me out of the salon. "I knew you and I were going to be the best of friends. The first time I saw you I said to myself, 'Self, that chick and you are gonna make Redemption your bitch.' And you know what? I was totally right!"

What had started as a tutorial on how to apply makeup to highlight what they called *my natural beauty* turned into a kind of game where we tried to outdo each other by drawing names out of a hat and giving that person a ridiculous makeover.

By the end of it, we were drunk off our asses and looked like drag show rejects. Aurora's phone had come out at some point to document the evening for posterity before Lark's fiancé, Clay, finally showed up some time after ten to pick them up and take them home.

"Good Christ," he grunted the instant my front door was whipped open. "What did you guys do to yourselves?"

Lark skipped/staggered over to her man, making the lopsided pigtails on her head bounce around like crazy. "We gave each other makeovers," she slurred, throwing her arms around his neck and puckering her smudged red lips for a kiss.

Clay smiled indulgently and leaned down, not giving a single damn that he was about to get makeup all over himself. Watching the two of them together gave me a pang of envy that tempered my drunken state a bit.

She batted her clumpy lashes up at him and asked, "Do I look pretty?"

"Always, baby. Most beautiful girl I've ever laid eyes on."

His arms looped around her waist so he could pull her tighter against him and my heart gave a little squeeze. What I wouldn't give to have a man look at me with such love and adoration.

And just like that, my mind circled back to Stone. What would it feel like to have him look at me the way Clay looked at Lark? Would I be able to survive something that swoon-worthy? My gut told me no, but damn, it sure would be nice to experience.

"All right, you lovebirds. Knock it off before you make me hurl," Aurora ordered, breaking up their romantic moment.

The girls gave me drunk, enthusiastic hugs, talking over each other as they decreed we needed to do another girls' night really soon before Clay finally managed to drag the two lushes out the door.

I tottered into the kitchen and forced myself to suck down two full glasses of water before heading for my room and collapsing on the bed, still covered in hideous makeup.

I didn't even care that I didn't have the coordination to wash it off, or what that could possibly mean for my poor skin come morning. I was too busy riding the high of a fantastic day.

I had new clothes. New hair, and despite how I currently looked, thanks to my new friends, I now knew how to do my makeup.

It truly had been the incredible girls' day that Lark had promised, and I couldn't wait for more.

Chapter Ten

STONE

I woke up that morning feeling like a hole had been punched right through my chest. Even all these years later, the pain was still so acute it tore through me like a jagged blade. It still took me by surprise just how hard this day hit me after so much time had passed, but just like the year before—and the one before that, and the ones before that—it never got any easier.

I couldn't be at home today, the solitude felt like a physical weight pressing down on my chest, slowly crushing me, so I'd climbed on my bike and gone into work. I kept to myself, cranking up the volume on the speaker to muffle the voices of the other guys working alongside me at the garage. I buried myself in work and tried to drown out the memories swirling around in my head.

Alice In Chains had been blaring through the Bluetooth speaker when my phone began to ring, cutting "Down In A Hole" off, mid-chorus.

Without having to look, I knew who was calling me. It was the same thing every year. Wiping my hands clean of grease and dirt, I pulled the phone from my back pocket and swiped to answer. "Hey, sweetheart."

A sweet, quiet voice laced with sadness carried through the line. "Hi, Stone."

Lyla Keller had been like family to me for years when I lived back in San Francisco, and the reason we were so close was all because of her older brother, Will Tolliver.

Not long after taking off from Redemption, I'd landed in a big city with no family and no friends. I was on my own for the very first time, and at first, it had been a serious shock. Truth be told, I wasn't sure I would have stayed had I not met Will.

He'd been a mechanic at the garage I'd just been hired on at, and I knew the moment I met him that he was different. Where I was hard and quiet and kept to myself, Will was the life of the party. Everyone he came into contact with instantly liked him. It was like he'd decided he was going to be my friend, whether I liked it or not, and he set about making that happen almost immediately.

In no time at all, we'd grown close, and as the loaner in a brand-new place, he'd taken me under his wing, so to speak. I spent Thanksgivings and Christmases with the Tollivers, being brought into the fold like I'd always been one of them.

They'd become a surrogate family to me, and Will had become my brother, so much so that blood didn't even factor in. I cared for the dude just as much as I cared for Shane. The worst day of my life was the day he'd died, and each year, when the anniversary of his death rolled around, it was another bone-rattling blow. I felt the pain all over again, just as strongly as the day it happened.

"How you doin', honey? You good?"

She sniffled through the phone, and I felt a sharp stab in my chest. "I'm okay. It's hard, you know that, but Mace is here, and he's doing a good job at taking care of me," she said of her husband.

Mace was the lead guitar player for the famous rock band, Civil Corruption. He and the rest of the members had grown up with Will, the five of them thick as thieves from childhood all the way into them becoming adults.

What no one knew until years later was that Lyla had been in love with Mace since she was just a girl, but he'd refused to go there, dreading what it could potentially do to his and Will's friendship.

As sad as it was, it was Will's death that had finally pushed them together, but now they were happily married, with a gorgeous little baby girl, and I was glad they were able to lean on each other on a day like this one.

"He doing okay?" I asked, knowing Mace would be hurting just as bad as the rest of us.

"Yeah, we're all okay over here. You don't need to worry about us. I'm more concerned with how *you're* doing."

Moving out of the bay and into the forecourt away from all the noise so she could hear me better, I answered, "You got nothing to worry about. I'm all good."

There was a pause through the line, and I knew she was doubting me. "You sure?"

I couldn't help but smile. That was just Lyla. Will was

her blood, her protective big brother, but she had such a big heart, she was worrying more about me than thinking about herself. "Yeah, Ly. I'm good. Promise."

"Okay. Well, if you're sure . . ."

"I'm sure, sweetheart."

"How's life in a small town treating you? Done any cow-tipping or mudding recently?"

A low chuckle rumbled from my throat. "I don't live in some podunk town, dollface."

"If you say so," she said with a giggle. "So, what's new with you? Any lucky lady in your life yet? Has the hard-as-stone Stone settled down with his biker babe yet?"

"Christ, Ly," I grunted with humor. "Not this again." She was just as bad as Shane when it came to giving me shit about settling down. But even as I said it, I couldn't help but think about Willow. Especially how goddamn sexy she'd looked driving Big Red the other day . . . after she'd gotten the hang of it, of course. I'd been too stressed to appreciate her beauty behind my wheel before that.

Goddamn it, Stone, I silently chastised. *Get that you of your fucking head, already.*

"No one is meant to be alone for their whole life, Stone, especially not someone as incredible as you."

While she meant the words to be a compliment, it still rankled. I'd known pretty much all my life that relationships and all the chains that came with them were never in the cards for me. I'd never been shy about admitting that to the people in my life; I just wished they'd actually believe me.

"Trust me, babe, if I meet a woman who knocks me on

my ass enough to make me want to put a ring on her finger, you'll be one of the first calls I make."

That seemed to be enough to appease her. "And if that day ever comes, I might just have to force Mace's ass on a plane so we can fly down there for a visit."

"You ever feel like doin' that, darlin', you guys have a place to stay."

I could hear the smile in her voice when she said, "I might just have to take you up on that."

The subject shifted back to Will after that, and we spent some time reminiscing about the good times that I'd been trying to forget all morning long. Each memory was like a knife to the chest, but I knew it was what Lyla needed, and I wanted to give that to her.

Finally, a few minutes later, the call started to wrap up, and a wistfulness filled her voice as she whispered, "I miss you, Stone."

My voice lowered, growing gruff. "I miss you too, sweetheart. I just want you to know that no matter how far apart we are, you're in my heart, and you always will be. You're family."

She sniffled again. "Same goes for you. And if you need me for anything, I'm just a phone call away."

My chest clenched painfully. "Same, dollface."

We said our goodbyes a second later, and I hung up, spinning on my boot to head back toward the garage. When I lifted my head, I saw Big Red pulling into the forecourt. Willow parked close by the office and climbed out dressed in a pair of light gray joggers that showed off that incredible ass, a plain light blue t-shirt with a pair of flip flops on her feet. Her hair was bundled up on top of her head in a messy knot, but it didn't take away from her beauty.

My dick immediately stood at attention, and the skin over my muscles grew tight as she shaded her eyes from the sun with her hand and did a casual sweep of the parking lot.

She did a doubletake when she spotted me, clearly not expecting to see me, and lifted her hand in an awkward wave. Instead of turning toward the office, she changed course and took a few steps in my direction . . . only to stutter-step to a stop before whipping back around and lunging back into the truck to grab whatever it was she'd forgotten.

Fucking adorable.

A second later, she popped out with my helmet in her hand. The past two times I'd been with Willow, I'd been so consumed with thinking things I had no business thinking—namely, how much I wanted her and couldn't have her—that the helmet hadn't even been on my radar, and I'd left it behind twice.

I stayed rooted in place as she got closer, unable to move as she hit me with a shy, nervous smile. "Um . . . hi."

Friends. Just friends, I reminded myself over and over as a grin pulled at my lips. "Hey."

She shifted from foot to foot silently for a few beats, her sky-blue eyes studying my face in a way that made my skin prick. It was like she could see deeper than just the surface and sensed something there.

She cocked her head to the side, her brow furrowing. "You okay?"

"Yeah. I'm good."

She took a step closer, those shrewd eyes narrowing even more. "Are you sure? You seem . . . I don't know; upset or stressed out, maybe."

I tried not to let my face relay the shock I felt at her insightfulness. One of the reasons people called me Stone was because they couldn't get a read on me. I'd become a pro at keeping my feelings hidden behind a rock-hard mask of indifference, so the fact she could see through that mask blew me away.

I opened my mouth to feed her the lie that everything was fine when the words just fell out of their own accord, without any permission from me. "Today's the anniversary of a close friend's death. It's always a rough day for me."

Sympathy washed over her delicate features instantly. Her free hand came out, her fingers wrapping around my forearm. "I'm so sorry," she breathed, her voice dripping with emotion. "You shouldn't be here, Stone. You should have taken the day off to just deal."

I figured I'd already started, so I might as well just keep spouting the truth. And honestly, there was something about confiding in Willow that felt different than talking to Lyla about it. Something almost . . . freeing. "It's actually my day off, but I'm not a big fan of being alone today. I came in to get away from the silence at home. If I'd stayed there, I'd have just drunk my weight in whiskey until I passed out."

The sadness was still there, swimming in her eyes, but there was something else there that I couldn't quite put my finger on. At least until she spoke next.

When she let go of my arm and clasped her hands together, I had to grind my teeth against the heat she'd left behind and the idea that I wanted that touch back. "I get it. My mom died six years ago. The anniversary of that day always sucks."

I wanted to reach out to her but clenched my fists to keep from doing just that. "I'm sorry about your mom, babe."

"And I'm sorry about your friend." She shrugged and gave me a tiny smile. "I know there isn't really anything that'll make you feel any better today, but if you ever need to talk, I'm here."

Christ, she was undoing me. "Thanks, mouse. I appreciate that."

As if remembering why she'd walked over in the first place, her eyes flared and the hand holding the helmet thrust out, nearly smacking me in the chest. "I brought this for you," she said quickly. "I didn't want you to go another day without it. That motorcycle was a lot of fun, but you really need to wear that," she rambled.

I took the helmet and let out a chuckle. "Thanks, sweetheart."

She took a step back, shifting from foot to foot. "Well, I guess I'll let you get back to . . ." she threw her thumb over her shoulder, "you know. Work and stuff." She kept moving back as she pointed to the helmet I was now holding. "Be sure to wear that," she said in a semi-scolding tone. "Safety first."

One corner of my mouth hooked up in a smirk as she stumbled a little, tripping over her own feet before quickly righting herself. "Got it."

"Okay. Well . . . have a good day."

With that, she spun around, hustled back to Big Red, and climbed inside.

It was the damndest thing, but after just a few short minutes in Willow's presence, I suddenly felt better than I had all damn day.

Chapter Eleven

WILLOW

I'd been a bundle of nerves as I got ready for work Monday morning. The high I'd been riding from my shopping trip with the girls had finally worn off, leaving me questioning everything.

I worried the clothes were too flashy. I worried that my hair looked ridiculous with the new cut and highlights. I'd done my makeup exactly how Lark and Aurora had taught me, but now I worried that it was too much.

I stared at my reflection for a good twenty minutes, debating if I should wash my face and change into my old clothes simply because that was more comfortable. I'd been a wallflower for so long that trying to step out into the light was terrifying.

Like she had psychic powers and knew exactly what I was about to do, my phone pinged with a message from Lark before I could pull the trigger.

Lark: *You better not come to work in your old frumpy clothes. If* *you do, I'll tell Aurora and she'll come and kick your ass. Grab me a venti caramel macchiato on the way in? Thankssomuchloveya!*

That was all the encouragement I needed to keep from crawling back inside my comfort zone. Thirty was just around the corner, and I was determined to keep the promise I'd made to myself and start living. And my new look was the start of that.

The truck only stalled out a couple of times when I was trying to back out of the driveway, but as soon as I kicked the platform espadrilles off my feet, I had a much better feel for the pedals.

Note to self: don't drive a standard transmission in anything but flats.

I headed into town, bypassing the closest coffee shop, The French Press, which was just a little too pretentious and high priced for me, and pulled the truck into the parking lot of my favorite place, Hot Java.

The atmosphere there was more laid back, and they weren't so snooty that they price-gouged their customers just because they felt they could.

With a fortifying breath, I shut off the engine and climbed out of the truck, only realizing once my feet hit the asphalt, that I was still barefoot.

"Hellfire," I cursed under my breath, as I bent to grab my shoes from where I'd kicked them under the bench seat. I hopped from one foot to the next as I strapped them on, tripping over myself and nearly landing on my ass before I caught myself on the doorframe.

I cast a quick glance around to make sure no one had witnessed my latest fumble while silently cursing my clumsy nature. It was a wonder I hadn't broken every bone in my body at least three times in my nearly thirty years. It was so bad that my dad used to tease about needing to cover me in bubble wrap before sending me out into the world.

My sisters had both been on the track team in middle school and had gone on to be cheerleaders in high school. But my severe lack of coordination had meant sports and cheering were totally out of the question for me.

Needless to say, PE had been my most hated period all through school.

As I headed into the coffee shop, I couldn't help but think that I was taking my life into my own hands—and possibly a few innocent bystanders'—by wearing such high shoes, but I knew if I'd worn flats with this outfit, Lark would lose her mind when she saw me.

Aurora bought these shoes with their light taupe straps specifically to go with this outfit. The cropped jeans were a nice dark color that hugged my behind and thighs. My top was a delicate, flowy chiffon that had string that tied around my waist to keep the material nipped in. The blouse was a pretty blush color with a pattern in white and pales blue that the girls said made my light-colored eyes really pop.

I took careful, slow steps through the door to make sure I didn't trip again and joined the back of the line already formed at the register by the early morning crowd just as my phone pinged with an incoming text.

Pulling it out of my purse, I saw my sister Elaina's name on the screen and let out a sigh, knowing that if she was texting instead of calling, it was because she needed something from me and didn't feel like dealing with an argument.

Elaina: *Hey, Will. Noticed Dad's fridge and pantry were looking a little light last night. You mind hitting the grocery store tonight on your way home? I have book club, so I don't have time.*

Of course she doesn't, I thought bitterly. I was quickly coming to learn that if anything inconvenienced Elaina's day-to-day life in any way, she just wouldn't do it. The more time that passed, the more my sisters leaned on me to pick up their slack when it came to helping our father, the angrier I got. The more of their shit I swallowed, the worse that storm brewed inside me.

I wanted to text her back and tell her it was her turn to pick up groceries for Dad, but I knew it was pointless. She'd refuse, and the only person who'd pay for it was him. So I clicked reply and began typing.

Me: *Fine. I'll do it this time, but I'm going to need you to pay me back. With my car in the shop, money's a little tighter than usual.*

The message I got in return made my blood boil.

Elaina: *If money's so tight, maybe you shouldn't have gone on that shopping spree last weekend.*

"Because God forbid I do *anything* for myself," I huffed under my breath as I closed out the screen and stuffed the phone back into my purse, that storm growing into a tempest.

"Um, I think you're next," a voice spoke from behind me, pulling me out of my angry red fog.

My head shot up to see that the line had in fact moved as I'd been messing with my phone—something I hated when other people did it, so I kind of felt like an asshole just then—and the girl at the counter was waiting for me to step up.

"Oh, God. I'm sorry," I said, shuffling forward while looking over my shoulder at the same time to apologize to the man behind me. "I didn't mean—" That was a huge mistake. My balance was thrown off immediately, and midway through my apology, I rolled my ankle and started going down.

I would have been kissing tile if not for his quick reflexes. Before I had a chance to faceplant, a pair of surprisingly strong arms circled my waist like steel bands, and a second later, I was pressed against a nice, warm chest with an impressive amount of muscle.

"Whoa. You okay there?"

"Uh . . ." Heat crawled up my chest and neck to my cheeks as I tipped my head back and met his gaze. He didn't have anything on Stone in my eyes, but that didn't mean this man wasn't incredibly handsome. He *absolutely* was. Where Stone was all hard and rough, this guy was fresh and clean cut. He was dressed in a pair of slacks and a button-down shirt that was open at the collar and tucked in. His shoes were shiny, and his sandy blond hair was styled back away from his face. If I didn't have a thing for a certain inked mechanic, I would have swooned hard over this guy for sure. "Sorry. What?" His green eyes sparkled and his lips curved upward with amusement.

His chest vibrated against mine as he said on a chuckle, "I asked if you were okay."

"Oh. Oh! Yeah. Yes. I'm—I'm fine. Thanks."

The man lifted his brows high on his forehead. "You sure?"

Realizing that he was still holding on to me and that we

were squeezed together, I took a step back to put some space between us and force his arms to drop.

"Yeah. Thanks. You know, for catching me. That would've been bad."

"I imagine it would have really hurt."

I let out a snort-laugh as I thought back to the dive I took out of Stone's tow truck last week. "Yes, well, if you can believe it, that wouldn't have been the most painful tumble I've taken recently. I'm a bit clumsy."

His eyes dipped down like he was looking me over, and I could have sworn I'd seen appreciation in his eyes as he said, "Nothing wrong with that." He extended his hand out to me. "I'm Alex."

I returned his handshake. "Nice to meet you. I'm Willow."

"Willow," he repeated, his smile widening, revealing two rows of nice straight white teeth. "Beautiful name. It's fitting."

Oh my.

"So, Willow, can I buy you a cup of coffee?"

"Oh, um . . . I'm actually buying for me and my co-worker—my friend," I quickly amended. It felt wrong to call Lark my coworker, especially after this past weekend. She and Aurora had cemented themselves as more than acquaintances, and I was thrilled about that.

He smiled again. "Then can I buy you and your friend a cup of coffee?"

My instincts were screaming for me to slink away and hide from Alex's attention. I wasn't used to having a man who looked like him focus so intently on me, and it was throwing me completely off balance. But instead of caving to my instincts, I pushed them to the back of my mind and grinned. "Sure. Thank you."

He moved in beside me at the register, giving me the lead to tell the girl behind the counter what I wanted. Once he paid and I had my coffees in hand, I turned back to thank him again.

"Not a problem. It was nice meeting you, Willow. Hopefully I'll see you around soon."

I couldn't remember what I said in return, but I was pretty sure it included a lot of blushing and stumbling over my words, as was my style. I moved out of the coffee shop feeling like I was floating on a cloud, and that sensation lasted all the way to the office.

Lark was waiting for me at my desk when I walked through the door and did a little hop dance the moment she saw me. "Oh my God, you look so hot!" she squealed, pulling her phone out of her back pocket. "Let me take a picture of you real quick to send to Rora. She's gonna flip!"

I stood there awkwardly as the shutter on her phone's camera sounded in rapid-fire succession. Once she finally lowered it, I walked the rest of the way to her and extended my arm holding her coffee. "Here you go."

"Ah, you're a lifesaver, hon. Thank you for this."

"Actually . . ." I pulled my bottom lip between my teeth and widened my eyes. "I didn't pay for it."

Her head quirked to the side in confusion. "Then who did?"

"The guy standing in line behind me." A smile slowly

parted my lips until it got so big my cheeks hurt. "I think—I think maybe he was flirting with me."

"Holy shit!" she enthused. "That's awesome! Was he cute? And he paid for *both* coffees?"

"First, yes, he was cute. Like, *seriously* cute. And he bought both coffees. He said my name was beautiful and fit me perfectly, and the way he said 'hopefully I'll see you around soon' made it sound like he actually did hope he'd see me around soon."

"Oh yeah, babe, he was definitely hitting on you. Did you give him your number?"

I bit down on my bottom lip. "Well, no."

"Why not?" Lark asked a little too loudly as her entire face drooped with disappointment. "If a hot guy flirts with you and buys your coffee, you're supposed to give him your number."

"But he didn't ask," I defended. Even if he had, I wasn't sure I'd have wanted to give it to him. "And I'm not—that is, I don't really—he wasn't . . ."

"He wasn't a certain scary-hot dude with tattoos and a motorcycle," she provided, plucking the words straight from my head.

I deflated a bit, plopping down in my chair, and slumped my shoulders. "That's pathetic, isn't it? It's not like he's given me any indication he'd be into me. I mean, he's been really nice lately, and he's helped me out of a few serious jams, and he taught me how to drive a stick last week, but that's all friend stuff."

"Hey," she started gently, coming around the front of my desk so she could lean her arms on the ledge, "you aren't pathetic. There's nothing to say that something won't happen between you and Stone. Sometimes friendship is the best building block for a relationship. And I know for a fact that he'd be lucky as hell to be with you."

"You're kind of awesome. You know that?"

"*Pfft.* Believe me, I know. I tell Clay every morning he should be thanking his lucky stars."

The door opened, and a second later a whistle sounded through the reception area, drawing Lark's and my attention to the door Laeth and Gage had just walked through.

"Damn, Will. You're lookin' nice today," Laeth said, his words setting my cheeks on fire.

I forced my head to stay up instead of bending my neck to hide behind the curtain of my loose hair.

"Thanks."

"That's more than we can say about you," Lark returned, looking the man up and down. "You look like shit run over."

She wasn't wrong about that. He was still wearing his sunglasses, which I assumed were hiding bloodshot eyes. His skin was sallow like he was sick, his hair was in disarray, and the stubble on his face was a good week past needing a shave. He looked rough, and not in the way I thought was hot on Stone.

"Partied a bit too hard last night," he said, spreading his lips into a cocky smile that more than likely got him laid regularly. Because even as wrecked as he looked just then, there was no denying that he was hot.

"Just like every night," Gage grunted next to him.

I didn't know exactly what was happening between my

bosses, but being a quiet observer, it was clear that Gage and Jensen both had a problem with how often Laeth was going out drinking and carousing. They weren't mad, though. The more I watched, the more I realized they were worried.

I wasn't sure what he was trying to escape night after night through the bottle and willing women, but I hoped he'd eventually let his friends pull him out of that darkness.

"Don't be jealous," Laeth teased. How he managed to still have swagger with a hangover was beyond me, but he sure as hell did.

"Not jealous," Gage grunted, shoving Laeth away from him. "You smell like a goddamn distillery. It's turning my stomach." He cast a look back over his shoulder, telling me, "You really do look nice today, Willow," before the two of them continued to bicker their way down the hall.

And I'd be lying if I said that didn't feel pretty incredible to hear from them.

Chapter Twelve

WILLOW

It had been a good day.

Actually, that was an understatement. It had been a *great* day. At least until I got to my dad's house to go through his kitchen and see what all he needed, only to discover that Elaina had seriously downplayed the need for food in his house.

I'd played it off that I was totally fine for my father's benefit as I stewed in my anger while making a grocery list that took up the front *and* back of the page.

By the time I got to the store, I was in serious need of an outlet, so I cued up the Pissed Chick playlist on my phone, stuffed earbuds in my ears, and got to work. I was halfway through shopping, Alanis Morissette wailing about how you oughta know in my ears, when I rounded the corner and my cart crashed into someone else's.

"Sorry, I—" The rest of the words died in my throat when I looked up and saw the cart I'd plowed into belonged to none other than Stone himself, the very man

I'd been thinking about nonstop since my talk with Lark earlier that morning. "Stone," I said on a gasp, sucking back the air that my lungs had expelled at the mere sight of him. "Hi."

He said something I couldn't hear over the music ringing in my ears.

I gave him an apologetic smile and yanked the buds out of my ears. "Sorry, I didn't hear you. What was that?"

The song had just reached the chorus, the volume so loud it carried several feet, and I could tell from the grin on his face that he definitely heard it. "Wow. Didn't take you for an Alanis fan," he said in that gravelly rasp that always made my skin tingle and pressure build between my thighs. What could I say? The man gave great voice. I didn't know if male phone sex operators were a thing or not, but if they were, he could make a freaking *fortune*.

"Oh, uh, yeah. Sometimes. I have a playlist I like to listen to it when someone's made me ragey."

On cue, the song ended and the next queued up; this time it was Rage Against the Machine's "Killing in the Name."

His eyes went big at the sound of it. "You're just full of surprises, mouse."

I giggled awkwardly, my face flaring with a blush when it morphed into a snort. "Oh, uh . . . yeah." Scrambling through my purse for my phone—I finally found it at the bottom, of course—and hit pause. I really liked that song, so I'd have to start it from the beginning.

When I looked back at him, a crease had formed between his brows, and those light brown eyes were scanning me from top to toe—or at least from top to waist where the cart cut me off. "You look different."

Well, that wasn't really the response I'd been hoping for, that was for damn sure. The compliments I'd received from the guys at work, as well as the little thing with Alex in the coffee shop earlier that morning, had fueled me all day long, making me feel pretty damn good. But one frown and a not-so-positive remark, and just like that, I felt myself run out of gas and sputter to a stop.

"Um . . ." I looked down at myself and placed my palm on my belly to hold the pain in. "Yeah. Lark and Aurora took me shopping over the weekend. I got some new stuff."

His eyes were pointed at my chest, that furrow growing even deeper. "Oh."

That was it. Just *oh*. Talk about a blow to a woman's confidence.

Pasting a bright smile I certainly wasn't feeling to my face, I gripped the handle of my cart in a death grip and steered it to the side. "Anyway. It was good running into you. Uh, I should really . . ." I threw my thumb over my shoulder, even though I was walking in the other direction. "Things to do, you know?"

"Yeah. Sure. See you around." I took a step to pass him when he spoke up again. "Meant to ask, how's the truck holdin' up?"

"It's good. Thanks again for giving me a loaner. It was a lifesaver."

"Glad I could help." His eyes returned to mine, and for a blink I could have sworn he was going to say something else. Instead, he jerked his chin up in a silent goodbye and walked past me, those motorcycle boots of his thudding on the linoleum floor with every step he took away from me.

Well, so much for a relationship built on the foundation of friendship. It was as if the strides we'd taken the day he helped me remember how to drive a stick had never happened.

I stupidly thought that at the very least we'd become friends. Looked like I was *very* wrong.

Stone

Clutching the socket wrench tighter, I put more of my weight behind it as I tried to get the last mounting bolt off the carburetor, but the rusted piece of shit didn't want to budge.

"Goddamn it," I groaned as I pulled harder. "Come off, you stupid son of a bitch." As if sensing the shitty couple days I'd been having could get just a bit worse, the wrench decided to lose purchase and slip off the bolt, causing me to fall forward and slice the back of my hand open.

"Motherfucker!" I shouted, hurling the wrench across the garage. I headed toward the small bathroom I'd had rebuilt at the back of the garage. When I first bought the place, it hadn't been more than a small closet with a toilet that didn't work. It wasn't much of anything to write home about now, but at least it was clean and functional.

Chief followed after me, sitting on his rump just outside

the open door and staring at me as I grabbed the first aid kit from under the sink and went about cleaning the cut on my hand.

"Don't look at me like that," I told him, knowing those beady eyes of his were full of judgment. "It was an accident. Shit happens."

Truth was, it wasn't so much an accident as it was pure carelessness on my part. Ever since my run-in with Willow at the grocery store three days ago, I hadn't been able to focus on much of anything. I kept picturing her in that new getup of hers. If I thought she looked good in those workout clothes, the woman was a goddamn knockout when she did herself up.

At first I hadn't even recognized her. She'd been wearing a bit more makeup than usual, and all that long hair had been loose, hanging down her back in a silky curtain. And the image of having it wrapped around my fist as I sank my cock into her filled my head almost instantly. The erotic imagery only got worse from there.

Her bee-stung lips were slick with the palest pink color, and I found myself wondering what it would taste like if I were to close the distance between us and kiss her.

The top she'd been wearing wasn't very revealing, but it draped just enough at the front that I was able to see a hint of cleavage. Just like that, my dick stood at attention like I had all the self-control of a teenaged kid seeing his first pair of tits. It was pathetic.

And *Christ*, had she smelled good. All sweet and warm, like honey and sunshine.

I'd had to get the hell out of there before I did something stupid like slam her against the endcap and shove my tongue down her throat.

Walking away from her hadn't helped in the slightest, because when I looked back before she disappeared down the next aisle, I caught a glimpse of her ass and legs in those jeans of hers. The image of Willow on her knees in front of me as I coated those naked globes with my cum almost did me in.

For fuck's sake, the goddamn woman wasn't even my type! But the more time that passed, it was getting harder and harder to convince myself of that.

With my hand properly doctored, I moved back over to my latest restoration—a sweet 1970 Chevelle SS that I was bringing back to her former glory—and bent back over the open hood just I heard the sound of tires coming up my drive.

Chief stood, staring out along the property on alert until my sister's car came into sight. Being the good guard dog he was, he let out a single bark when Shane stepped out.

"Down boy," I ordered gently. He didn't hesitate to sit and thump his tail against the ground as he watched her grow closer. "She's welcome. At least until she gets on my damn nerves. Then you can run her off."

"Nice," Shane deadpanned, having gotten close enough to hear me. "Is that any way to greet your favorite sister?"

"It is when you're a pain in the ass. And you're my only sister, so try not to give yourself too much credit."

She rolled her eyes and patted Chief on the head as she passed him by. "The Chevelle's really coming along. Looks great."

"Thanks," I grunted as I gave the bolt that was making my life so damn difficult one last crank. It finally loosened and unscrewed the rest of the way. "So what brings you by? And where's the little monster?"

"Your sweet, precious nephew is spending some quality time with his daddy so Mommy can have a break. And as for your other question, can't a sister just come by to visit her big bro she hasn't seen in a while?"

I stood to my full height and grabbed the shop rag out of the waistband of my jeans to wipe the grease and dirt off my hands. "Since when do you come by just to hang? You always have an ulterior motive, so spit it out. As you can see, I'm busy," I said, pointing to the car that still needed a ton of work.

Partnering with Cannon had been a great move business-wise, but it hadn't left me with a whole lot of free time to work on my own projects, so when I had the rare day off, I spent hours out here, getting as much done as I could.

Moving to the '36 Harley Knucklehead I was also trying to restore, she hopped up on the seat and made herself comfortable, and I knew by the smug grin on her face that she was most definitely here to annoy the shit out of me.

"Busted. You know me so well, Gavin," she teased, using my real name just to mess with me. No one had called me Gavin since I was fourteen and discovered that my life was basically going to be shit until I was old enough to get the hell away from my mom and build a life for myself. "I am here for a reason."

Leaning against the side of the car, I crossed my arms

and ankles, settling in for whatever was to come. "All right, then get to it."

"Scoot and Caroline are planning a family dinner this Sunday," she said, speaking about our aunt and uncle. They'd been the ones to take us in when our mom bailed for good. I'd basically been old enough to go off on my own at the time, but Shane was still just a kid, six years old, and I didn't have the first clue what it took to take care of her, so I'd gone to live with my aunt and uncle too, so I could watch what they did and try to copy, giving my baby sister a better shot at a good life than I'd had when I was her age.

She'd stayed with them until she was old enough to go out on her own, but as ashamed as I was to admit it, I hadn't lasted nearly as long. Only a few years after Mom bailed, I'd taken off as well, needing to get the hell out of this town and away from the memories.

I owed those two people more than I could ever pay back for helping both of us when we needed them, but I was sad to say that I'd seriously dropped the ball since coming back.

"And before you try to make some excuse, attendance is mandatory," she added, her tone leaving no room for argument. She was dead serious. "They miss you, big bro. The least you can do is grace them with your presence for one evening. Not to mention, Brantley's been talking my ear off, asking when he's gonna get to see Uncle Stone."

A smile pulled at my lips and pinched my cheeks. Christ, I loved that kid. I missed him too, and I really needed to step up and do a better job of being there for him. "All right. I'll be at the dinner. Happy?"

She shrugged casually. "I've got a great life, so I'm always happy."

It was nice to hear her say that and to know from the expression on her face that it was true. Shane hadn't always had it so easy. It had been a bumpy road to get to that happy, for her and Jensen both. There was a point when I hated the man for breaking her heart when they were younger. But he'd come back. He worked his ass off to win her trust, took his lumps, and more than made up for the hurt he caused. I was glad that they'd worked everything out and were a family again.

"Well, since that's done, you can go. Like I said, I got shit to do."

Shit that did *not* include jerking off to the memory of a certain awkward wallflower turned bombshell. I'd taken care of that particular issue this morning—twice—before heading out here.

Fuck, I was a mess.

"Not just yet. There's one more thing," Shane said way too fucking gleefully as I groaned and dropped my head back.

"Jesus, you really are a pain in the ass. What is it?"

"I noticed your helmet was on Willow Thorne's desk at work a few days back, and when I asked about it, she said you gave her a ride into work."

I had a feeling I knew where she was going with this, but I tried not to let show the sudden tension locking up the muscles in my shoulder. "Don't make a thing out of this, Shane. It was hot as hell outside that morning, and she was walking to work because her car's a piece of shit. It's not that big a deal."

"Maybe," she said calmly. *Too* calmly. Suspiciously calmly. "But you see," she started again, and I knew she was about to lower the boom. "I already know that you and Jensen talked once, and you told him that you'd never had a woman on the back of your bike and had no intention of *ever* putting one there. So I know that you giving Willow a ride on the back of your bike, when I know for a fact that you've told other women there's no way you'd take them for a ride when they asked, is a *very* big deal. Whether you're willing to admit it or not."

Fuck. I'd have to remember in the future to never drink with my piece of shit brother-in-law again. It made us both too goddamn chatty, and apparently he ran back and told his wife everything we talked about. The gossipy little bitch.

"Shane. It's not—"

"And before you tell me it's not what I think it is, I'll also mention that I saw Big Red in the parking lot of Hot Java the other morning, and you'll never guess who climbed out of the driver side just as I drove past." She arched her brow like a villain in an action movie who was just about to reveal that he'd hidden the last bomb in the basement of a school building. "Or maybe you do."

"Shane," I said in warning.

But of course, my sister didn't listen for shit. "I'm sure you can imagine my surprise at seeing someone driving your baby like that. Especially when you threatened bodily harm to your entire family if any of us so much as touched that truck without your permission."

I dropped my arms and clenched my fists, feeling the muscle in my jaw begin to tick. "She couldn't afford a rental and the garage was out of loaners. She needed a ride while her car was being fixed."

"Uh huh. I'm sure that's all it is."

"You wanna stop tap dancing around your point and fucking get to it already?"

"I'd love to, thanks." She lifted her index finger in the air. "First, you give her a ride on your bike when you've sworn never to have another woman on the back of it." Her middle finger joined the first. "Then you let her drive your precious Big Red all by herself. There's only one conclusion I can draw from all of that."

"Don't say it."

Again, she didn't listen. "You *like* her," she singsonged. "You *like her* like her."

"What are you, twelve?"

"One might even go so far as to say you *lurv* her."

"That's enough," I barked, losing my cool for no good reason. "Whatever you've got goin' on in that head of yours, just stop. There's nothing happening between me and Willow and there never will be, so just drop it."

I felt like a piece of shit as I watched my sister deflate, but I couldn't let her continue down the road she was currently on.

"You know, you could do a whole hell of a lot worse than Willow Thorne. She's sweet and thoughtful and kind—"

"She's not my type," I grunted, turning back to the Chevelle and burying my head back under the hood.

"Yes, because all those skanky biker bitches are so much better."

"Drop it, Shane," I clipped.

She pushed off the Knucklehead and started toward me, coming to a stop on the other side of the car and slamming her hands down on the rusted metal. "No, I'm not gonna *drop it*. Why are you acting like it's such a terrible thing if you like someone? Your views on relationships are seriously fucking warped, big brother, and you need to get over your shit or you're going to be alone for the rest of your life."

I stood up so I could glare at her across the raised hood. "The fact you can say that to me, living with the shitty excuse of a mom we both had, not to mention the worthless pricks that were our fathers, seriously blows my mind."

"You aren't Carley," Shane snapped so loud Chief let out a low whine. "You aren't her, and you aren't your father. You're a good man, Stone. You deserve happiness."

"Yeah, well, it's not in the cards for everybody."

"It could be for you if you'd just get your head out of your ass and go for it."

"Well, that's not gonna happen, so let it the fuck go."

Knowing we both shared the same unflinching stubborn streak, she must have sensed that she wasn't going to get anywhere with this conversation, because she sighed and dropped her head in defeat. "Fine. But when you're old and gray and hunched over from arthritis in every bone, don't come crying to me that you don't have anyone to help you wipe your ass or lift you off the toilet. I'll be busy with *my family* while you're getting old and crusty all alone."

"Thanks so much for the imagery," I grunted.

"You're welcome," she snapped back, spinning on her heel and starting for her car, calling over her shoulder as she walked away, "I still love you, even though you're a freaking idiot."

I fought back the smile that wanted to pull at my lips and grumbled, "Love you too."

"And you better not bail on family dinner or I'm gonna kick your ass!"

With those loving parting words, she climbed into her car and backed out.

I looked down at Chief, quirking a brow and lifting my arms. "Where the hell were you, man? I said to get rid of her if she started to annoy me."

He let out a dog groan as he slid to the floor, falling over onto his side and promptly passing out.

"So much for man's best friend."

Chapter Thirteen

WILLOW

Today was the day. It was my time. I'd woken up this morning with a sense of determination. I was thirty years old. My twenties were officially behind me, and it was time to start living.

Taking risks. Putting myself out there. New Willow's life started today, and as I looked at my reflection in the mirror, a sense of confidence washed over that, until today, had been completely foreign to me.

Sure, things with Stone had gone absolutely nowhere. It had been three weeks since I'd crashed into him at the grocery store, and after a promising start of . . . well, I wasn't quite sure what . . . friendship maybe? I'd certainly been hoping for more, that was for damn sure. Anyway, all I'd gotten was radio silence.

But that was okay. Or at least that was what I kept telling myself.

It was probably—okay, definitely—delusional, but I couldn't help but think there was still time to build that foundation of friendship Lark had talked about that could hopefully lead to something more.

For now, I was going to celebrate this day with a nice dinner at the Cattleman, a fancy steakhouse, with my sisters and their families.

I wore the soft, fitted jersey knit dress I'd gotten with the girls during our shopping trip a few weeks ago. I'd gotten a bit better at wearing heels lately, so I'd decided to go a little more daring and attempted a pair of strappy gold stilettos that I thought looked good with the navy dress.

After an unsuccessful YouTube tutorial and subsequent call to Aurora to have her talk me through it on FaceTime, I'd successfully curled my hair into long, fat curls. My makeup was still soft and subtle since I wasn't a fan of my face feeling cakey, but all in all, I thought I looked pretty damn good. After a quick selfie to Lark, she agreed.

My car was still in the shop, so I hopped in the loaner truck and drove to the restaurant.

"Hi," I said to the hostess as I stopped in front of her stand. "Reservation under Thorne?"

She scanned through the iPad resting in front of her. "I'm sorry, ma'am, but there's no reservation under that name."

"Oh, um . . . well, my sister was the one who was supposed to make it, so maybe look under Harrison?"

She did another scan. "No, I'm sorry."

I felt some of that excitement from earlier deflate. "Okay, uh . . . I'll just call her and get this squared away."

The hostess gave me a placating smile as I stepped away

from her stand and moved out of the way for the couple waiting behind me.

The front of the restaurant was starting to get crowded, so I headed outside as I pulled my phone from my purse and called Elaina.

It took five rings before she finally answered, "Hello?"

"Hey, it's me. I'm at the restaurant right now. What name did you make the reservation under?"

There was a long pause before she spoke again. "What reservation?"

My heart leaped up and lodged itself in my throat. "The reservation at the Cattleman," I told her. "For my birthday dinner? You were supposed to call and make one, remember? Are you guys on your way?"

I knew what was coming next before she even said anything. "Oh my God, Will, I completely forgot. I'm so sorry."

"You forgot to make the reservation or you forgot my birthday?"

There was another pause, and this one was like a punch to the stomach. "I'm so sorry, honey. I don't know how this slipped my mind."

I closed my eyes and pulled in a deep breath, willing the tears that were burning the backs of my eyes to disappear. "So you guys aren't coming." It wasn't a question.

"I'll make this up to you, I swear. I'm really sorry. But you guys have fun okay? Enjoy dinner, and we'll celebrate another night. How's that sound?"

"Yeah," I croaked. "Whatever. That's fine."

I wanted to scream at her that it *wasn't* fine, that her

forgetting something as big as my thirtieth birthday really hurt my feelings, but there was no point. She'd think I was overreacting and give me a hard time for being upset, so instead of getting in a fight with her, I hung up and tucked my phone away, deep breathing to keep my emotions at bay before heading back into the restaurant. There wasn't time for me to throw myself a pity party. Crissy and her family would be here any minute now, and we didn't have a table.

I moved back to the hostess stand, feeling a lot less confident than I had when I first got here. "Hi, sorry about that. Looks like she forgot to call ahead, but is there any way I could get a table for five?"

She consulted something on her iPad before looking back at me with aggravation clear in her expression. *You and me both, sister*, I thought to myself.

"We have a table, but we can't seat you until your whole party arrives."

Shit. "They'll be here any minute. I swear."

"I'm sorry. That's the policy. You can have a seat while you wait," she offered, dismissing me and waving the next diners over before I'd even had a chance to step aside.

I managed to squeeze myself into the only empty spot on the crowded bench that ran along the wall and waited for the rest of my family to get here so the night could hopefully be salvaged.

Five minutes turned into ten. Ten turned into fifteen, and I was just about to call Crissy when she came scurrying through the door in a seriously disheveled state.

I shot up and waved her over, scanning the entrance behind her for my niece, nephew and brother-in-law. "Hey, where's everybody else? They won't seat us until the whole party's here."

She stopped in front of me and blew her bangs out of her face. "I'm so sorry."

Oh God. Not again.

"Aiden got a stomach bug from some kid at school, and it's making its way through the whole house right now."

"Oh no. Crissy, I'm sorry. So it's just the two of us then?" *Man*, that hostess was going to hate me.

"I can't stay," my sister said, checking the time on her watch. "I wanted to run by to give you your birthday present, but I have to get back. Phil was hugging the toilet as I was heading out the door, so I need to get home to the kids."

As far as excuses went, it was definitely better than forgetting altogether.

"Cris, you didn't need to do that. You should have just called. I would've understood."

"Are you kidding? My baby sister's turning thirty. That's a big deal. I wanted to make sure you had your present before your birthday was over." She looked around the entryway. "Where's Elaina?"

"Oh, um . . ." That burn in my sinuses came back. "She forgot."

Crissy's face pinched up like she'd just sucked on a lemon. "You've got to be kidding me."

I shrugged, my heart clenching in my chest. "Wish I was."

"All right. Then I'll stay. I'm sure Phil and the kids will be fine for a couple hours."

"No, you don't have to do that," I insisted. "Really, it's fine. They need you, so you should go."

"But—"

I reached out and squeezed her arm, giving her a smile that felt stiff and brittle. "Seriously, go home and take care of the kids. It's all good."

She looked like she wanted to continue arguing, but eventually gave in. "I'm so sorry, babe. I'll make this up to you." She shot forward and pulled me into a tight hug. "Happy birthday, sweetie."

"Thanks," I said past the lump that had formed in my throat as we pulled apart.

She handed over a festive gift bag that had tissue paper sticking out of the top. "I swear, Willow. I'll make this up to you."

My smile was a little more genuine this time around. "Not necessary. Now go home. And give your family my love once they're all less pukey."

"I will," she said with a giggle, taking a single step back. "And Willow?"

"Yeah?"

"You look really pretty tonight. The new clothes suit you."

She left after that, and I headed back to the hostess stand. Having witnessed the scene between my sister and me, the agitation on the woman's face had morphed into pity, which was even worse.

"I appreciate you holding the table, but it looks like I'm not going to need it after all."

"You could have a seat at the bar," she offered. "We still serve our full menu there. And first drink is on the house."

I appreciated the offer, but at the moment, I couldn't imagine anything worse than eating my birthday dinner alone at a five-star restaurant.

"Thanks, but I'm just going to head out. Have a good night."

"You too," she called after me. "And happy birthday."

Chapter Fourteen

WILLOW

The downstairs lights of my dad's house were still on when I pulled up in his driveway, and I breathed a sigh of relief that he might still be awake. After the epic failure that was supposed to be my birthday dinner, I needed my dad something fierce. He had a gift for making me feel better, no matter how down I was.

"Dad?" I called as I stepped inside the house and closed the door behind me. I could hear the television playing in the living room, but that was it. When I turned the corner and peeked in, I found him asleep in his old, worn recliner.

He looked so peaceful when he was sleeping. For him, sleep was a relief. It was the only time he didn't have to battle his own mind. It was the only time he found peace. Not wanting to wake him, I slinked across the carpet to shut off the TV, but when I got closer, I saw a familiar brown leather album resting face down on his stomach.

With gentle hands, I grabbed the remote and turned off the television before reaching for the album.

It was open to a page with a glossy 8x10 photo of my mom and dad on their wedding day. I stood there for a solid minute, looking down at it as my heart clenched and throbbed, clenched and throbbed.

They looked so damn happy. The love shining in their eyes as they stared at each other never failed to steal my breath every time I saw this photo. It was just one of many photos of the two of them with that very same look in their eyes.

Their marriage wasn't perfect. I wasn't sure such a thing even existed. But they loved each other with their whole hearts.

Their love was so big and so strong that six years after her death, my father still pulled out their wedding album from time to time when he was missing her fiercely.

Moving backward toward the couch, I sat across from my sleeping father and started flipping through the pages, looking at picture after picture of my parents in love.

God, I wanted that. I wanted a man to look at me the way Dad had looked at Mom. I wanted to love someone with all my heart and have them love me back just as much. My dad used to tell us that Mom was his everything, and that was what I wanted. I wanted to be someone's everything.

I sniffled back the tears I'd battled all evening as I flipped through the album, carefully studying every picture as I told myself that what they had was exactly what I wanted.

"You look just like her. You know that?"

My head shot up at the sound of my dad's voice. "Sorry. I didn't mean to wake you."

"You didn't, pumpkin." He straightened out of the recliner and came over to the couch to sit beside me. "Out of all three of our girls, you're the one who looked the most like your mother from day one."

I gave him a look. "I don't know about that. Mom was a knockout."

He chucked me under my chin, lifting my gaze to his. "Precisely. Pure beauty inside and out. Just like my baby girl."

My smile trembled as I laid my head on his shoulder and confessed on a whisper, "I miss her."

"I know you do, sweetie. I miss her too."

We sat there in silence for I don't know how long, looking through the album at all the happy memories inside. My mom might not have understood me, but she loved me without conditions. Her attempts to change me hadn't come from a bad place. She just didn't want me to be hurt. That was all. She was scared that me being different would lead to pain. But once she accepted me for me, I never felt anything but unconditional love.

"It's getting late. You should head up to bed. It's a school night."

I curled my lips between my teeth and bit down to keep the sob climbing up my throat from breaking loose. My dad came and went so fast it gave me whiplash. One minute I'd have him, and the next he'd be gone, just like that. I couldn't let him see me upset. In this state, he wouldn't understand

and all it would do was agitate him and make things so much worse.

Lifting my head, I looked at him with a forced smile. "You're right. It's getting late. Why don't you go up to bed and I'll shut everything off down here?"

He leaned in to press a kiss to my forehead. "Okay, pumpkin. Love you."

"Love you too, Daddy. Goodnight."

I waited a few minutes for him to get upstairs and into bed, knowing it wouldn't take long for him to fall back to sleep. He'd always been the type that could pass out as soon as his head hit the pillow.

Once I thought it was safe, I carried the photo album back to the bookshelf beside the fireplace and slid it into place. I made sure everything was locked up tight before shutting off all the lights and heading out to the truck.

I sat in the silent cab as my mind whirled in a million different directions. I could go home after such a terrible night, but I didn't want to. I didn't want the night to end on such a sour note.

This was supposed to be a rebirth of sorts for me. It was supposed to be the beginning of something. I couldn't let it start off this way.

The bright colors of the gift bag caught my eye, and I reached over to pull Crissy's present into my lap. I removed the tissue paper and dug down into the bag before my fingers curled around the items inside.

There was a gift card to the spa Aurora and Lark had taken me to with written orders to pamper the hell out of myself.

Inside the box was a skincare set from Sephora that I knew for a fact had cost a small fortune because I'd been eying it myself but couldn't afford it. The set came with all kinds of serums and creams and masks for optimum pampering. It was an incredibly thoughtful gift, and I really loved it.

I tore open the envelope to the card, flipping the card open and reading the message scrawled in my sister's swirly, elegant handwriting.

Here's to the big 3-0 and new beginnings! Grab life by the balls and live it, little sis. Love you!

Beneath that, her kids and husband had signed their own names with smiley faces and other flourishes.

I smiled as I tucked the card back into the envelope and set it aside, placing everything back into the bag while the words Crissy had written played over in my mind. After the night I'd had, her pep talk came at the most advantageous time. I'd desperately needed it.

I *wanted* to grab life by the balls and live it. And, damn it, that was exactly what I was going to do.

I kicked off my shoes, shoving them under the seat so I could feel the pedals better, and put the truck in gear.

Reversing out of my dad's driveway, I pointed the truck away from my house and started in the opposite direction with a specific place in mind. I'd have been lying to myself if I said I wasn't going with the hopes of running into Stone. But whether or not he was there wasn't going to change the fact that I was stepping out of my comfort zone tonight. I was done being the wallflower.

I'd only been inside Bad Alibi a few times since I became

legal to drink, and each time my anxiety at being surrounded by so many people had forced me to leave within the first half-hour of arriving.

But not this time.

Pushing away the discomfort I felt at seeing how crowded the parking lot was, I navigated around the other cars until I found an empty space in the back. I parked the truck and slid my fabulous heels back on before climbing out and slamming the door shut.

"You can do this," I whispered to myself as I pulled in a fortifying breath and squared my shoulders. "You can go in there, have a couple drinks, and have fun, damn it. And you will *not* trip on your heels while walking across this parking lot."

The bar was so loud when I first pulled the door open, I had a brief moment of doubt that I could do this. But instead of letting it rule me, I stepped inside and slowly made my way toward the bar, keeping my eyes pointed forward so I didn't stumble and fall flat on my face in front of all these people.

The long U-shaped bar near the back was crowded with people, but I managed to find an empty barstool near the end, and hoisted myself up.

The bartender stopped in front of me, scanning me up and down with a vague sense of familiarity in his eyes. "Willow? That you?" he asked, surprise written across his craggy features.

"Hey, Buck" I greeted. I might not have come to the bar often, but I still knew a lot of these people from seeing them around town. Buck owned Bad Alibi with his wife, Darla, and even though we weren't close, I still knew them well enough to know I liked them both. That was one of the things about living in a small town, everybody seemed to know everybody.

"What can I get you, darlin'?" he asked while pulling the hand towel from his shoulder and using it to wipe down the bar directly in front of me.

"Um, I'm not really sure. I've never been a big drinker. What would you suggest?"

He gave me another look before answering. "Well, based on your fancy get up I'm assumin' tonight is something special? We're more of a whiskey and beer place, but if you want, I could mix you up a margarita."

I gave the big, burly man a bright smile and nodded my head. "A margarita sounds great, thanks."

"You got it, darlin'." He got to work on my margarita while asking, "So what's got you all dolled up tonight? Special occasion?"

"Well, it's actually my birthday," I confessed, feeling my face flush with heat.

His gaze returned to mine, his eyes widening with bewilderment. "And you chose to spend it *here*?"

I couldn't bring myself to admit that my sisters had bailed on me and that my father, the only person who would have cared under normal circumstances, didn't remember what day it was because his mind was slowly failing him. I simply shrugged and gave him a grin I hoped didn't look as fake as it felt. "I figured this is as good a place as any, right?"

"Can't argue with that," Buck returned, dumping the concoction he just mixed together into a cocktail shaker and giving it a nice hard shake. "In that case first drink's on the house," he said as he poured the margarita into a glass. He stuck a straw in the top and slid it in front of me, shooting me a wink before knocking his knuckles against the scuffed wood. "Happy birthday, darlin'," he said as he took a step back. "Holler if you need anything else."

With a friendly smile, he turned on his boots and headed down the bar to take care of the other customers, leaving me alone with my birthday drink. I took the first sip, the citrusy tartness exploding on my tongue as I sucked the liquid down.

It had to have been one of the best margaritas I'd ever tasted. Before I knew it, half the drink was gone. Feeling a little bit lighter, I spun around on my stool and scanned the bar, recognizing faces here and there scattered throughout the crowd.

I grew disheartened the longer I looked around and didn't see his face. But when I eventually glanced to the section where the pool tables were, one step up from the main bar area, I spotted Stone sitting at a clump of tables that had been pushed together. And he wasn't alone.

My heart sank as I watched him pull a gorgeous blonde onto his lap, making her giggle at something he said.

She was all curves and long, wild hair. Based on how revealing her outfit was, she was comfortable in her own skin, and didn't mind showing as much of it as she could legally get away with. In other words, she was absolutely nothing like me.

Chapter Fifteen

WILLOW

My heart suffered a million tiny paper cuts as the woman bent to whisper something in his ear. But the pain grew to be too much when I saw her tongue peek out and run along the cord at the side of his neck.

Spinning back to face the bar, I stared down into my glass, silently willing it to fill itself up.

As if sensing my need, Buck reappeared a second later. "Get you a refill?"

I gave him an appreciative look and answered, "Yes, please. That would be great."

"Put it on my tab," a voice said behind me.

I spun to face the guy standing just off to my left. He had several days' worth of stubble coating his strong, square jaw, and his thick black hair was long enough that it curled up around the collar of his plain white T-shirt. The first thing I noticed was his deep, dark blue eyes. The second thing was the leather vest over his shirt that sported a familiar patch sewn to the front. This man was a part of the Iron Wraith Motorcycle Club based in Ashland, one town over from Redemption.

Their club had a bit of a seedy reputation, but it was mainly based on stories from when the club was first founded years ago, before I was even old enough to remember. Lately, they'd been pretty quiet, but people still crossed the street or turned in the opposite direction when they saw a club member coming their way. It was still known far and wide that you didn't fuck with the Wraiths.

"Thanks, but you don't have to do that."

"Didn't do it because I felt I had to, sweetness. I did it because I wanted to. Mind if I sit?"

I looked to the stools on both sides of me, or more specifically, to the people sitting on them. "There isn't really—"

"Dude," the man said, tapping the shoulder of the guy on the stool to my right. "Find somewhere else to sit."

My cheeks heated when the man shot up without any argument and took off.

"There." Hot Biker Guy smiled at me again as he sat down in the recently vacated chair. "Problem solved."

"Wow," I said with a short laugh. "That's a handy little trick. I bet you find the best parking spots at the mall too, huh?"

"Probably would if I went to the mall, but I'd rather have my fingernails peeled off while getting a root canal with no anesthesia."

A laugh burst past my lips before I could tamp it down, ending in a loud, indelicate snort. "Oh God," I groaned, covering my face with my hands. "That's so embarrassing."

I jolted when his long fingers wrapped around my wrists and pulled my hands away. "Nah. It was cute as fuck." Those dark blue eyes looked me over, leaving a trail of heat in their path. "So what's your name, gorgeous?"

Okay. This guy had just bought my drink. He'd kicked the man sitting beside me off his stool so he could sit with me. And he'd just called me gorgeous. I didn't think I was too far off the mark in thinking he was flirting with me, and while he wasn't Stone, he was still hot as hell. And besides, Stone was currently sucking on some blonde's tongue, probably without a single thought of me in his mind.

It wouldn't kill you to use this guy to brush up on your flirting skills, I thought to myself. *Or even* develop *some flirting skills.*

Deciding that was a smart plan, I extended my hand to the hot biker and gave him my name. "I'm Willow."

He took my hand, but instead of shaking it like I thought he would, he flipped it over, bringing it up so he could place a kiss on my inner wrist. Was the move intimate and possibly too familiar? Yes. But there was something about this dude; he executed the move perfectly, sending goosebumps across every inch of my skin.

"Nice to meet you, Willow. I'm Roe."

He dropped my hand and I pulled it back into my lap, still feeling the lingering tingles where his lips had been as I cocked my head to the side. "Row, like rowing a boat?"

His chuckle was deep and heady. "Nah, darlin'. Roe as in short for Monroe. My parents were assholes when it came to namin' me."

"Roe," I repeated, testing the name out on my tongue. "It's unique; I like it. Well, thanks for the drink, Roe."

He lifted up the beer I hadn't noticed he was holding, and clinked it against my glass. "My pleasure, sweetness. So, what are we celebrating?"

I opened my mouth, about to tell him it was my birthday, when an angry voice cut through our conversation. "Stand up and walk away."

We both turned to find a furious-looking Stone standing behind us, glaring at Roe with so much rage it was a wonder the skin didn't melt right off his bones.

"Stone—" I started, but Roe interrupted me.

"Don't think I will, man." From the look on his face, Roe was about as happy with Stone's order as Stone was at seeing him sitting next to me.

Oh shit.

The muscle in Stone's jaw clenched so tight I could see it twitching beneath what was now a short beard covering his jawline. "Won't give you a second warning, *man*."

Oh *shit*.

Roe pushed to his feet, but not to move away. Instead, he took a step closer to Stone, getting up in his face in a way I *really* didn't think was smart. "We got a problem here?"

"Not if you get the fuck away from her and forget she exists. You don't do that, then, yeah. We got a big fuckin' problem."

"Stone, really. It's okay—" I attempted, but he shot me a look so murderous it made me snap my mouth shut.

Oh shit!

"You stay out of this," he ordered on a growl, his finger pointing in my face. It had to be said, I really wasn't a big fan of that.

"How about you go back to the bitch that's been crawlin' all over your lap, and mind your own fuckin' business."

It *also* had to be said that I wasn't a fan of men referring to women as bitches either, even if the woman in question was one, which I couldn't know for certain, seeing as I hadn't talked to the curvy blonde Stone had been with earlier.

"Uh, Roe, just to point out, that woman might not be a bitch. For all we know, she's really sweet."

His dark blues came back to me and for a split second the fury melted away and he smiled at me. "Nah. Had that chick a few weeks ago, and believe me, gorgeous, she's a raging bitch."

Oh. Well in that case . . .

Just like that, the standoff between the two men continued like I hadn't said a word.

"Willow *is* my business, asshole," Stone clipped, those words making my back shoot straight. Since when had I become any of his concern, because for the past few weeks, he hadn't acted like he even knew I existed. "You got five seconds to walk away, or I'm gonna make you."

That was *not* good. From his hard, granite expression, I had no doubt he meant it. Roe wasn't exactly a lightweight; he had more than his fair share of muscle and stood a couple inches over six feet, but Stone was a mountain of a man, and I wasn't sure I liked Roe's odds. I also didn't like the fact that these men had drawn the attention of most everyone in the bar. I'd been all about stepping out of my comfort zone tonight, but that didn't mean I was ready to be the center of attention, standing right in the middle of the freaking spotlight.

A group of men all wearing the same patch as Roe came sauntering up to join the fray. The big man at the front of the group spoke up, and when he did, I got the distinct impression he was the one in charge: there was something about his vibe and the way the other men stood at his back, almost like they were waiting for his command. I looked down at the leather covering his chest, and sure enough, the patch resting over his left pec read President. "We got a problem?"

"Tell your boy to back the fuck off, Pope, or we're gonna have a serious fuckin' problem."

The man, now known as Pope, gave his full attention to Stone. "She belong to you?"

Wait. *What?*

"As far as you and your crew's concerned, yeah."

Roe's lips curled up in a sneer. "Lacey know that?"

"Don't you worry about Lacey."

I could only assume Lacey was the "bitch" that Roe had a few weeks back and that Stone was—from what I could tell—gearing up to have tonight.

Gross.

Pope spoke again, and what he said next surprised the hell out of me. "Back off, Roe. He claimed her so you need to stand down."

Again. *What?!*

Roe's nostrils flared, his eyes narrowed on Stone, and for a moment I thought he was going to defy his president's orders. But after a few tense, terrifying seconds, he jerked his chin up in acknowledgement of his leader's order.

He shifted his attention to me and that panty-melting smile returned. "Was good meeting you, sweetness. Your situation ever changes"—he tipped his chin at Stone in indication—"feel free to look me up."

I really wasn't sure what to say to that, so I went with, "Uh, thanks?"

He shot me a wink that would have made my knees wobble if I'd been standing, and I thanked my lucky stars just then that I wasn't. "Any time."

Pope did that chin jerk thing to me, then to Stone, and with that, the group of bikers turned and moved away.

I whipped my head around to Stone and started, "What in the world was—?" but my question cut off with a yelp when he grabbed me by the wrist and yanked me off the stool. I barely had the wherewithal to grab my purse and had to jog to keep up with his long-legged strides as he pulled me toward the exit.

"Wait!" I called, tugging at my hand. "I didn't pay for my drink!"

"I'll handle it," he grumbled as he put a big hand to the glass and pushed the door open with a hard, angry shove.

I stumbled over my heels in an effort to keep up with him as we hit the sidewalk outside. "Stone, just wait a second. You're going too fast."

All of a sudden, he stopped on a dime, dropping my

wrist and spinning around on me with an expression so fierce I was surprised he wasn't breathing fire. "Have you lost your goddamn mind?" He barked so loudly I jumped a bit and took an unsteady step backward. "What the fuck were you thinking, talking to that guy? Do you even know who he is?"

"His name's Monroe," I answered stupidly. "But he goes by Roe for short, because he doesn't like his name and thinks his parents are assholes for giving it to him."

Stone took a menacing step toward me, and for the first time ever, I actually found myself feeling a little afraid of him. "I don't give a shit what his name is. I asked do you *know who he is*?"

I shook my head in confusion. "I-I don't understand what you're asking."

"He's a fucking Wraith, Willow!" he boomed.

I wasn't sure why I snapped just then—no, that wasn't true. I knew exactly why. I'd been on tenterhooks all night. Seeing Stone with that woman was the icing on the craptastic cake that had been my birthday, and him yelling at me was the final straw.

"Stop yelling at me!" I yelled back, lifting up on my tiptoes to get in his face.

"I'll yell at you all I fucking want if it means you'll get your head out of your ass! You don't fuck with those guys ever, Willow, but especially not when you're that far out of your goddamn league."

Okay, wow. Well, that really fucking hurt.

The tears I'd been battling against all damn night finally proved to be too big an adversary for me. One broke free and slid down my cheek, followed by a second, then a third.

"Fuck you, Stone," I whispered, my voice wobbling with emotion as I forced them past the lump in my throat. "How do you know he was out of my league, huh?"

Understanding registered in his eyes, and the whiskey-brown filled with remorse. "Mouse, that's not what I meant—"

"At least he was nice to me," I continued, unable to hold the words back. "At least he didn't pretend I didn't exist. Unlike *some* people."

His eyes filled with pity that made me want to cry even harder, but I refused.

"Willow—"

I let out a bitter laugh that miraculously didn't come out as a snort. "You know, I honestly didn't think this night could possibly get any worse."

"What are you talking about?" he asked, but I was already on a roll and going too fast to stop.

"First I get stood up by one sister. Then the other's whole family is sick, not that that's her fault, but it still meant I didn't get to have my fancy dinner. Then my dad —" I choked down a sob as sadness washed over me. "Still, somehow you managed to make an already shitty birthday that much worse." I tipped my head back and yelled up at the sky, like I was calling to a higher power. "How is that even possible?"

"Shit. Babe, I didn't realize it was your birthday."

I lowered my head and shook it sadly. "It doesn't matter."

"Yes, it does," he declared. "Come on. Let's go back inside. Let me buy you a drink to celebrate."

I shot him a narrow-eyed look. "I was *already* having a drink to celebrate until you stormed up, acting like a total caveman. What the hell was that?" I jabbed my finger in his face. "You had another woman crawling all over you. Why did you have to do that? Roe was being a perfect gentleman. You had no right!"

"He was trying to get in your pants," he snapped back, his words firing through the quiet night air like a gunshot.

I threw my arms out wide and cried, "*So what?* It's none of your business what I do or who I do it with!"

He took a step closer and clenched his teeth. "Everything having to do with you *is* my business."

I drilled my finger into the solid wall of his chest. "And that! What the hell is that, huh? You *claimed* me in front of them? What bullshit! You acted like I actually meant something to you, and we both know that's a lie."

"It's not a lie," he insisted, and something about the way he said those four words gave me pause and sent a ripple across my skin. "You're my friend, mouse. I *do* care about you whether you believe it or not."

Grab life by the balls and live it.

The words my sister wrote on that card suddenly meant more in that very moment than they had when I first read them. I wanted to be more than this man's friend. I wanted what my parents had. I didn't know what the future would hold, but I did know that I at least wanted a shot to see if I could have that with him.

But I'd never know if that was possible unless I acted.

Unless I grabbed life by the balls and started living.

So I did just that. Closing the space between us, I fisted the front of his shirt and jerked him down at the same time I lifted up on the balls of my feet.

Then I crashed my lips against his.

Chapter Sixteen

STONE

THE PAST THREE WEEKS HAD BEEN MY OWN PERSONAL version of hell. I'd been doing everything in my power to avoid Willow while still thinking about her more than was healthy.

It hadn't helped that I'd been pushing shit aside at the garage so I could work on her damn car, either. The problems that had kept it from running had been fixed weeks ago, but I hadn't been able to bring myself to call her and give it back. I hated that fucking car, and I hated the thought of her driving it. It was a deathtrap on four wheels.

Cannon had been having a field day, giving me shit for paying out of my own pocket to fix everything wrong with that car so Willow could at least get enough of a trade-in for a hefty down payment on a new one. But even his constant ragging hadn't been enough to make me stop.

On top of that, there was also the inconvenient fact that at least once a day, I'd been fucking my own fist to the image of her in my mind. I pictured her each and every way I wanted to fuck her, and it never failed that, within only a few minutes, I'd come so damn hard I'd see stars. It had gotten to the point I was actually worried about chafing.

I'd come to the bar tonight looking for any available pussy to sink my dick into in the hopes it would clear my head of images of Willow fucking Thorne. I thought I'd found the solution to my little—okay, not so little—problem when a blonde I'd seen around the bars here and in the neighboring towns came up and started hitting on me.

All it had taken was a bit of innuendo before she was practically falling into my lap, and in no time flat, she was running her tongue up my neck and whispering in my ear all the things she wanted me to do to her.

And. It. Did. Nothing.

My traitorous dick didn't so much as twitch. The chick's tits were right up in my face and she was basically dry humping me right there in the middle of the bar. If anything, the erection I'd been sporting for the past few weeks thanks to Willow had deflated like a popped balloon.

She was wearing too much makeup. Her powdery perfume was suffocating me and didn't smell anything like sunshine. Her clothes left too little to the imagination. Her hair was too . . . blonde.

A million and one reasons why I couldn't get it up for this woman ran through my head at lightning speed, but the main thought that I kept shoving to the very back of my brain, stuffing it down until a steel trap door slammed over it and locked shut, was Willow.

I'd been just about ready to tell the chick it wasn't going

to happen, when I looked toward the bar and lost every bit of air in my lungs.

I hadn't thought about it; I just reacted. I'd shot to my feet so damn fast that the girl in my lap nearly tumbled to the floor. Before I could blink, I was across the bar, going toe-to-toe with the asshole sitting next to Willow.

It was as if my brain had temporarily malfunctioned. All I could see was red. All I could think was that this fucker had just had his hands on her, that he was sitting way too goddamn close.

It was a true wonder that things hadn't escalated to an unpleasant point, but the next thing I knew, I was dragging Willow out of the bar, wanting—no, *needing*—to get her as far away from that asshole as humanly possible.

How the two of us had started fighting was beyond me, but when tears started to spill from her sky-blue eyes, every ounce of anger I'd been feeling disappeared. Those protective tendencies I'd tried to bury so deep, the ones I found myself fighting every time she was around, came roaring to the surface at the sight of those goddamn tears.

I'd been wracking my brain, desperately trying to come up with a way to make her feel better when, between one breath and the next, she was fisting my shirt and her lips were on mine.

It took my brain too long to catch up to what was happening, but once it registered Willow's soft lips and the gentle, almost timid sweep of her tongue along the seam of my mouth, all rational thought flew out the window.

Acting solely on my baser instincts, I tangled my fingers in her hair, jerking her head back so I could get better access. Her lips parted and I drove my tongue inside, letting out a groan as the citrusy sweet flavor of her drink and something else distinctively Willow exploded on my tongue.

Christ, she tasted better than I ever could have imagined, and as I fed from her mouth like a starving man, that erection that had been MIA earlier with Lacey came back with a vengeance.

Her needy little whimpers fueled me on. The way she dragged her nails across my chest and latched onto my shoulders, like she was trying to fuse herself to me, made my balls tighten.

I was completely lost in all things Willow when, seemingly out of nowhere, the door to the bar opened, and a group of drunk assholes came staggering out. Just like that, the spell was broken.

I ripped my mouth and hands away and stepped back like touching her had just burned me. She staggered forward a little bit, slowly blinking her glassy eyes, and looked up at me.

"Stone—" she started, taking a step closer, but now that the haze of lust had worn off a sense of panic took its place.

I had this terrible habit when I felt like I'd been backed into a corner of lashing out at the person nearest, and before I could stop myself my mouth opened and the words came spewing out.

"What the fuck was that?" I asked in a tone a whole hell of a lot harsher than I'd intended.

She blinked away the desire and looked up at me in confusion. "I thought—"

"Thought what?" I barked. "That I wanted you to shove

your tongue down my throat in the middle of a goddamn parking lot?"

That's exactly what you wanted, asshole, my brain screamed. But I was beyond thinking with that. Right that second, I was functioning on pure adrenaline.

Her delicate features fell into a frown. "You kissed me back," she said in a voice so soft and quiet I had to strain to hear her.

She wasn't lying. Not only had I kissed her back, but I'd taken over completely, and fuck me if it hadn't been the best goddamn kiss of my life. But that didn't matter. I needed to put a stop to this now, no matter how much my body rebelled at the thought of it.

Those hearts were back in Willow's eyes, and I knew that if I didn't shut this down now, she'd get the wrong idea. Despite the fact I wanted to fuck her more than I wanted my next breath, I wasn't the man for her. I didn't do relationships, and that was never going to change. If I took this any further, she'd end up getting hurt, and I couldn't stand the thought of being the one to cause her that kind of pain. *Better a little in the beginning than crushing her heart later down the road*, I told myself.

She took a step toward me, lifting her hand like she was going to reach out and touch me. I grabbed her wrist before she could make contact, but it was too late. Just the feel of her soft skin beneath my rough, calloused fingers sent a pleasurable jolt of electricity through my whole body.

Instead of letting her see how she really affected me, I dropped her arm like it had given me a painful shock. "Willow, stop," I gritted through clenched teeth.

"I-I don't understand." That blush faded from her cheeks, leaving her face unnaturally pale.

"Look, this isn't going to happen. I can't give you what you want."

The skin between her brows puckered in a frown. "How do you know what I want?"

I could feel the pity etched into the lines of my face as I looked down at her, and I hated myself for what I was about to do. But it had to be done.

"Because it's written all over your face. Listen to me, babe. I'm not the man for you, all right? You want something big, and I'm never gonna give you that."

I watched as she drew her shoulders up straight and lifted her chin high, and Christ, I respected the hell out of her strength right then. "You're right," she admitted in a hushed voice. "I do want something big. Someday. But what I want even more is to live. You kissed me back, Stone. I felt it. You can't deny there's something here."

Fuck me, but she wasn't going to make this easy.

"It's not gonna happen, Willow. You need to let this go."

"But—"

"You aren't my type," I snapped, and before I could stop them, the words came pouring out. "You saw that woman I was with inside. That's what gets me going, babe. Not some shy, quiet librarian type who blushes every time she makes eye contact with someone. Move on. Find some nice, unassuming guy who works as an accountant or some shit. But you need to get your head out of the clouds, because this here"—I waved my hand between us—"it's never gonna happen."

I was a fucking asshole. The very worst kind of person. Standing there, seeing the crushed expression on her face, I knew right then I was no better than the piece-of-shit mother I'd been cursed with. She'd been gone almost as long as she'd been around, but the filth that was Carley Hendrix was still managing to infect me.

Willow Thorne deserved someone so much better than me, better than the man my parents had turned me into.

She deserved to have someone look at *her* with hearts in their eyes, and no matter how badly I wanted her, I knew I'd never be that man.

This is for the best, I tried telling myself. The problem was, I wasn't sure I believed it.

Her chest stuttered on a broken breath as she took a step backward, putting some distance between us and taking that fresh, sweet, warm scent with her.

"Fuck you, Stone," she whispered, shaking her head as another tear fell from her beautiful eyes. "Fuck you."

With that, she spun around on her heels and walked away from me. And I was left standing there, feeling like I'd just been gutted.

And I only had myself to blame.

Chapter Seventeen

STONE

I woke up Sunday morning with a hangover from Hell. After the scene with Willow in the parking lot of Bad Alibi Friday night, shit had continued to roll downhill at breakneck speed. I hadn't bothered to go back inside after she walked away from me. The reason I'd gone there in the first place was moot.

It had become glaringly obvious that my dick wasn't going to work for anyone but her. The one goddamn woman I couldn't have.

I'd driven my miserable ass home and proceeded to drink myself into oblivion in an attempt to wash her shattered expression from my mind.

It hadn't worked.

If anything, the alcohol had only amplified the memory—or maybe exaggerated it. Either way, I'd been trapped in a recurring cycle, replaying that terrible conversation and seeing her face crumple over and over again. I'd gotten so damn blitzed that I hadn't even staggered out to my garage to work on the Chevelle.

To add insult to injury, I'd chugged back so much whiskey Friday night and most of Saturday, that just the thought of my drink of choice made my stomach lurch. I had a feeling I was off the stuff for a good long while.

My eyes were so damn gritty it felt like they were coated in sand. My mouth tasted like a dumpster fire, and I currently had a death metal band playing in my skull.

With a groan, I swung my legs over the side of the mattress and made my way into the bathroom. I needed to piss like nobody's business. There was just one problem.

Standing over the toilet, I pulled my sweats down and . . . nothing.

I looked down at my hard dick and let out a weary sigh. "You've gotta be fuckin' kidding me," I cursed at my erection that had nothing to do with the usual morning wood and everything to do with the dream I'd been having of Willow that damn near ended in a mess on my sheets. "This is all your goddamn fault. Get your shit together so I can take a leak already."

I stood there for a good five minutes, waiting for the hard-on to go down so I could piss. Finally, it got with the program. I did my business, splashed water on my face, and headed downstairs for a much-needed cup of coffee.

With a fresh pot brewed, I poured myself a cup and sucked that first gulp back, hoping it would help make me feel somewhat human.

I was halfway through my first cup—it was going to be

at least a three-cup morning if I wanted to function—when my cell chimed with an incoming message.

Shane: *Don't forget family dinner tonight at Scoot and Caro's. You bail and I'll kill you.*

Goddamn it. Dinner with my family was the last thing I needed today after the shitty weekend I'd just had.

I knew there were a million excuses I could have made to get out of it, but something told me that Shane's threat was very real. She wasn't bluffing. If I bailed, the police would have to organize search parties to find my body buried somewhere in these woods.

I swiped my thumb across the screen and typed out a short reply. *Got it.*

Finishing off my first cup, I poured a second and looked down at where Chief was watching me expectantly. "Yeah, all right," I muttered with a roll of my eyes. "I forgot that in this household, you come first."

His tail thumped against the floor once like he agreed with me in his own dog way.

I dumped a scoop of food in his bowl, refreshed his water, then took my mug and headed back upstairs.

A long, steaming hot shower helped a bit in setting me back to rights, and by the time I got out, dressed in a pair of jeans and a T-shirt I'd found on the floor that smelled clean enough, and headed out to the garage to spend a little time on the Chevelle, I was feeling relatively normal. In spite of the lingering throb behind my eyeballs. I could have popped a couple aspirin, but I figured this was my penance. It was my own damn fault I felt like I'd been run over by a tractor-trailer, after all.

I hooked my phone up to the Bluetooth speaker I had set up in the garage, scrolled to my playlist, and got to work.

Five minutes in, karma decided it wanted to give me a bitch slap in case I'd forgotten what a prick I was, and Rage Against the Machine's "Bulls on Parade" started cranking out of the speaker.

Just like that, I recalled how Rage was screaming out of Willow's earbuds when I ran into her at the grocery store. I'd been shocked to hear her listening to something like that. It just seemed so out of character. Then again, I was quickly discovering that the woman was full of surprises.

I couldn't bring myself to skip to the next song, so I let it play out as I bent over the engine compartment and got to work.

I worked straight through lunch without even noticing, and if it hadn't been for the alarm I'd set going off when it was time to leave, I'd probably have kept going well past dusk.

I let out a sharp whistle, calling Chief, who'd been crashed out on the dog bed I kept out here for him, and together we headed inside.

I washed up really quick at the kitchen sink and tossed Chief a treat before heading out the door and climbing on my bike.

The second I came rumbling up Scooter and Caro's driveway, their front door opened and my nephew came rushing out with all the speed and energy of a tornado.

"Uncle Stone!" he shouted as he launched himself at me. I barely had time to climb off my bike before I had to hold my arms out to catch him.

Swinging him in a circle, I tossed him up in the air, eliciting a hyper squeal before bringing him back down and resting him on my hip.

"Hey there, monster. How you doin'?" I asked as I carried him up the walkway and toward the door he'd just rushed out of.

"Good! Can you take me for a ride on your bike?"

I arched a brow at him as I pulled the screen door open and stepped into the house. "You ask your mom?"

"Yes," he answered so fast I couldn't help but be suspicious.

"Really?"

His face fell in a frown so cute I had to bite my lip to keep from laughing. "No. 'Cause I know she won't let me."

"You got that right, kid," Shane said, coming out of the kitchen while wiping her hands on a dish towel. "You already have to wear a helmet in the house because you keep plowing into walls. You aren't getting on a motorcycle until you're bigger."

"You know, you could just put carpet down to prevent that from being an issue," I told her as I put Brantley back on the ground. In an instant, he took off like a shot down the hallway, skidding and sliding on the floors. A second later, we heard a loud bang that made my sister and me wince. "I'm okay!" he called out right after.

"Less traction means he's less likely to slam into the wall every time he runs around a corner."

"Believe me. It's something I'm considering."

"At least we know the kid'll probably have a promising

career as a pro football player. Christ knows he can take a hit to the head."

She moved in close to me on a giggle and raised up on her tiptoes to place a kiss on my cheek. "Glad you could make it."

I gave her a quick squeeze before letting her go so she could take a step back. "I told you I would, didn't I?"

She gave me a skeptical look. "Yeah. And I'm sure my threats didn't have anything to do with it, huh?"

I hooked one side of my mouth up in a smirk as I threw my arm over her shoulder and began dragging her toward the kitchen where all the delicious smells were coming from. "Never said that. You're downright fucking terrifying."

"Amen to that, brother," Jensen declared, extending his arm to hand me the beer he'd just pulled out of the fridge.

My stomach twisted unpleasantly at the sight of it, but I took it anyway, giving my brother-in-law a fist bump in greeting before twisting off the cap and taking a sip as Shane moved into her man and punched him lightly in the gut as he pulled her against him.

"Watch it," she threatened playfully.

Aunt Caroline entered the kitchen a second later and threw her arms out. "You're here!" she exclaimed as she rounded the island for a hug. Her excitement made me feel like absolute shit. I'd been living in the same town as my family for close to a year now, but I saw them so infrequently that something like showing up for a family dinner was cause enough for a celebration.

I really needed to do better.

"Hey, Aunt Caro," I said as I leaned down to wrap my arms around her.

Uncle Scooter came by next, clapping me on the back. "Glad you could make it, son. Now let's eat before my stomach starts munchin' on my liver, already."

As long as I'd been gone, sitting at their table for a meal still felt as familiar as drawing in breath. Back when Shane and I had lived with them, we'd eaten dinner at this very table every single night. I hadn't appreciated the purpose behind it back then, being a jackass of a kid with my head up my own ass. But looking back, I knew what they were doing when they made us eat with them every night and tell them every aspect of our day.

They wanted us to know we belonged. That this was our safe place. And I'd only realized I'd taken that for granted once it was too late.

Like always, the meal passed with good conversation and a ton of laughs. The food was fantastic and worked wonders on my stomach, which had been battling me all damn day.

I was comfortably full and totally relaxed when my uncle decided it was the perfect time to drop the hammer.

"So, Stone, Fletch told me he spotted you outside Bad Alibi Friday night with your tongue down that Thorne girl's throat. What's that about?"

I'd just taken a sip of my beer and proceeded to choke as every set of eyes at the table shot to me.

"You were *what?*" Jensen asked, looking rather unhappy.

"I *knew* it!" Shane shouted. Unlike her husband, she had a shit-eating grin on her face.

"Eww, gross!" was Brantley's reaction. "Why would you wanna put your tongue in a girl's mouth? Girls are nasty!"

"I'll explain when you're older, son," Jensen told him.

"Christ," I grunted once I was able to breathe again. "Can anyone in this fu"—I swallowed down my curse when Shane shot me a murderous look and jerked her chin toward her son—"in this town keep their mouths shut?"

"It's Redemption, son," Scooter said with a shrug, like that explained it all. "It's a small town, and you were right out in the open. What did you expect?"

"So does this mean you're together now?" Shane cut in, practically vibrating in her chair. "You're officially a couple?"

"Of course not," Jensen said, like it was the most ridiculous idea he'd ever heard. "He's not even her type."

I completely understood the whole protective vibe he had going on, probably better than most. But that didn't mean it didn't piss me off to hear him say that. And believe me, I saw the hypocrisy in that.

Shane let out a snort and looked at her man. "Oh, honey. It's sweet how oblivious you are. Willow's had a thing for Stone practically from the moment he stepped foot into town."

And it just kept getting worse.

"She's a sweet girl," Aunt Caroline stated, nodding approvingly. "You could do a lot worse."

"Look, guys, it isn't like that. We aren't together."

Just like that, the atmosphere shifted.

"So Fletch saw you with someone else?" my sister asked in confusion.

"No. He saw me with Willow. And we did kiss, but it was a mistake, and I stopped it before it went too far."

"Ah, shit," Jensen muttered, flopping back in his chair and scrubbing at his face as Shane's eyes narrowed into vicious slits.

"And you expect to get points for that?" she snapped sarcastically, sending a chill down my spine. "If it was such a mistake, why the hell did you kiss her in the first place?"

"I—" couldn't answer that question. "It's complicated, Shane."

"So let me get this straight. You've known all this time that she's had a serious crush on you, but even though you knew you had no intention of going there with her, you kept doing nice things that could potentially give her the wrong idea, like giving her rides and loaning her your truck while her car's being fixed—"

Jensen's eyes widened. "You loaned her Big Red? Dude! What the hell?" He looked at me like I'd just betrayed him.

Before I could attempt to defend myself, Shane continued. "*Then* you kiss her, out in the open for anyone to see, in the middle of the parking lot of the most popular bar in town, during one of their busiest nights of the week. Do I have it right so far?"

I opened my mouth, but my aunt got there first. "Oh, Stone," she admonished with a shake of her head.

"I didn't do anything wrong!" I defended. "*She* kissed *me*."

"So you pulled away instantly?" Shane asked in a tone that said she already knew the answer to that question.

When I clamped my mouth shut, she let out a sigh. "You really are an asshole, you know that?"

"Mommy said a bad word!" Brantley shouted.

"It's okay this one time," Jensen assured him, shooting daggers at me. "Uncle Stone *is* an asshole, so Mommy can say it, but you can't."

"You realize you just crushed that poor girl, right?"

"I—I didn't mean to," I finally confessed. But it didn't matter, because no matter my intentions, no matter my reason for shooting her down, I'd still hurt her.

This was going to go down in history as the worst fucking weekend ever.

Chapter Eighteen

WILLOW

"That son of a bitch," Aurora hissed between her teeth. "He's dead. That's it. I'm gonna kill him so dead. And I've watched like a bazillion murder mystery movies and serial killer docs and all those true crime channels, so I totally know how to do it and get away with it. His body will never be found. You have my word on that."

So, the whole grabbing-life-by-the-balls thing had started off pretty rocky, but it was okay. All right, it wasn't okay. It sucked something fierce, and the sting of Stone's rejection still left my skin feeling raw and exposed. But I did my best to pull myself up by my bootstraps—whatever that meant.

I gave myself the weekend to wallow in my sadness. I ate all the junk food and watched movies that made me cry until my eyes were red and nearly swollen shut. Then, when Monday morning rolled around, I got dressed in one of my nicest outfits and spent extra time on my hair and makeup, wearing it all like armor, then headed off to work, determined to keep my head up.

Apparently I hadn't done as good a job at it as I'd hoped, because it took no time at all for Lark to realize something was wrong. After work, she and Aurora had all but dragged me to a local sandwich shop for dinner, and at their insistence, I dove in, telling them about the whole disastrous event, starting with dinner with my sisters and ending with Stone's devastating rejection.

I considered it a win that I hadn't started crying again when I relayed the story to them, but that was probably because I'd run my tear ducts dry over the past couple of days.

Lark reached over and patted Aurora's arm. "All right, easy there, psycho. I'm all for hurting the bastard, but I'm thinking more along the lines of a nice, hard junk punch. Not something that could get us put away for life."

Aurora gave her a sour look. "Did you *not* hear the part where I said I'm basically a genius at getting away with murder? Your lack of faith in me really hurts."

She rolled her eyes at Aurora and looked back at me. "Just ignore her. I'm so sorry, honey."

I looked down into my glass, stirring around the lemon wedge in my water. "It is what it is, right? I'll be fine."

"Yeah. You will be," Aurora said with a serious expression. "You know why? Because you're a beautiful, brilliant glowing ball of sunshine and kitten fur and rainbows, and he's just a big crap cloud."

"Poetic," Lark deadpanned.

"I thought so. Anyway, he's an asshole, and he doesn't deserve you."

"She's absolutely right." Lark nodded in agreement. "You can do so much better than him."

Aurora lifted a finger. "Also, I'm sorry to say this baby cakes, but your sister is an asshole. She's out. I'm your sister now, and I'll do right by you, sugar."

Lark gave her a disgusted look. "It doesn't work that way, Rora. And that's still her sister."

Aurora's face took on an air of haughtiness. "Not anymore. I just decreed it."

God, I loved these crazy-ass women.

"And I also have a brilliant idea to help you get over Sir Asshole McDouche Nozzle."

I was almost scared to ask. "Oh?"

"Yep!" Aurora beamed with so much excitement you'd have thought she discovered the cure for erectile dysfunction. "We're gonna get you laid!"

"Oh my God, Rora!" Lark cried. "That's a *terrible* idea! She just had her heart broken. Trying to set her up with some random hookup isn't going to make things better!"

It really wasn't. And I really wasn't that type of woman.

Aurora pouted at Lark. "Why do you always have to ruin my fun?"

Lark rolled her eyes on a laugh. "You're ridiculous."

"I think you mispronounced amazing."

I decided it was time to break in before things escalated and they got into a hair-pulling match. "I appreciate any and all suggestions, really. But I think for now I just need a little time to lick my wounds. I'll get over it. Believe me, it's not the first time I've had a crush on a guy who didn't feel the same about me. It'll just take a little time." Or at least that was what I was hoping.

The only thing I could really do was continue on with life as normal and swallow down the pain.

A quick glance at my watch showed that it was already past six. "Sorry to cut this short," I started, reaching into my purse to grab my wallet. "It's getting late and I still need to check on my dad."

Aurora's hand shot out, her fingers wrapping around my wrist to stop me. "Don't worry about it; I've got it."

"You don't have to—"

She cut me off with a wave of her hand. "If you haven't realized it already, I like to take care of my besties. Dinner is on me. Go take care of your dad and we'll talk to you later."

I put my wallet back in my purse and pushed the chair back, rising to my feet while giving my new friends a bright smile. It was the first time in days I'd actually felt good. "Just in case I haven't told you already, you guys are the best, and I'm so glad I met you both."

Lark looked up at me with a smile before reaching out to take my hand and give it a squeeze. "The feeling's mutual, babe."

Aurora nodded solemnly. "What she said."

I bent to place a kiss on both their cheeks before turning and heading out of the restaurant. The sight of the loaner truck parked at the curb made my blood begin to boil. It was just another unwelcome reminder of Stone, and I needed to get rid of it as fast as possible. I'd have to take care of that tomorrow, though. My dad needed me tonight.

Pulling out of the parking lot, I pointed the truck toward my father's house and started in that direction. The door was unlocked when I got there, and I let out a sigh of frustration that he hadn't remembered to lock it, yet again.

I pushed the door open and stepped inside. "Dad?"

A loud crash came from the second level. With my heart in my throat, I ran up the stairs as fast as my heels would allow, grabbing the newel post at the top of the staircase as I whipped around in the direction of his room. "Dad? Are you okay?"

I came to a screeching halt just inside the doorway. My heart nearly fell to the floor at the state of his bedroom. All the drawers had been pulled open, the contents strewn across the floor. The clothes had been ripped out of the closet and were scattered all over the place among broken hangers. The sheets and comforter had been ripped off the bed and it looked like the pillows had been thrown around without a care, knocking picture frames and knickknacks off the dresser and nightstands.

In the middle of all the chaos, the broken glass and porcelain, was my dad, looking harried, his eyes wide and manic, his face red with exertion.

"Where is it!" Dad yelled.

"Dad, stop!" I cried, lifting my hands palms out. "Just don't move, okay? You're barefoot, and there's broken glass everywhere."

His wide gaze shot to mine, and I barely recognized the man looking back at me. "You," he hissed, his rage-filled eyes boring into me like laser beams. "You did this. You stole it! You're one of them, aren't you? Get out of my house!"

He lunged toward me like a raging bull, like he didn't even recognize who I was.

I stumbled backward, hitting the wall in the hallway with my arms held up in front of me. "No, Dad. It's me! It's Willow!"

"You're one of them!" he continued to scream, his fury so acute his cheeks were actually starting to turn purple. *"Get the fuck out! I'll kill you!"*

Before I had a chance to react—or duck—his arm swung wide, the back of his hand connecting with my cheekbone so hard I stumbled sideways, falling to the floor as starbursts formed in front of my eyes.

It wasn't him, I knew that. This was one of his episodes. The worst he'd ever experienced. He never in a million years would have hit me if he'd been in his right mind. My dad was a loving, big-hearted person. He'd never take his hands to anyone. Hell, he hadn't even been able to bring himself to spank us when we were kids.

But the man who'd just struck me wasn't my father.

I tried my best to remain calm despite the tears rushing from my eyes. The main goal right now was to calm him down. Maybe that would get him back. But even if that didn't happen, I couldn't risk him hurting himself. I didn't give a shit about myself. I had to keep him safe.

With one hand out in a placating gesture, I carefully pushed to my knees. "It's okay, Dad. You're safe. It's all right, I promise."

"No!" he shouted so loud it made my ears ring. "No, you're one of them. I won't let you take me!"

Before I could get to my feet, he turned on his heel and

darted back into the bedroom. A second later I heard the bathroom door slam, and fear so thick I thought it might choke me, saturated my blood.

"Dad!" I shouted, running into the bedroom. I headed straight for the bathroom door. Reaching for the knob, I gave it a jostle, trying to get it open. But he'd locked himself inside.

Calling him dad wasn't working, so I decided it was best to use his name.

"Jon? It's okay, Jon. Come on, you can open the door. You're safe, I swear. No one's going to take you, you have my word." I knocked on the door, trying my best to sound calm, but I couldn't keep my voice from trembling.

"Please, just open the door. Everything will be okay."

"Get the fuck out of my house!" he yelled through the solid wood. I heard him rustling around inside the small bathroom. It had been a while since I last checked his medicine cabinet to make sure nothing dangerous was inside, and the panic clutching my chest just then threatened to take me to my knees.

Remembering that I dropped my purse on the floor just inside the front door, I ran as fast as I possibly could down the stairs into the entryway. Dropping down to the floor, I wrestled around inside the bag, digging for my phone. As soon as I found it I scrolled to Crissy's name and hit go.

She answered on the second ring. "Hey sis, what's up?"

"Crissy," I started frantically, my hands shaking so hard it was a wonder I could keep the phone to my ear. "I'm at Dad's. I need you to get here now. He's having an episode;

it's really bad. He's locked himself in the bathroom. I need your help . . . *please*."

She didn't hesitate before saying, "I'll be right there. Give me ten minutes."

Before she could disconnect the call I spoke up. "Bring Phil," I told her, hating what I was about to say. "He's in a rage. He's violent, Criss. I don't think we can handle him ourselves."

There was a brief pause before my sister sniffled through the line, and I knew without having to see her face that she started to cry. "All right," she said, her voice cracking over those two words. "I'll grab Phil. We're on our way now."

The call disconnected and my hand dropped like the weight of the phone in my palm was just too heavy to keep my arm up. Sagging all the way to the floor, I gave in to the sobs tearing at the inside of my chest, desperate to get out.

I wasn't sure how long I stayed there on the floor, but it felt like no time had passed at all, yet at the same time it seemed as if an eternity had ticked by.

The front door burst open and Crissy and Phil came rushing inside. My sister looked down at me with wide, pain-filled eyes. "Where is he?"

I lifted my trembling hand and pointed toward the stairs. "His bathroom," I croaked. "He's locked himself in."

Phil moved first, picking me up off the floor before taking the stairs two at a time with Crissy and me hot on his heels.

I stumbled halfway up the staircase, my heel catching in the carpet runner. I paused briefly, just long enough to rip my shoes off and throw them down the stairs before heading back up to my father's room. Phil was already outside the locked door, knocking, his calm, soothing voice attempting to coax my father out.

Crissy stood just inside the bedroom door, looking in my direction, waiting for me to catch up. Her face filled with sadness as she reached up and caressed my cheek, careful not to touch the spot where our father had hit me. "Are you okay?" she asked, tears filling her eyes and spilling over onto her cheeks.

"It's not his fault," I told her, my chest hitching on a sob. "He's not himself."

"I know, Will," she whispered. "I know." She took my face in her hands and pulled me close, resting her forehead against mine. It was something she hadn't done since we were teenagers, and the tender move made my heart shatter.

I heard the bathroom door creak open and pulled away to see my dad had unlocked it and opened it just a crack. Phil was talking to him in a hushed tone that seemed to be working.

"Why don't you head home?" Crissy suggested, drawing my attention back to her. "We'll handle this. Go home and try to relax, maybe put some ice on your cheek."

I wanted to argue, and she must have seen it on my face because she spoke again. "You do more than your fair share for him, honey. It's our time to step up. We'll take care of him. Calm him down, and take him back to our place for the night, okay?"

I didn't have the energy to fight her. Not anymore. Instead, I nodded and let her pull me in for a hug before turning and heading back downstairs.

Moving on autopilot, I gathered up my shoes and purse from the floor and drove myself home. Once I got inside the door, the silence beat against me so hard it stole my breath. I didn't want to be alone, not after what had just happened.

I could call Lark, but I didn't want to interrupt her and Clay's evening. Pulling my phone back out, I checked the time on the screen and realized barely an hour had passed since I last left her and Aurora. It felt like forever ago.

I scrolled through my contacts and hit call when I got to Aurora's name.

"Hey there, my savory little pork dumpling."

"R-Rora?" I stuttered as I crumbled. "C-can you come over? Something happened with my dad. I-I don't want to be alone."

She didn't even hesitate.

"I'll be right there, and I'm bringing an overnight bag, vodka, and ice cream."

I might have failed when it came to my romantic life, and my family life might have been falling apart at that very moment, but at least when it came to my friends I was winning.

Chapter Nineteen

STONE

It was the Tuesday after that disaster of a family dinner, and I wasn't feeling any better about myself or what I'd done to Willow.

After being laid into by pretty much my whole family, I'd sequestered myself in the kitchen just long enough to do the dishes—brownie points—and then get the hell out of there.

My guilt had been eating at me to the point I'd been calling Shane, trying to get her to talk to me. Of course, the bride of Satan wasn't taking my calls. I'd told myself I'd done my part; I'd reached out. The next step was up to her. But the truth was, she wasn't the relationship I needed to fix.

Lunchtime rolled around, and I decided to hop on my bike to make the short trek from Banks Body and Auto Repair to Elite Security to see if Jensen wanted to grab a bite. I could have called him and had him meet me somewhere, but I'd have been lying if I said I didn't have ulterior motives for wanting to go see him directly. Specifically, a particular brunette I hadn't been able to stop thinking about since that kiss that had rocked my goddamn world.

I could still taste her on my tongue days later. Christ, I'd thought her hair was silky before, but after having my hands tangled in it, I knew it was the softest thing I'd ever touched. She's smelled like heaven, tasted like sugar, and felt like sin pressed up against me.

Fuck, I was so screwed.

I parked my bike in the empty spot closest to the entrance and headed inside. The relief I felt when I first walked through the door was short-lived. The cool air conditioning was a nice contrast to the heat outside, but the reception desk sat empty, the computer monitor black.

I stood rooted to the spot for a few seconds, looking around, waiting for Willow to appear out of thin air. When the reception area remained empty and quiet, I decided to head down the hall toward Jensen's office.

"Yo," I called out, knocking my knuckles against the wall of glass that made up the front of his office.

My brother-in-law lifted his head and waved me in. "Hey man, what's up?"

I moved into his office, bracing my hands on the back of one of the chairs that sat facing him. "Not much. Just wanted to swing by and see if you wanted to grab lunch." I hooked a thumb over my shoulder. "You know your reception area's empty? Willow at lunch or something?"

He rocked back in his seat, making the chair squeak as he scrubbed a hand down his face. "Yeah, I know. Willow called in this morning. She's out the next few days, and it didn't even take us half a day before shit here started falling apart. I'm gonna have to skip lunch man, but thanks for asking."

I didn't hear anything he said after *she's out the next few days*. "What happened?" I asked, my fingers clenching the back of the chair so hard the skin on my knuckles turned white. "Is she sick? She tell you what's wrong?"

He arched his brow and gave me a flat expression. "You asking because you care? Because that really wasn't the impression I got on Sunday. And I have to say, I'm not a big fan of you fucking with Willow. She's a good woman. She deserves better."

I couldn't murder my brother-in-law. Shane would be pissed and Brantley would probably never talk to me again. "Yes, I'm asking because I care," I gritted out between clenched teeth. "You know, I'm not a heartless prick. I fucked up. I know that. But I never meant to hurt her."

He looked at me skeptically. "Whatever. If you must know, she's said she had some personal things she needed to take care of. If it makes you feel better, it didn't sound like she was sick."

That didn't make me feel any better. A voice in the back of my head was shouting out, desperate to know what personal things. Was she okay? Was it something with her dad? Did she need someone to take care of her?

But I didn't have the right to know the answers to any of those questions. Hell, I didn't even have the right to ask them, because I'd fucked everything up.

"Okay, well then I guess I'll head out and leave you to it." I started for the door, but before I could take a step out, my body turned back around like it was functioning without any authority from me. "If you hear anything—"

He cut me some slack and nodded. "I'll let you know."

The sense of relief that gave me was irrational and staggering. "Thanks, man."

"No problem. Just don't tell Shane I agreed, yeah? Honestly, I love your sister, but sometimes she terrifies me."

I got that. More than he knew. "Yeah, brother. I won't say a word."

With that, I turned on my boot and started back down the hall toward the exit, feeling a heaviness in my chest that refused to go away for the rest of the day. And I knew it was all because I didn't get to see *her*.

Willow

I'D GONE from never taking a single sick day to missing nearly an entire week of work, but there was no way in hell I was going to be seen around town, sporting a dark, ugly bruise that would make people ask questions.

I'd waited until it had faded enough that makeup could cover the majority of it before risking a venture into town. Lark and Aurora had been amazing, coming by every day after work with takeout from different restaurants around town, but I was running seriously low on food, and had used up the last of my coffee this morning, so a trip to the grocery store was necessary.

My heart was still hurting too much to care about putting any effort into my appearance, so I'd slipped on a pair of yoga pants, a long, slouchy T-shirt, and thrown my hair up into a messy bun on the top of my head. The only makeup I'd bothered with was the concealer I used to cover the purple and yellow smudges on my cheekbone. It covered everything up, for the most part, but there was still a dark violet crescent moon starting right at the inside corner of my eye that showed through. Fortunately, my sunglasses covered it, so it looked like I would be one of those douchey people who wore their sunglasses indoors.

I'd spent the past few days worried about my father and desperately wanting to see him, but Crissy and I had both agreed that I needed to wait until the bruises were completely gone. He'd blame himself, and that would just send him into another spiral.

For the time being, she and Phil had picked up the slack for me when it came to taking care of him, cleaning up the mess he'd made of his bedroom that night, running him to doctor's appointments to have his meds adjusted, preparing his dinners, keeping him company.

I was missing him like crazy, but I was so grateful to my sister for being there when he needed someone the most.

I headed out the door toward that damned truck I was quickly coming to hate because it reminded me of *him*—the interior even smelled like him, for crying out loud. I had a constant, glaring reminder of what went down sitting in my driveway, and I was over it.

Hell, I was over pretty much everything at this point.

After the week I'd had, I was fully embracing the righteous indignation coursing through my body. I was a woman scorned. I was hurt and angry and sad, and I was sick and tired of taking people's shit!

As soon as I stepped outside, my eyes narrowed behind my sunglasses at the offending hunk of metal like it had personally betrayed me.

"That's it," I said to the truck as I stomped up to it. "You're gone. Today."

Yanking the door open with a bit too much force, I climbed in and plopped down on the seat. Before I could get the key in the ignition, my cellphone rang. I pulled it out and let loose a frustrated sigh as Elaina's name scrolled across the screen. I hadn't spoken to her since she blew me off on my birthday a week ago, and at this moment, she was second on the list of people I had no desire to talk to. Stone Dickface Hendrix had the number one spot, and he probably would for the rest of eternity.

Swiping my thumb to answer, I lifted it to my ear and gave her the same kind of greeting she usually gave me when I called her.

"Elaina, now's not a good time. I'm just getting in the car to—"

"This'll only take a second," she interrupted.

Rolling my eyes heavenward, I silently asked for a bit of patience as I said, "All right. What is it?"

"I know it's last minute, but I need you to cover for me with Dad's dinner tonight. I forgot that my friend Lois from book club and I made plans to meet for drinks tonight. I'll make it up to you, I promise."

Like I hadn't heard those words before.

I gripped the wheel with my free hand, squeezing so tight my knuckles cracked as I hissed through the line, "No."

Silence filled the line for several seconds before her voice returned, full of bewilderment. "What do you mean, *no*?"

"Last I checked, that word only had one meaning, but if you require further explanation, here it is. No, I will not cover for you. You made a commitment to Dad long before you made stupid plans to have stupid drinks with a stupid friend, and you're going to uphold your end of the deal that you, Crissy, and I made."

"What the hell—?" she started to argue, but I wasn't finished. Not even fucking close.

"Even if I wanted to help your spoiled, self-entitled ass out—which I do *not*—I couldn't. It's obvious you've been too busy in your own little world, not giving a shit about anyone else, so I'll fill you in on some of the things that have occurred in the past few days."

"Now, you listen to—"

"No!" I barked through the line. "*You* listen, Elaina. For once, you're going to hear what I have to say, because it's important. On Monday, Dad had one of his episodes, only this time, he was extremely violent. I got the brunt of that, and until the black eye he gave me heals, I can't see him."

That was met by her sharp intake of breath on the other end of the call, and I knew I had her full attention.

"If he sees the bruises, he'll ask questions. If he finds out the truth, it'll kill him. You know that. He never once raised his hands to us, and if he knows he hit me . . ." I swallowed down the lump that had suddenly formed in my throat. "You know what that will do to him."

"I-I know," she whispered, her voice holding so much pain. "Oh God, Will. I-I don't know what to say. I'm so sorry."

The sudden and unexpected shift in her took some of the wind out of my sails, and it took me a moment to get my bearings. "Thank you."

"Is he okay? Are *you* okay?"

Well I certainly hadn't been expecting that. "Crissy's been taking care of him, and she said he's doing okay. She took him to the doctor and they adjusted his meds to see if that would help. As for me . . ." I thought about how to answer that and decided the truth was the best option. "I've definitely been better, but I'll be okay."

"Willow, I—"

Vulnerability wasn't necessarily one of Elaina's strong suits. She'd always been the hardest of the three of us. I'd never doubted that she loved me, she just tended to be incredibly selfish.

"It's all right," I said softly. "But he needs you, okay? *I* need you. I'm struggling. This is really hard on me, and sometimes I need my big sister to hold me and tell me it's going to be okay."

I could have sworn I heard tears in her voice when she said, "I'm sorry I've been such a shitty sister to you."

"Well, you haven't *always* been shitty," I teased and felt a sense of relief when a short laugh carried through the line.

"I'll do better. I promise. From here on out, the three of us are a team."

I felt moisture hit my eyes, but for the first time in a

week, the tears swimming in my vision weren't due to sadness. "I'd like that."

"I'll let you get back to what you were doing, but we'll talk soon, yeah? And I'll take care of Dad tonight."

"Thanks, Elaina."

"Don't thank me, sweetie. It's my job. I—I love you. You know that, right? I'm sorry I've done such a shitty job of showing it."

"I love you too. We'll be okay. All of us."

We rang off a short while later, and as I put the key in the ignition and started the truck, I actually felt like those words were true. We would be okay. Maybe not today or tomorrow, but we'd find our way there.

As I backed out of the driveway and started toward town, a fire lit in my belly from the conversation with my sister. I decided I'd stop by Banks Body and Auto Repair before hitting up the store.

I was getting my car back and severing the very last connection I had with Stone Hendrix.

Chapter Twenty

WILLOW

My heart beat like a bass drum in the center of my chest as I turned into the parking lot of the garage. The adrenaline was rushing through my veins so fast and hard it felt like they were vibrating beneath the surface.

I slowed the truck, scanning the cars and motorcycles parked all around the lot, looking for one in particular, and breathed a sigh of relief when I didn't spot Stone's familiar bike anywhere.

Looked like, for once, luck was on my side, and it appeared I'd shown up on one of Stone's days off.

"Thank God," I breathed to myself as I steered the truck to the empty spot right outside the office.

I climbed out, mindful to leave my sunglasses on, and stepped out of the heat and into the air-conditioned waiting area.

The older woman behind the counter looked up and me and smiled. "Hi. Can I help you?"

I moved up to the desk and placed my palm on the cool

surface. "Yeah, hi. I'm Willow Thorne. I'm here to pick up my car. The Honda Civic?"

The woman's demeanor shifted, and something flashed across her face that I couldn't quite put my finger on.

"Oh, um, hold on. Let me check something real quick."

She stood up and rounded her desk, heading for a door to my left that led out into the garage.

Too jittery to stand still, I paced the office while I waited, looking at the different pictures of old muscle cars and advertisements hanging on the walls.

When the door opened again, I turned to find the office assistant coming back in with Cannon Banks following after her.

"Hey, Willow," he greeted in a pleasant tone, a smile on his face. "So you're here for your car?"

"Yeah. And to return the loaner."

His brows dipped down into a deep V, confusion filling his eyes. "Willow, that truck you've been driving isn't one of ours."

It was my turn to be confused. "What do you mean? Stone said it belonged to you guys."

He shrugged while wiping his hands clean on a white towel. "He asked about a loaner for you, but we didn't have any at the time. That truck out there is Stone's personal vehicle."

What? He'd given me his own truck to drive?

I shook my head to clear the confusion. It didn't matter: not whose car I'd been driving, not why he'd lent it to me or lied and said it belonged to the garage. None of that mattered.

"Okay, well, still. I'd like my car back."

I suddenly got the distinct impression that Cannon was all kinds of uncomfortable. "It's actually not ready yet."

"How is it not ready? Stone said it would only take a couple weeks to fix and it's been a month."

He reached up and scratched the back of his neck. Yep, *definitely* uncomfortable. "Yeah, it did. I mean—the initial issues anyway. But he's been working on some other things."

My stomach plummeted. I couldn't possible afford for him to make any more repairs. "He didn't discuss additional work with me," I said in a panic. "I don't have the money—"

"I believe he was planning to cover the costs."

What in the actual hell?

"Maybe you should come back tomorrow when he's here. He can explain it to you."

Pfft. Like I'd ever in a million years do that. I was quickly losing my cool, which was a completely foreign feeling for me, and one I honestly didn't like all that much. "Does the car run in its current state?"

"Well, yeah, but—"

"Then I'd like it back, please. Now."

"I can't do that."

A tick formed in my eyelid. Thank God for the sunglasses. "You can't give me *my* car? Why the hell not?"

"Because even though it runs, it isn't exactly street legal at the moment, and, well, Stone told me I couldn't," he added with a shrug.

"He said you couldn't."

"Yep."

My head was about to explode. "Why?"

"I really think you should talk to him, darlin'."

The plan had been to avoid him until one of us died of old age or got run over by a car or something, but, in a split second, my plans changed. "Oh, I intend to," I answered on a growl that sounded almost feral. "Give me his address."

I'd expected some pushback on that, but Cannon didn't hesitate to turn around and scrawl the address on a sticky note. Guess he figured the asshole deserved a sneak attack almost as much as I did.

"Thanks," I snapped, yanking the Post-it off his finger and whipping back toward the door.

"Not a problem. Give him hell, darlin'."

Stone

I was bent over the open hood of the Chevelle when I heard the deep rumble of a very familiar engine coming up my drive. Knowing exactly what truck was driving up—and shocked as hell to be hearing the sounds of it—I stood tall and grabbed a rag to wipe my hands clean as I moved to the open bay door.

Chief joined me, cocking his head and looking out into the distance just as Big Red came into view. The tires spit up dirt and gravel. I basically lived in the wilderness, so there wasn't an actual driveway, more of a worn-down path made by years of cars driving along the packed dirt and gravel.

The truck stopped beside where I'd parked my bike, and a second later Willow swung out, slamming the door so damn hard that I winced at the mistreatment of my baby.

But as quickly as my concern for Big Red came, it disappeared the instant I caught sight of Willow.

Despite going to Elite Security more than once this week, I hadn't caught a single glimpse of her. She hadn't been there Tuesday when I first showed up. Or Wednesday. Or Thursday. I'd have gone back today as well if Jensen hadn't threatened to tell Shane that I was acting like a crazy stalker.

I hadn't been able to help myself. I knew what I was doing was all kinds of fucked up, especially after how I'd shot her down a week ago, but the desperate need to see her —even if she refused to speak to me—had come to life in my chest, turning into this vicious clawing thing that wouldn't loosen its grip on me.

She stormed toward my garage, and even though a ridiculously large pair of sunglasses covered a majority of the top half of her face, I could tell she was pissed about something.

I'd seen her flustered, nervous, shy, heartbroken, and upset, but I'd never seen her pissed. Maybe there was something seriously fucking wrong with me, but for some reason, I found it hot as hell.

All that long hair was piled on top of her head. Her long, slender legs were encased in tight yoga pants that were *really* fucking working for her, and even though the T-shirt she was wearing was baggy and hung low, the white material was very thin, nearly see-through, and the collar draped off one shoulder, revealing a soft girly pink bra strap.

I expected her to stagger to a halt when she spotted Chief sitting next to me—most people did. If you didn't know him, he looked menacing and scary as hell—but she didn't. Instead, she stopped a foot away, those sunglasses pointed right at me, and extended her hand, almost like it was second nature for her to let my dog give her a sniff, doing it without a single thought. She barely seemed to notice when Chief stood and gave her palm a happy lick because she was too busy snapping at me, "I want my car back, now."

The urge to reach out and touch her was so damn strong, I had to cross my arms over my chest to keep from reaching out. "It's not done yet."

Something told me that fire was flashing in those sky-blue eyes of hers just then, and I was a little pissed I couldn't see it for myself because of those stupid sunglasses.

She slammed her hands down on her hips and curled her top lip up in a snarl that looked too cute for words. I bet her nose was scrunched up too, but again—stupid sunglasses. "Only because you're working on a lot more than you initially told me you'd be doing."

Well shit. Apparently she'd stopped at the garage and talked to Cannon. The betraying bastard.

"It needed to be done," I grunted, lifting my chin higher. I wasn't going to apologize for going behind her back and fixing every problem that piece of shit had. "It was a goddamn death trap."

"It was just fine!" she exclaimed, losing control in front

of me for the first time ever. There was no nervous stuttering, no blushing, no hiding behind her hair. Apparently anger overrode all those nervous ticks of hers.

That's something I'll have to keep in mind for the future, I thought before I could stop myself.

"I can't afford all these repairs you're making—"

"I'm paying for it, so it's nothing you need to worry about."

She let out an adorable little huff at being cut off. "No the hell you are not," she gritted. "I don't need your handouts. And while we're on that particular subject, I know the truck is yours." *Fucking Cannon.* I was going to choke the bastard to death. "I don't know why you felt the need to lie to me about that, but I'm not some sort of pathetic charity case. I'm a grown woman more than capable of taking care of herself."

That was a direct hit to that place deep inside me where my protective instincts were locked away.

"Is that right?" I asked menacingly, uncrossing my arms to prop my palms on my hips as I took a step closer to her. The longer we stood there arguing with each other, the more I hated those fucking sunglasses, because they were preventing me from looking into those baby blues. "That why you've been driving around all this time with airbags that don't even fuckin' work?" I growled.

When I'd been taking shit apart and discovered that malfunction, I'd seen red. She could have been in an accident, and the one goddamn safety feature in that rust bucket she called a car would have been worthless. She could have been seriously hurt. Or worse.

"Well, I didn't know the airbags didn't work!" she defended, throwing her arms out at her sides.

"Doesn't matter, because now they do."

"Then give me my car back. I'll work out some sort of payment plan with Cannon so you and I don't have to speak to each other."

Okay, now I was well into pissed, and quickly starting to lose my grip. "You're not paying for shit," I grunted. "You're not getting that car back. And will you take those goddamn sunglasses off? Yelling at you while you're wearing them is really fucking with my flow."

"Well, suck it up!" she shouted. "And if you don't give me that Honda back *today*, I swear to God, I'm going to sue the shit out of you!"

"When I finish fixing it, I'm going to sell it for a fair price. Then I'm going to help you get a great deal on a dependable car and use the cash as a down payment."

Her chin jerked back and I had to assume her eyes had gone wide. "Have you lost your mind?" Each word of that sentence rose a decibel until she was practically shrieking.

"Goddamn it. No!" I barked. "I haven't lost my mind!" I reached for the sunglasses just then. "And take off those fucking glasses."

"Stone, no—" she started to shout in panic, but it was too late. The moment I saw that black eye, I did what she'd just accused me of and lost my mind.

"What the fuck is that?" I hissed so quietly the hairs on Chief's back stood on end.

With her eyes unobscured now, I could see the panic swimming in the blue depths. "Don't worry about it."

"Someone hit you?" I asked, that deadly low tone turning into a rumble.

She steeled her spine and narrowed her eyes at me, but now that I could see her whole face, I could tell it was all an act. "It's none of your business."

"Like fuck it's not!" I boomed. "Someone fucking hit you, Willow, and you're gonna tell me who it was!"

"Why?"

"So I can beat the shit out of them for putting their hands on you!" Something primal and savage was building up inside me, boiling over. It was something that screamed *mine*. Someone had put their hands on what was mine, and I was going to kill them for it.

"All the more reason not to tell you," she replied, her voice beginning to tremble with fear at the shift in me. "Besides the fact that it's none of your business."

"Everything about you is my business," I snarled. "Fucking *everything*. And if you don't tell me, I'm going to tear this whole goddamn town apart if that's what it takes to get a name."

With each word I spoke, her eyes got wider and wider until the panic on her face was all I could see. Then she did something I didn't see coming; something I thought would never happen again.

Instead of giving me the asshole's name, she lunged at me, wrapping her arms around my neck and slamming her lips against mine.

And just like that I snapped.

Chapter Twenty-One

STONE

That primal force inside me took over the moment her lips touched mine. There was no hesitation this time. I didn't freeze. I might not get another chance at this, and I'd be damned if I wasted this one. There was no way in hell.

She might have been the one to initiate, but I'd taken over before my arms had finished closing around her.

With one hand fisted in her hair, I pulled her neck back, giving myself perfect access, and forced my tongue inside, desperate for another taste of that sweetness I'd gotten last week, the sweetness I'd been dreaming about for the past seven days.

I didn't take it nice and slow. I didn't savor. I plundered. I was a man possessed.

Willow let out a muffled yelp when I reached down and grabbed her ass cheeks, giving them a hard squeeze before I jerked her off her feet. She had no choice but to hold on as I swung her around and carried her back into the garage.

The sharp bang of the hood slamming down filled the

air, but I barely heard it over the blood rushing through my ears as I dropped her onto it.

The move nearly pulled our lips apart, and the tiny little growl she let out as she fisted the material of my shirt and yanked me back to her before I could get too far away made my dick throb.

Grabbing hold of her hips, I jerked her back down the hood and wedged one of my thighs between her long legs, applying pressure as I rocked her against me. She ripped her mouth from mine and let her head fall back on a needy groan as she took over, riding my thigh all on her own.

She wanted this as badly as I did. I could smell her arousal, feel the heat of it between the layers of our clothes.

"Stone," she whimpered, wanting something, but not knowing what, or maybe she did and she just wasn't the type of woman who felt confident enough to demand it.

I was about to change that.

"Say it," I growled into her ear before nipping at the column of her neck. I kept a firm hand on her ass, urging her to keep rocking, while I dragged my other hand up to cup her perky round tit and give it a squeeze.

"Oh God," she cried, her coordination thrown off for just a moment at the dual sensations of pleasure.

"You want me to make you come, baby?" *Say yes. Please God, I'm begging you, say yes.* "You want me to make you explode? I'll do it, mouse. All you have to do is ask."

I pulled my face out of her neck and looked down at her. The sight of that bruise would have sent me over the edge into a rage if all the blood that normally fueled my brain wasn't currently making my cock swell painfully.

"I'll make it so goddamn good, you'll see stars."

"Stone," she whispered, her hips rolling faster. "Please."

Christ, she was beautiful like this. Her hair was a tangled mess, half of it falling out of that bun thanks to my ministrations. Her skin was flushed. Her eyes were glassy, her pupils dilated. Her lips were swollen and pink, which made me wonder if her pussy looked the same.

Reaching up, I pulled the elastic from her hair so it would all fall past her shoulders. "Sorry, baby. Not good enough. You have to say the words." It might have been cruel to make her beg, but I wanted to hear those words drip from her kiss-swollen lips almost as badly as I wanted to fuck her. And, *God*, did I want to fuck her.

I couldn't remember a time in my life when I'd wanted a woman more than I wanted Willow. I wanted to fuck her until her muscles gave out and she'd feel me between her thighs for days every time she moved. I wanted to pull those yoga pants down, bend her over the hood of my car, and spank her ass until my handprint turned pink on her ivory skin. Then I wanted to bury myself inside her until she came around me, screaming my name, and pull out to paint those cheeks with my cum, marking her in the most animalistic way.

Her chest hitched on a stuttered breath. "Stone," she breathed, that sweet voice of hers so quiet. "Make me come."

That was all it took. My movements were a blur after that, and before I knew it, I had her spread out on the hood of my Chevelle in nothing but a lacy pink bra that held her tits up beautifully, and a matching thong.

If I thought she was beautiful before, it was nothing compared to how she looked right then. She was a goddamn vision. She took my breath away. All that perfect, creamy skin was begging me to defile it.

Dropping to my knees right there at the front of the car, I pulled her farther down the hood until her hair splayed out around her. I'd have given anything to have my phone on me just then so I could snap pictures. There'd never been a more tantalizing, erotic sight in the history of the world than this one.

Palming the insides of her thighs, I spread her legs apart as far as they'd go. The pink of her panties was a bit darker with wetness right over her slit, and the sight of it made my mouth water.

Hooking the material with my index finger, I pulled it aside, getting my first peek at those slick pink lips. Sure enough, they were as swollen and needy as I'd imagined. I was about to fucking *devour* her.

Her thighs trembled beneath my palms, and I could hear the quick, frantic breaths she was taking just before she pushed up onto her elbows and looked at me with wide eyes. "What-what are you doing?"

The smile that pulled at my lips was downright wicked. "What's it look like? I'm about to eat your pussy until you come all over my face."

"I don't—" Shy, nervous Willow had suddenly made a reappearance, and if anything, that made my dick even harder. "That is, I can't . . . you know. Not like this."

Challenge. Fucking. Accepted.

"You can't come?" I teased, loving the way her skin

pinked even brighter with a blush at my crude language. But if the way her eyelids lowered to half-mast and her tongue snuck out to trace her bottom lip was any indication, she loved it when I talked dirty. She nodded, pulling that lip between her teeth to bite down, and I let out a groan. "Then you were with the wrong men because I'm about to get you off so hard you'll scream my name."

With that, I dove in, feeling starved. I swiped my tongue the full length of her slit and let out a moan, instantly hooked. She tasted like the sweetest ambrosia, the thickest, richest honey. Using my thumbs to pull her lips apart, I fucked my tongue inside her so I could coat my mouth with that addictive taste.

Heaven. That was what Willow Thorne tasted like. Pure. Fucking. Heaven.

"Oh my—oh *God*," she cried as she collapsed back onto the hood. Lifting my gaze so I could enjoy the view while I devoured her, I watched as her back arched and the pads of her fingers dug at the metal, trying to find purchase. "*Yes*. Stone, yes, baby."

Jesus, that was the hottest sound I'd ever heard.

She pulled her knees up, bracing her heels on the bumper for leverage so she could grind against my mouth while I traveled higher up and sucked her clit between my lips before flicking it with my tongue.

"*Oh!*" she yelped, her head shooting up and her eyes widening like she just experienced something for the first time. Those assholes she'd had in her past clearly didn't appreciate what they had with her if they didn't do everything in their power to get her off every way imaginable and as many times as possible.

Her hands moved, her fingers tangling in the hair at the top of my head and twisting hard. At the sting in my scalp, my cock twitched, letting me know it wasn't going to last much longer as Willow wrapped her long legs around my neck and lifted her hips even higher. With her grip on my hair, she held me exactly where she wanted me and rode my face like she'd been born to do this.

That quiet, unassuming woman was a fucking wildcat once she got going. It was just another layer I desperately wanted to peel away in the hopes of discovering what was inside. Nothing about her was what it seemed.

Needing to get her off so I could fuck her, I added my fingers to the mix, plunging two inside of her as far as they'd go. I twisted to make a come-hither motion right against that silky spot that would set her off at the same time I scraped my teeth against her swollen nub, and that was it.

She let out a sharp, keening cry that quickly turned into my name, just like I'd promised her. I didn't let up as she undulated against my face, gripped my hair in an iron fist, and flooded my mouth with her release.

I lapped it up, sucking at her lips and licking her clean as she came down from an orgasm that left her panting and splayed out on my hood like her whole body had turned to jelly.

"Not done with you yet, mouse," I growled as I quickly rose to my feet while wiping her arousal off my face with the back of my hand.

That taste had guaranteed I'd be an addict for life, and

I had no fucking problem with that. But if I didn't get inside of her in the next few seconds, my head would explode.

Her lazy, lust-drunk gaze traveled down the front of me, stopping at my fly as I ripped my jeans open and pulled my cock out. Her chest shook on a broken breath and her eyes widened slightly as she took it in.

I didn't think I'd ever been this hard before. As I wrapped my hand around the base and stroked up, it was almost painful. "You like what you see?"

She licked her lips and nodded. "Uh huh."

"Good. Then hold the fuck on." Reaching down, I ripped her thong off and jerked her up to sitting, sliding her even farther down the hood until her ass was practically hanging off. We were chest to chest, pressed so tight together not even sunlight could get through. I lifted one of her knees, bringing it up to wrap high over my hip, bent my knees to line myself up with her opening, and plunged in fast and deep.

She cried out in shock, her eyes bugging wide. Christ, she was so tight. Tighter than I ever could have imagined.

As difficult as it was—and it just might have been the hardest thing I'd ever had to do—I stilled, giving her time to adjust to my size.

Letting out a slow, agonized exhale, I rested my forehead against hers and squeezed my eyes closed, willing the pressure building in my balls to let up so I could make this last, make it good for her too, because it was already perfect for me.

Her body trembled against mine, and my arm around

her waist, the one that was holding her pinned against me, clenched a bit tighter.

"You okay?" I asked, needing to hear her say it before I could move.

"Yes," she breathed, digging her nails into my shoulders.

"I didn't hurt you?"

She shook her head in quick, jerky movements. "No. God, please. Move Stone. I can't take it."

That was all the reassurance I needed. I pulled nearly all the way out before pounding back in.

"Harder," she panted, her breath rushing across my face.

"Fuck me. My little mouse is wild, isn't she? You like to be fucked hard, baby?"

"Yes. Please. Don't stop."

Not a chance in hell of that happening.

I slammed into her, over and over, feeling the walls of her slick heat clench and ripple. She was close, I could feel it. Thank God, because I didn't know how much longer I could hold back.

"So fucking tight," I grunted with each thrust. She began snapping her hips in time to match mine, chasing her next climax. "Jesus, your pussy's like a glove, baby." I was fucking her so hard sweat was coating both our bodies. "Never felt anything more perfect."

She sucked in a sharp gasp. "Stone. Oh God. I'm—" I could tell by her eyes that the intensity building inside her was overwhelming.

Fisting her hair to keep her head in place and her eyes

on me, I ordered, "Give it to me, Willow. I want to feel you come around me."

"I'm coming!" she cried out, and just like that, her cunt clamped down around me in a vise grip, the ripples pulling me in and spurring on my own release. I didn't have a chance of holding back as those inner muscles squeezed.

I bit out a curse as my balls exploded. That pleasure/pain combination threatened to take me down as I let go deep inside her, spurt after spurt.

I'd never come so hard or so long in my life. I grunted as each thick ribbon shot out of me and deep inside her. By the time there was nothing left, I was breathing so hard I felt like I'd just run a marathon after smoking an entire carton of cigarettes. It took forever for me to catch my breath.

My hold on her didn't loosen in the slightest as I finally came back down. Taking stock of everything that had just happened, the realization hit me that I never wanted to let her go.

Chapter Twenty-Two

WILLOW

It took hardly any time at all for the fog from the endorphin high I'd been riding to wear off, and once it did the realization of what had just happened hit me like a bolt of lightning.

Things had gotten way out of hand before I could think to put a stop to it. I'd wanted to make him stop asking questions, that was all. I hadn't meant for things to escalate the way they had when I first kissed him. My only thought was: *do something to shut him up, Willow!*

If I'd been in my right mind at the time, after how badly the last kiss had ended, I *never* would have tried for a second. But desperation was a fickle thing.

Stone let out a slow, chopped exhale that whispered across my skin, bringing me back to the present, most specifically to the fact that he was still holding me so tight I was molded against him. He still had hold of my leg right behind my knee, keeping it hitched up and draped over his hip. While I was completely naked except for my pretty pink bra, he was still fully dressed. But the most crucial thing at that moment was that he was still inside me and he was still hard.

How the hell was that even possible?

He straightened, putting a small gap between us, and slowly began to pull out, causing me to gasp. I'd never felt so tender after sex in my life, but I guess being ravaged until I'd had two of the strongest, most intense orgasms of my life would make me a little sensitive.

My gaze shot down to where we were connected, and a whole new sense of panic washed over me, sending a chill across my naked skin despite the summer heat. I hissed as I watched his glistening length slip out. His *bare* glistening length.

My gaze darted back to his, my breathing escalating by the second. "You didn't use a condom."

His gaze flared, but only for a second. His expression remained calm, almost serene as he asked, "You on the pill?"

"Well, yes. But—"

He interrupted me. "I'm clean. That's not something you have to worry about with me. I've never gone ungloved until now. Never lost control like that before."

My head twitched to the side. I was taken completely by surprise. But still, I couldn't let myself react to that, and I certainly couldn't admit that the knowledge that I made him lose control felt good.

Nope. It didn't. Not at all.

I opened my mouth and spit out the first words that popped into my head. "I have to go."

His chin jerked back in confusion and his eyelids narrowed. "What?"

I gave his chest a shove, forcing him backward and hopping off the hood of his car. "I have to go," I repeated as I scrambled for my clothes. My panties were ruined thanks to Stone, but I managed to locate my pants and shirt, and dressed as quickly as I possibly could.

"What the fuck are you doing?" he asked as he tucked his length back into his jeans. He pulled the zipper up but didn't bother with the button.

"I shouldn't have come here," I told him as I struggled with my shirt, getting it stuck over my head before I finally managed to yank it down and cover the rest of myself. "This was a huge mistake."

"Are you kidding me?" he asked in a tone that was almost a snarl.

When I forced myself to glance back at him, his expression radiated pissed-off alpha male. Something about that look on his face reignited my own anger, the very anger that had fueled me to drive out here and confront him in the first place.

"Why in the world would I be kidding you?" I snapped. "You made it very clear last week that you had no interest in me."

"Pretty sure the fact I just came inside you so goddamn hard I'm *still* seeing stars might prove otherwise."

I brushed my hair back from my face and lifted my chin. "You mean how maybe the shy, quiet librarian type who blushes every time she makes eye contact with someone does get you going after all?" I asked sarcastically, throwing his words from last Friday back in his face.

He flinched, regret quickly pouring over his features as he recalled the nasty words he'd hurled at me that night. "Baby, it's clear we need to talk—"

We really didn't. And I was so done with this.

"I'm not your baby," I informed him. "And we have absolutely nothing to talk about. This"—I waved my hand toward the car hood he'd just fucked me on—"never should have happened, and it's a mistake I intend never to make again."

"That's bullshit, and you know it, Willow. You kissed me first," he barked.

I threw my arms out in frustration. "To shut you up! Not because I wanted *that* to happen. After last time, I was hedging my bets that you'd pull away, hurl a few more insults at me, and send me on my merry way just like last time!"

He paused, inhaling deeply as he propped his hands on his hips and dropped his head like he was silently counting to ten in order to calm himself. A second later, his amber eyes locked with mine. "That was the best fucking sex I've ever had. And you can deny it until you're blue in the face, but I know it was the best for you too. You can't just walk away from something like that."

"That's *exactly* what I'm going to do," I returned. Not wanting to give him a chance to say anything else, I spun around and started out of the garage. The sight of that truck reminded me why I'd come here in the first place. I didn't slow down as I looked back over my shoulder and called, "And I want my car back, Stone. I'm dead serious."

"That's not gonna happen, sweetheart," he called back, his tone full of arrogance that made my blood start to heat.

I whipped back around and hit him with my most vicious glare. The bastard was standing with his feet planted shoulder width apart and those thick tattooed arms crossed over his chest. The air he was giving off was like he was just daring me to argue. The dog I'd completely forgotten about was now standing at his master's side.

"Oh yes it damn well will!"

"Not a chance in hell."

I clenched my fists at my side and felt a growl vibrate up my throat. "*God*, I hate you," I barked at him, and for some inexplicable reason, the corners of his mouth hooked up in a smile.

"Really? 'Cause you sure as hell didn't just fuck me like you hated me."

"Gah!" I threw my head back and screamed at the heavens before turning back around and storming the rest of the way to the truck. I climbed in and peeled out of there as fast as I could, the whole time every move I made sent a twinge between my thighs and reminded me of what I'd just done.

STONE

. . .

I HAD a feeling I was taking my life—or at the very least, the safety and wellbeing of my testicles—into my own hands as I made my way up the porch steps toward the front door. After the brain-melting release I'd had with Willow a few hours earlier, I *really* didn't want any part of my groin at risk, but I didn't have much choice.

My knock on the door was greeted with the sound of a dog barking. A second later, Clay pulled it open with one hand while keeping hold of his chocolate Lab's collar with the other. "Stone? Hey, man. What's up?"

I held out my hand for his dog to sniff so he'd calm down, and sure enough, after a few seconds, he got bored with the new guest. Clay was able to release him, and he didn't hesitate to turn tail and head back inside the house.

"Hey. Sorry to just swing by like this. Hope I'm not interrupting anything."

"Nah, it's cool. You want to come in?"

I reached around and scratched the back of my neck, feeling an uncomfortable tightening in my gut. "Thanks, but it's probably best I stay outside. I'm here to talk to Lark."

Understanding flicked across his expression, followed quickly by a smart-ass grin. I knew then that Lark had shared just how big a dick I was with her soon-to-be husband. He knew I was on his woman's shit list, and he didn't feel bad for me in the slightest. "All right, brother. I'll go get her and leave you to it." He started to turn but stopped to look back at me. "Stay on your toes, man, she's a wily one. Don't take your eyes off her. And protect your manhood at all times."

I offered him a flat expression and a dry, "Thanks."

With a snicker, he walked back inside and shut the door behind him. Two minutes later, the door opened again, this time swinging so fast it gave me a start. Lark stomped out, hip cocked and arms crossed over her chest. The look on her face made my balls shrink up just a bit, and Clay's words of warning came back to me.

"What the hell are you doing here?" she asked, practically spitting fire.

I figured there was no point in dancing around the subject, so I came right out with it. "I know you and Willow have gotten really tight, so I know you know who gave her that black eye, and I want to know who the fuck it was."

Her mask slipped for a second, and I caught sight of her shock before she schooled her features and tilted her chin up almost defiantly. "How do you even know about that?"

"Doesn't matter how I know," I replied. "I just know. Tell me who it was. Please," I tacked on when she arched an eyebrow, looking like she was seconds away from ripping into me.

"If you want to know anything regarding Willow, I suggest you ask *her*. It's not my place to air her personal business."

I gritted my teeth and counted to ten, trying to control the frustration rushing through my veins. "I did ask her. She wouldn't tell me. That's why I'm here."

She rocked back, her eyes filled with suspicion, narrowing into beady little slits. "When did you see her? She hasn't gone anywhere since—" She caught herself, clamping her mouth shut and rolling her teeth between her lips.

"Look, there's stuff you don't know about, and like you

said, it's not my place to share it with you. But things between Willow and me are very different now—"

"Different how?" she broke in, her features awash with skepticism.

I knew I had to give her something if I had any hope of getting her to talk. "Different in the sense that she's mine," I said, causing her eyes to flare. "Even if she denies it, even if it takes me a good long while to convince her, she's mine now, and someone put their fucking hands on her. I can't let that stand."

Her demeanor changed significantly. She seemed to deflate right in front of my eyes.

"Stone, you need to let this go—"

"The fuck I do," I clipped.

"It's not what you think, okay? Willow's already having a hard enough time as it is, and running around town trying to exact justice in her name isn't going to help. If anything, you're just going to make it worse. *You need to let this go*," she repeated, stressing each word.

"That's not going to happen," I grunted. "This son of a bitch has to pay."

She let out a sigh, like she was carrying the weight of the world on her shoulders. "It's not that simple." She shook her head and grumbled to herself under her breath, "I can't believe I'm about to do this," and for the first time since stepping up on her porch, I felt a tiny glimmer of hope.

"The only reason I'm about to tell you any of this is because I'm afraid you're gonna go off half-cocked and make everything so much worse."

Her words were doing little to comfort me.

"And I swear to God, if Willow hates me because of this, I'm going to make it my life's mission to burn your world to the freaking ground."

I fully believed she had the tenacity and can-do attitude to pull something like that off. "Christ, Lark. Just tell me."

"Her dad is sick," she started, that initial declaration doing nothing but confusing me. "Like, really sick."

"What? Are we talkin' cancer or something?"

"Alzheimer's. And it's progressing really fast. Sometimes he doesn't know who Willow is. Sometimes he thinks she's her dead mother. But Monday night was really bad. She and her sisters have been splitting shifts, going to take care of him. Making him dinner, keeping him company, that sort of thing. Anyway, Willow went over there that night, and he was in a paranoid rage." My gut sank to the floor, because I had a feeling I knew where this was going, and it wasn't going to be good. "He thought she was someone else, someone who had come to take him away, and he hit her. He wasn't in his right mind. She had to call her sister and brother-in-law to help calm him down."

Reaching up to rake a hand through my hair, I turned to the side, staring out, unseeing, at the view from their porch. "Jesus," I hissed.

"Yeah. To say it messed her up pretty badly would be a serious understatement. She hasn't been able to see him since, because if he gets a look at that eye he'll freak out just as bad as you did. And if he finds out he's the one who gave it to her . . ."

She looked at me expectantly, and I didn't hesitate to finish her sentence for her. "He'll hate himself."

"Exactly. And she'll do anything to prevent him from that kind of pain. But in the meantime, not being able to see him *and* knowing he's going downhill fast is killing her. She's strong as hell, stronger than most women I know. But I don't know anyone who wouldn't fall apart if they were living with what she's living with. The fact that she hasn't is just a testament to how incredible she is."

Didn't I know it. I'd thought there was more to Willow than met the eye, and each day more and more layers of her were peeled away.

Feeling a heaviness in my chest I didn't know what to do with, I turned back to her. "Thanks for telling me," I said before moving to the steps and taking them down off the porch.

"Don't make me regret it, Stone," she called after me. "She's one of my best friends. Please don't mess that up."

Looking back over my shoulder, I assured her, "I won't. I promise."

But as I climbed back on my bike and sped off, I couldn't help but think. I wouldn't mess things up for her, but as for me . . . had I fucked everything up so bad I couldn't possibly come back from it?

Chapter Twenty-Three

WILLOW

Rolling up my mat after disinfecting it and wiping it clean, I carried it over to the wall of cubbies and stowed it inside.

Aurora's Saturday evening yoga classes weren't nearly as packed as the ones earlier in the day, and I desperately needed to talk to her and Lark after what had gone down with Stone and me the day before. The bruise was still there, but with a thicker coating of concealer, I'd been able to make it look more like it was just a dark circle from lack of sleep. Not that that was too far off the mark either. But with all the emotions swirling around inside me, I couldn't stay locked up in my house, with only my thoughts as company, for another second.

The classroom was quickly emptying, the people with Saturday night plans eager to get on with their night, leaving just the three of us behind.

"Hey, my colorful kumquat," Aurora said as she and

Lark came over to stand by me. "So what did you think? You like your first class?"

"I always feel so calm and relaxed afterward," Lark added before lifting her water bottle to her lips and taking a sip. "I'm really glad you decided to come with me."

I gave her a smile that felt a little wobbly. "Yeah, me too. I really liked it." That wasn't a total lie. I had liked the class a lot, and I was sure I'd feel more centered or whatever if it hadn't been for the fact that every time we moved into a new position, I'd feel a twinge or subtle ache between my thighs, reminding me again and again and again of what went down and how *brilliantly* Stone had used his wildly impressive erection.

Aurora's forehead crinkled and her head cocked to the side. "Your face is getting all red. You okay?"

"What? Yeah! Yes, I'm totally fine. Absolutely. It was a great class."

Oh no.

"She's rambling and getting all high-pitched," Lark said to Aurora as they both looked at me suspiciously. "She's hiding something from us."

"You hated it, didn't you?" Aurora asked, her expression falling like I'd just informed her that her favorite brand of chocolate was being discontinued.

"What? No! Of course not!"

"Then what aren't you telling us?" Lark demanded to know.

"I had sex with Stone yesterday," I blurted out in rapid fire. "That's why I'm all blushy and stuff. I had sex with him yesterday, and those positions just made me . . ." I shifted uncomfortably, pressing my thighs together to try and ease that incessant throbbing. "I still feel . . . well, you know."

"Holy shit!" Aurora cried. "Willow Amelia Thorne, you saucy little pink flamingo! Look at you!" She lifted her hand in the air, and I gave her a weak high-five, still unsure how I felt about the whole situation. "I'm so proud," she fake-sniffled, wiping at a nonexistent tear. "I feel like my baby's all grown up and getting laid."

"Rora," I said with a sigh, "we've had the whole middle name conversation already."

"I'm just trying different ones on for size until I can find one that fits you."

"I already have a middle name."

She waved her hand in the air and scrunched her nose. "Eh. We can talk about that later."

Deciding it was pointless to get into that particular argument with her, I moved on. "I'm not really sure you should be proud of me right now. I don't necessarily think this news warrants excitement," I admitted. "Other than freaking the hell out, I honestly don't know how I feel about what we did."

"Hmm," she hummed thoughtfully, lifting her hand and tapping her chin like she was giving my situation some serious thought. "Mm-hmm. Mm-hmm. I see."

I shifted my gaze to Lark, realizing she'd been surprisingly quiet after my confession. I'd expected *some* kind of reaction from her, but I was surprised to see her features awash with what looked a whole lot like worry, and maybe a bit of guilt.

"Honey, what's wrong?"

"I—" She stopped and dragged her bottom lip between her teeth, and for a second, I thought she might actually start crying. "I did something. And I want to tell you, but I'm really scared you'll get upset and hate me forever."

"Oh, Lark." Moving toward her, I wrapped her in my arms and squeezed her tight. "I could never hate you; it's literally impossible."

She pulled away with a sniffle, batting at the lone tear that had fallen from her eye. "You say that now, but you don't know what I did."

"Just tell me. Whatever it is, we can work it out."

She pulled in a fortifying breath, her eyes dancing around the room like they were unable to keep contact with mine. "Stone showed up at my house yesterday. He was really upset and saying all this stuff. He wanted to know who had hit you. I told him it wasn't my place, but he wouldn't let it go. I was worried he was going to make things harder for you."

"Oh shit," Aurora breathed. Meanwhile, I couldn't seem to pull enough oxygen into my lungs.

"I didn't want to, but I ended up telling him what happened with your dad." Another tear fell, and the sadness in her eyes tore at my chest. "I'm so sorry, but I was scared he'd find out on his own and get the wrong idea. He was really mad, Will. I didn't want him to try and track your father down—"

I cut her off, reaching out to take both her hands in mine. "It's okay," I assured her. "I'm not mad."

She blinked slowly. "You—you're not?"

"No. I'm not. It's not like you were gossiping. You had a

really good reason for telling him the truth. I get that, and I can't tell you how grateful I am that you had my back like that."

Her whole body sagged with relief. "Oh, thank God," she breathed. "I was so scared you were going to hate me forever."

I smiled and squeezed her hands. "Never gonna happen."

"Well, now that we've gotten the soap opera drama portion of the conversation out of the way," Aurora broke in, "can we please get to the important shit? How in the hell did this happen? I thought we were firmly in the I Hate Stone Hendrix and Plan to Cut His Dick Off camp. Not that I mind switching camps or anything, just color me curious."

"We were never planning to cut his dick off," Lark admonished. "You always take things to such a violent level! We were going to junk-punch him and hate him for eternity. That's it."

"Whatever," she said with a roll of her eyes.

I broke up their fight by telling them how everything happened, from my phone call with Elaina, to going to the garage to get my car, to driving to Stone's house to confront him and demand he give it back. I told them about the kiss that was only supposed to get him to stop asking questions.

"I don't know how it happened. It's like we both just . . . I don't know. I've heard people say things like 'it just happened' and 'I don't know how it started' and I used to think they were full of it. But now I get it. I went there planning to yell at him, and the next thing I know, I'm sprawled out on the hood of this old muscle car, and he's down on his knees in front of me."

"No. Freaking. *Way*! You did it on the hood of a muscle car?" Aurora asked, her voice rising with each word until she was practically squealing. "That's like my ultimate *Fast and Furious* fantasy! Ugh! I'm so jealous of you right now."

I felt the heat return to my cheeks, a slow smile pulling at my lips as I thought back to it. "It was pretty hot," I had to admit. There was really no point in lying about that. "But after we finished—"

Lark lifted her hands, palms out. "Wait, wait, wait. Something tells me you're leaving out some crucial details."

"Yeah," Aurora agreed vehemently. "Like his dick size."

"Or if it was any good," Lark added.

"Or how many orgasms you had," Aurora ticked off on her finger.

"Or—"

"Okay, okay! I get it." I closed my eyes and pulled in a fortifying breath. "I don't know the exact size; all I can really tell you is it was *big*. Yes, it was good. It was *really* freaking good. I had two"—I paused in contemplation—"or it could have been three. Or two, but the last one was just super long—"

"Oh my God, I hate you so much right now," Aurora whined. "Seriously. I need to get laid. It should be illegal to live in a town with this many hot men and not get the D on a regular basis."

Lark giggled but brushed her off. "Okay, so what happened afterward?"

And this is where it got messy. "Well, I freaked out."

She nodded in understanding. "Rightfully so, given the last thing he'd said to you."

I jabbed my index finger at Lark. "Exactly! So I freaked out, told him it was a huge mistake, and started getting dressed."

Both women were looking at me with wide, enthralled eyes. "What did he say to that?" Aurora asked.

"He didn't like it. He got really pissed. Said it was the best sex he'd ever had, and I'd be lying if I claimed differently, and told me I couldn't just walk away from something like that. He did a complete one-eighty from the week before. We started fighting, and I told him I hated him." My face got so hot, I knew my skin had to be bright red. "He got this smirk on his face and said I didn't fuck him like I hated him. Then I basically jumped in the truck and got the hell out of there."

Neither of them said anything for the longest time, and after a while my whole body started to tingle like there were ants skittering around beneath my skin. "Will one of you please say something?" I cried when the silence got to be too much for me. "You're making me really anxious!"

"I—Wow," Lark murmured.

Then Aurora added, "That was so freaking hot, I think I just came a little."

I let out a pathetic groan. "That's not helping."

"Well, what is it you want us to say, babe?" Lark asked.

"I don't know," I exclaimed, throwing my arms in the air. "Maybe agree with me that I was right and it was a colossal mistake."

For the first time since the conversation started, Aurora grew serious. "We can't do that, honey."

My bottom lip poked out in a childish pout. "Why not?"

"Because I'm not sure it was. Yes, he hurt you, and he's an asshole for that, but obviously something changed for him."

Lark spoke up. "Or maybe it *didn't* change, but he finally decided to stop lying to himself."

I'd considered all of that myself over the past twenty-four hours. Problem was, it only made that storm of unstable emotions inside of me that much stronger.

"I saw it on his face when he came to talk to me yesterday," Lark continued. "He was ravaged at the thought of someone hurting you. He looked like he wanted to tear the world apart and set it on fire. When I told him the whole story, it was like his heart broke right then and there. A man doesn't react like that if the woman doesn't mean something to him in a *very* big way."

"The fact that he'd even go there and face Lark's wrath in the first place, just to get the truth, speaks volumes," Aurora stated. "Raging hot sex aside, there's something much more there. But you're the one who has to decide if it's worth going after."

God, why did my friends have to be so reasonable? "I put myself out there once already. You guys know what a big deal that is for someone like me. I've always been the girl who hides away in a corner."

Lark gave me a sympathetic smile. "Yeah. Until now. You aren't that girl anymore, Willow. Sure, you can still be shy and get flustered, but it's totally adorable. And you don't give yourself enough credit. You're tough as nails. You can take a few lumps."

Aurora's expression grew fierce. "And if he's a dick to you again, you can dole out a few lumps of your own."

Lark nodded in agreement. "You aren't saving yourself any pain by ignoring your feelings for him, sweetie. They aren't going away. That kind of stuff doesn't fade over time. All you're doing is cutting yourself off from the possibility of anything good happening. Look at me and Clay. If I'd let the past dictate our future, there's no way I ever would have given him another chance. And if I hadn't, I'd be miserable right now."

She had a point. She and Clay had the very definition of a rocky start. And Lark had endured the kind of heartbreak I couldn't even imagine. What happened with Stone was peanuts in comparison.

"Look, it's not like you have to make a decision today or even tomorrow," Aurora told me. "You've been through a lot lately. Give yourself some time, sit with your feelings. You'll eventually come to a decision."

Sit with my feelings. That didn't sound like bad advice.

"Have I mentioned lately that I love you guys?"

"Aw!" Aurora opened her arms wide. "We love you too, my little string bean. Now come on, bring it in for a group hug."

And just like that, my two friends managed to lift a huge weight off my chest and make everything a little bit better.

Chapter Twenty-Four

STONE

I stood on Scooter and Caroline's back deck, the neck of a half-full beer bottle dangling from my fingers as I rested my forearms against the banister and stared out at the trees and mountains beyond their property line.

I'd been summoned to another Sunday family dinner, and while this one had gone a whole hell of a lot better than the last, I was still feeling off-kilter. If my mind wasn't replaying the scene with Willow on the hood of the Chevelle —it was guaran-damn-teed I was never getting rid of that car after that—I was thinking about everything Lark had told me.

I couldn't imagine what she was going through, having to care for a loved one who sometimes didn't even recognize her face. It had to kill her. She really was so much stronger than I'd ever given her credit for, which made me feel like even more of an asshole for what I'd done to her.

I'd convinced myself she had too much baggage, that she required someone to protect her from the big bad world, and that I wasn't up for that much responsibility, when the truth was, she didn't need anyone to take care of her. She had it in hand just fine. Hell, she was handling shit better than I would if the shoe was on the other foot, that was for damn sure.

And as far as protecting her went . . . well, that instinct wasn't going away no matter how long I ignored it or how deep I tried to bury it. That baser instinct was pushing all others to the background.

And I'd fucked it all up by pushing her away.

On that thought, my chest clenched painfully tight. I massaged at the ache with my free hand as I silently berated myself for being a world-class dick.

"What's got you standing out here, staring off into the distance like a broody teenage vampire?"

I'd been so lost in thought that I hadn't heard the back door slide open, but at my sister's words, I twisted my neck and shot her a bewildered look. "What?"

She joined me at the railing, letting out a frustrated sigh. "Why will none of the men in my life watch *Twilight*, for crying out loud?"

"Because we don't want our balls to shrivel up to the size of raisins and sink back up into our bodies."

She rolled her eyes and bumped her shoulder against mine before bending down to copy my stance and lean on the banister. "Whatever. So why are you out here alone, looking all stoic?"

"Just thinking," I replied, turning my unseeing gaze back out across the yard.

"Let me guess . . . about a certain sweet brunette with a

tendency to blush?" I shot her a side-eyed look, and she smiled smugly. "Jensen told me you went by his office almost every day last week to try and see her."

"Goddamn it," I grunted, lifting my beer and taking a swig. "That man of yours really can't keep his mouth shut. He has to be the worst gossip in this fucking town."

"I heard that," Jensen called through the screen door. "And I am what I am. Town gossip keeps my woman happy and happy wife, happy life. You'll get that when you and Willow settle down."

Shane started laughing while I let out a mumbled curse.

"So? Am I right? You're out here all messed up over Willow, aren't you?"

I didn't bother lying. After all, what was the point? "Yeah. I am."

Silence enveloped us for so long that I figured she'd decided to drop the subject, but when she spoke next, her insightfulness took me by surprise. "You've spent so long letting the memory of our mom dictate every important decision in your life, big bro. Aren't you tired of living in her shadow?"

"I'm not living in her shadow," I insisted, but something about what she just said struck a chord deep within me.

Her voice grew low and gentle with what she said next. The teasing Shane who liked to give me shit just to be a pain in the ass was gone. "I'm not stupid, Stone, I remember what it was like for you when we were with her. You were responsible for everything. Most of all me. That wasn't fair."

My protective instinct came raging to the surface. "I

didn't mind looking after you. You were my baby sister; it was my job."

She looked across her shoulder at me with a sad smile. "No it wasn't. It was hers, and she failed with both of us. Epically."

I remained quiet at that, the silence all the confirmation she needed to know I agreed with her. Carley Hendrix had failed both her children so astoundingly, she'd have gotten all the medals if bad parenting was an Olympic sport.

"She wore you so thin and used you up that by the time you were an adult, you were over it. I understand that, Stone. Maybe I didn't get it when I was a kid, but I get it now. Because you spent nineteen years of your life taking care of her, cleaning up her messes and owning up to *her* responsibilities, your well ran dry. I can't say it didn't hurt when you left, but, looking back, I understand now. You never had a life of your own. You had to live hers because she gave you no choice. You needed to leave so you could attempt to carve out something for yourself."

The fact that I'd hurt my baby sister, even if she'd forgiven me for it, even if she'd moved past it, still burned like a red-hot brand against my skin.

"I'll regret hurting you until the day I die."

"Don't," she whispered fiercely. "I don't want you to do that. You carried too much damn weight on your shoulders when you were a kid, and you're still doing it today. I'm not saying any of this because I want an apology. You gave that to me a long time ago, even though you didn't have to, and I gladly accepted it. Let that go, bro. I'm telling you all this now in the hopes of helping you pull your head out of your ass."

I snorted into my beer as I took another pull. "Shane Rose, the self-help guru."

She knocked into me playfully. "Hey, I'm damn good at it. If you'd just listen to me, I could fix your life in like two seconds."

I arched my brow and gave her a crooked grin. "That right? Okay, oh wise one. Hit me with it. What have you got?"

"Well, first of all, you need to stop thinking all relationships are like the ones you saw Carley spiral through when you were younger. Her dating life was a hotbed of crap because she was a shitty person who picked shitty men. I'm convinced it was a conscious decision on her part because she got off on all that fighting. But you look at every woman who crosses your path as a potential Carley when you have better examples all around you. You're just too stubborn to pay attention.

"Scooter and Caroline have been together since they were teenagers. Sure, Jensen and I had a bit of a rough patch"—she smiled when I shot her a dark look at how she'd downplayed what had gone down between them—"but look at us now. Look at all our friends. Cannon and Farah. Poppy and Jase. Lark and Clay. You have shining examples all around you that love isn't an albatross around a person's neck, slowly choking the life out of them, but you refuse to pay attention.

"No one said love was easy. It's hard as hell, but it's so worth it, Gavin." Her use of my given name wasn't sarcastic this time. She was using it as a way to drive her point home. "It's not a responsibility. It's a partnership. If you love someone, and they love you back, they carry half that load you've been dragging around. It may still weigh a ton from time to time, but that's okay, because the other person is there to take over and give you a break when it gets too heavy. *That's* what you've been missing out on, big brother. That's what I want for you. You've been dragging that weight behind you all this time. Don't you want someone to step in and give you a hand?"

"Christ," I grunted, clearing my throat in an attempt to dislodge the lump that had taken up residence there. "When the hell did you get so wise?"

She shrugged, a self-satisfied grin on her smug face. "One of us had to be the brains in the family. Lord knows it wasn't gonna be you."

I tipped one corner of my mouth up. "True. I got the looks, after all."

Her hand flew out, giving my arm a stinging slap. "If the decisions you've been making are anything to go by, all you got was the brawn. I'm the brains *and* the looks, asshole."

I chuckled as I rubbed at my sore skin. "Jesus, you're vicious."

"And don't forget that."

My sister might have been a pain in the ass, but she had a gift for being able to read me, and as though she sensed I needed a while to take in the heaviness of everything she'd just said, she kept quiet, standing beside me in companionable silence.

Finally, I spoke, asking the question that had been weighing on my mind for a while now. "How do you know when you love someone?"

She stared off like she was giving that some consideration while she pulled in a deep breath. "I'm not sure there's a definitive answer for that. It's something that can be different for everyone. I think you know you love someone when you look at them and feel a happiness you've never experienced before. When you think of them out of nowhere and can't stop from smiling. But I think, at the end of the day, you know when you realize you want to do everything you can to make them happy, that your sole purpose for being in their lives is to make each day better than the one before."

I silently finished off my beer while I thought on that, feeling something strange and foreign in my chest.

She'd struck that chord again, this time making it ring through my skull.

There was something so damn familiar with everything she'd just described, and now I knew there was no way in hell those feelings vibrating inside me were going away.

Chapter Twenty-Five

WILLOW

It had been a long day. If I had to guess, this day would go down in the history books as the Monday-est Monday ever.

I used to brush it off as a joke when the guys at work would tease me that they couldn't function without me. I was just a receptionist after all. Sure I did some paperwork and handled most of the filing, but it wasn't like I was performing brain surgery or something. It had always been nice to hear them say that, but I never really believed it.

Then I got to work this morning and realized they hadn't been exaggerating. Lark had done what she could in my absence, but she had her own responsibilities. The filing was an absolute disaster, and there were countless voicemails on my personal extension from unhappy clients. As shy as I was, I'd always been pretty good over the phone. Not having to see the person I was talking to face to face had made it easier, and apparently, our clients would much rather deal with me than the men who did the actual work they contracted Elite Security for.

I'd always liked Jensen, Laeth, and Gage, but I had to admit, when it came to bedside manner, the men were a bit lacking. They preferred to get the details of the job, do it, bill the client, and move on. Who knew that I was the rosy go-between that kept everything moving fluidly?

When the guys walked in earlier that morning and saw me sitting behind my desk, I'd almost thought Laeth was going to burst into tears of relief. "Thank fucking God," he'd whispered, his eyes growing a little misty.

"Never again," Gage had grunted. "We'll pay you anything you ask; just name the price. Anything to keep you from taking another day off."

"I don't think that's legal," Lark had intervened on my behalf.

"Don't care." He pointed his long index finger at me. "If you ever take a vacation, I'll quit. Hand to God." Then he'd spun around and stomped down the hall to his office and slammed the door.

I'd spent the rest of the day putting out fires. I'd appeased clients' concerns and smoothed all that over, then I'd spent the rest of the time cleaning up the filing that three grown men—who were all computer savvy, I might add—had managed to royally screw up.

By the time my day ended, I was exhausted and just wanted to go home and crash. I swung by and picked up some Chinese takeout for dinner on my way home, knowing there wasn't a chance in hell I'd have it in me to cook.

I was still driving Stone's truck around, but despite the

fact I wasn't as angry as I'd been about it the week before, I had yet decided how I felt about the whole situation. But that was okay. After my talk with Lark and Aurora this past Saturday, I felt a lot better giving myself time to decide how I felt.

I turned the truck into my driveway and slammed on the brakes at the sight of the familiar motorcycle parked next to my closed garage door. My eyes swung to the front porch, and I saw Stone sitting on the top step, his gaze pointed at me, and even from this distance, I could feel those whiskey-browns burning into my skin.

Pulling the rest of the way up, I threw the truck in park and killed the engine while I breathed deep, trying to keep calm as I grabbed the bag of food and climbed out.

He stood to his full, imposing height as I came up the walkway and stopped at the foot of the porch steps. "Hey," he grunted in greeting.

"What are you doing here?"

"We need to talk."

I really didn't have the energy to do this. As it was, just standing there I could feel myself starting to sag.

"Stone, I really don't want to fight with you tonight, okay? It's been a long day, and I'm tired."

He took a step down, surprising me by reaching out and brushing a lock of my hair behind my ear. "I'm not here to fight, mouse, I promise. There are some things I want to tell you." His eyes practically pleaded with me to hear him out. "But if now's not a good time, I'll wait. You can name the time and place. Just promise you'll hear me out."

I let out a slow, steady breath. He'd just given me an out

if I wanted it—sort of—but seeing him standing there, smelling that manly scent of his, I felt a pang deep within my chest.

You've missed him, dummy, my brain screamed at me. *Stop being an idiot and let him inside.*

I shifted in place for a second before meeting his intense gaze. "Are you hungry?" I asked, lifting the heavy bag in my hand. "I got Chinese and they always give me too much to finish by myself."

He hit me with a smile that made my core pulse. "That sounds great. Thanks."

He took the bag from my hand, holding it for me as I got my keys out and unlocked the door.

My house felt so much smaller with him standing inside of it. I tried not to let my nerves get to me as we silently plated our food and started eating, but I knew I was blushing furiously, because every time I looked down at his hands or watched his tongue peek out to swipe across his lips as we ate, I was hit with a fresh wave of arousal, knowing exactly how skilled that tongue and those fingers were.

I was halfway done with my meal and his plate was clean when I managed to summon up the courage to ask, "So what did you want to tell me?"

He cleared his throat, wiping his mouth with a paper towel before shifting in his seat to face me full-on.

"I'm not sure how much you've heard about me from when I lived here when I was younger, but my mom took off on Shane and me when I was nineteen."

I vaguely remember hearing something about that, but I'd only been around ten years old when that happened, and our families didn't really run in the same circles, so I didn't know much.

"I'm really sorry," I told him.

"It's okay. To be honest, her bailing on us was a blessing. Shane was only six at the time, but even when Mom was around, I was still the one taking care of her. Carley didn't have a maternal bone in her body. The only reason she had either of us was to trap our fathers into staying." He let out a bitter chuckle and shook his head. "Needless to say, that didn't work out too well for her, and just like when she left, Shane and I were better off without those assholes in our lives."

My heart splintered in my chest. "I didn't know."

"When we lived with her, she had a revolving door of men. And let me tell you, she could fucking pick them. Losers, every one of them. I grew up in a household where screaming and yelling and throwing things at peoples' heads was just a typical Tuesday night. Not only did I have to take care of Shane, but she was so worthless that I had to take care of my mom too. I got a job before it was legal for me to be working just so I could pay to keep the lights on and make sure Shane got fed, or to make sure I had bail money when Carley would do something to get her ass thrown in jail."

"Oh God," I breathed, the threat of tears for a young Stone burning behind my eyes.

He looked down at the table, his tattooed fingers idly tracing the patterns of the woodgrain. "Like I said, best thing to ever happen to Shane and me was when that bitch left. But by then, she'd already managed to fuck me up. I looked at all those men she had parading in and out of her life, and I told myself, that was never gonna be me. If that was what relationships were about, I didn't want a goddamn thing to do with them."

As hard as it was, I made sure not to let the pain of the blow he'd just landed show on my face.

"I'd spent my entire childhood and into my adult years taking care of people. Shane and I talked about it yesterday, and she described what happened to me in the best way. She said that Carley used me up. By the time I was grown, I'd been living my whole life for someone else, and I didn't think I had anything left to give. I was done. I didn't want the burden of taking care of another person. I just wanted to live my life."

"Why are you telling me all of this?" I asked on a croak, a whirlwind of emotions making my throat uncomfortably tight.

He met my eyes just then, and what I saw in them stole my breath. "Because what I said to you in the parking lot of Bad Alibi was all bullshit, mouse."

My eyebrows dipped in and my head canted to the side. "I don't understand."

He shifted his chair toward mine, leaning in so close he was all I could see. "I was lying to you to push you away because what I felt for you scared the shit out of me. Since I bailed on this place at twenty-one, I've been telling myself I wasn't a relationship guy, because being with a woman meant you had to live for her. You had to protect her, be the guy she depended on. And I couldn't do that. When I met you—the first time I saw you—every protective instinct inside me came roaring to life, so I told myself that nothing could ever happen between us."

"I don't need to be protected," I clipped, feeling my anger return as my hands clenched into fists. "I don't need to rely on anyone else to take care of me. I'm more than capable of taking care of myself."

For some inexplicable reason, my comment made him smile. "Trust me, baby. I'm well aware of that. You're so goddamn strong; I'm constantly in awe of you. Every time I think I've figured out who you are, you show me another piece, and I'm taken back all over again. You don't need protecting, but when it comes to you, those instincts won't let up. And I realized something a while back that scared the shit out of me and made me more determined than ever to stay away."

I could feel my heart racing and my hands trembling as I clasped them together and held them in my lap. "What was that?"

"That I never want that feeling to fade. Whether you need it or not, no matter how capable you are, I want to protect you. You blew everything I thought I believed out of the water. I was made to be the man you rely on, mouse. I never really felt like I had a purpose until I met you."

Oh God. My heart was in my throat, my mind spinning out of control. "What-what are you saying?"

Before I could react, he reached over and grabbed me by the hips, pulling me into his lap and taking my face into his big hands. "I'm saying I fucked up. I don't deserve it, but I'm asking you to give me another chance, because I want to spend my days trying to make each one of yours better.

You're mine, baby. You can fight me on that, but I'm not gonna stop trying to prove it to you."

You are not *going to cry, Willow,* I warned myself. *Get your shit together. The man you've wanted for a freaking year just claimed you as his.*

There was just one thing I had to know. "If I'm yours, what does that make you?"

He gave me that smile again, and that tightness between my thighs was accompanied by a rush of dampness that made me squirm in his lap.

"That makes me all yours, baby. For as long as you want me."

I wanted to tell him right then and there that I wanted him forever, but I worried it might be too soon for that. Besides, what he'd just given me was more than enough. By a *lot*.

That pulsing between my thighs morphed into a needy ache I couldn't deny. "Stone," I whispered, scratching my nails through the stubble on his jaw.

His eyes darkened and his nostrils flared. "Yeah, baby?"

"We've had two kisses by my count, and I was the one who initiated both of them. I think it's your turn to—"

Before I could finish, he fisted his hand in my hair, jerked my mouth down to his, and plunged his tongue inside. I loved that there was no slow, sweet buildup with our kisses. Stone wasn't a slow and sweet kind of guy. The way he kissed me made me feel like he was desperate for me, and that was the biggest turn-on I'd ever experienced. I didn't need slow and sweet. I needed him to be so crazed for me that he couldn't maintain control.

"Tell me something, mouse," he growled against my lips when we had to break apart in order to breathe. "Are you wet for me right now?"

I sucked in a needy gasp and nodded, because, *God*, was I ever!

He let out a primal sound that drove me wild. One second I was on his lap and the next he had us both on our feet. Grabbing me by the hips, he spun me around and pressed his chest to my back, using his chin to brush the hair off my neck. "Promise I'll go nice and slow next time. Take my time with you. But I need you too goddamn bad right now," his husky voice said into my ear right before his teeth nipped at my neck, making me shiver.

My lids fell to half-mast, unable to stay open all the way as I looked back at him over my shoulder. I didn't know who I was when I was with him, but something about this man brought out a side of me I'd never known existed. And I freaking *loved* it! "I don't want nice and slow. I want to feel you. After last time, I felt you between my thighs for days. I want that again."

His chest rumbled with appreciation. He wrenched my pants and underwear down to my ankles and pushed me so my chest was flat against the cool surface of the table. He caressed one of my bare cheeks. "Jesus, do you have any idea how long I've dreamed about this ass?"

"N-no," I whispered, my desperation growing until I was practically dripping. His hand disappeared for just a brief moment before returning with a stinging slap to my left cheek. I sucked in a gasp at the needles of pleasure that sent through me and lifted off the table.

"Stay down," he ordered on a snarl. I did what he said, pressing the side of my face against the wood. "Do you like being spanked, mouse?"

"I-I don't know," I answered, my brain too flooded with endorphins at the moment to tell. "I've never had anyone do that to me—Oh!" He smacked me again, this time on the other cheek.

"What do you think now?"

I felt uncomfortably wet and swollen between my legs. "Um . . ."

Smack. This time, he didn't ask. Instead, he reached down and slid his fingers across my slit and let out a growl. "Fuck me, you're so goddamn wet. Know what I think, Willow?"

"What?"

"I think you *love* this." He spanked me again. And again. Over and over until my ass cheeks felt like they were on fire and I was rocking back against him, silently begging for another.

I was so ready for him I thought I'd burst into tears at any second—or come from just this if he kept going. Either way, I needed a release or I was going to lose my mind.

"Stone," I called out on a whimper as his fingertips teased me again. "Please."

"Please what? Say the words."

"Please fuck me," I begged with no shame whatsoever. "I need you to fuck me."

He didn't make me wait; almost as soon as the last word left my lips, it was followed by a rush of air escaping my lungs when he buried himself deep. "Oh God, *yes*," I cried, some of the tension he'd been building inside of me releasing at the feel of him stretching me wide with his cock. But it still wasn't enough.

"This what you need, baby? You need me to fuck you good and hard?"

"Yes. *Please*."

He pulled nearly all the way out and pounded back in. "Like that?"

"Yes," I hissed, feeling myself tighten around him. "Again."

He didn't have to be told again. He began to fuck me so hard the legs of the table scraped against the floor beneath me. "In awe of you," he grunted as he powered in and out, building that pressure deep inside me with every thrust. "Every time I think I've figured you out, you show me a new layer I love just as much as the last."

"Don't stop," I pleaded, bracing my hands on the table and lifting up just enough to drive myself back against him every time he plunged into me.

"Not going to stop, baby. Never going to stop. This is the best pussy I've ever had."

"God, you feel so good," I said on a cry.

His fingers tangled in my hair and jerked, forcing me up so we were standing front to back. The new angle made everything more intense, and I cried out at the sensation. That hand in my hair yanked my head to the side so he could kiss and lick and nip at my neck, while his other hand traveled down to my center, his fingers spreading out in a V so he could cup where he was entering me. "Who's this pussy belong to?"

"You," I didn't hesitate to answer.

"That's right, baby. It's all mine. And who does this cock belong to?"

Oh God, that was hot! "It's mine, baby."

He growled against my neck. "Fuck yeah it is. Now give it to me baby, come all over your dick."

On his order, that pressure inside me snapped, and I careened headlong into the most powerful orgasm of my life. I cried out until my voice was hoarse, bucking against him as explosions went off inside me, one after another.

By the time I finally starting coming down, his thrusts had turned more frantic, his grunts echoing in my ears.

His hand moved from between my legs and returned to the center of my back, and once more, I found myself lying across the tabletop right before he pulled out and unloaded on my ass. His cum hit my skin, soothing the sting that still remained from his earlier spanking.

I arched my back and looked over my shoulder at him, wanting to see what he looked like as he came.

"Jesus fucking Christ," he gritted as he jerked himself violently, spurt after spurt pouring from him and landing on me.

Never in my life did I think I'd like something like that, but there was no denying it. That. Was. Hot!

When he finally finished, he collapsed over the top of me, taking my hands that were pressed to the wood and lacing his fingers through mine.

"In. Fucking. Awe."

Needless to say, the feeling was mutual.

Chapter Twenty-Six

WILLOW

Stone: *Dinner at my place tonight? I'll cook.*

I tried not to let the smile swallow my face whole as I read the text that had just come in. It hadn't even been a week since Stone and I had become an 'us'—it felt weird calling him my boyfriend. He just seemed too rough and badass to be referred to as my *boyfriend*. So what did that make him? My man? That worked for me—and I felt like I was floating; my feet still hadn't hit the ground.

Me: *You cook? *gasp** I shot back teasingly. The idea of him in the kitchen, preparing a meal for me, revved my engine in a very serious way. I'd have given anything to see that. However, it would have to wait.

We'd seen each other every night. Either he crashed at my place, or I'd stay at his with him and Chief. On the nights I slept over with him, we'd usually done takeout. But while my belly filled with butterflies at the thought of seeing him again —even though I'd seen him this morning—this was the first day since the incident with my dad that the bruise was officially faded enough for me to be able to visit him. I'd missed him more than words could say, so I'd already talked to my sisters, and we'd agreed that tonight was my night to be with him.

Stone: *Yes, smartass. I can cook. Pretty damn well too. And you play your cards right, I might consider cooking shirtless for you.*

Damn, that was some serious incentive, and my fingers actually hurt as I typed out my reply.

Me: *You make a very compelling argument. I really wish I could, but I'm making dinner for my dad tonight, and I'm excited to see him. Raincheck?*

The response that came through made my heart skip a little.

Stone: *I know you're excited, mouse. Have fun with your dad. I'll take you up on that raincheck.*

God, he really was perfect.

Me: *Thanks, baby.*

Stowing my phone back in my purse, I did my best to concentrate on work and keep my mind off all things Stone, no matter how hard it was.

Shortly before lunch, the door came swinging open, and Aurora came skipping in—literally skipping—with a huge smile on her face. "Feel like going to lunch?"

I gave her a curious look. "Why do I have a feeling you voiced a command as a question just to be nice and don't plan on taking no for an answer?"

"Because you, my exquisite little angelfish, are as smart as you are beautiful."

"Oh good, you're here already," I heard just before Lark rounded the front of my desk. "Let's go, guys. I'm starving."

Guess I was going to lunch.

I shut my computer down, grabbed my bag, and followed my two best friends out.

We hit the local diner, and I didn't even realize the change in me, the way I kept my head up and met peoples' eyes instead of hiding behind the curtain of my hair, until I reached the booth, after receiving—and more importantly, returning—several smiles and head nods from people I'd known all my life yet never really talked to.

It felt really damn good to know I no longer had to actively keep myself from retreating back into my shell. My mind had been so consumed with Stone these past few days that it took this trip to lunch with my girls to discover that stupid shell was gone for good.

Aurora and Lark waited until I sat, sliding into a booth right beside the window that overlooked the main drag through town before they both took the seat across from me so they could stare at me with strange googly expressions and their chins in their palms.

I rolled my eyes. "Just spit it out, already."

Aurora smiled so big I could nearly see all her teeth and batted her eyes, making her look a lot like a cartoon princess. "You seem in a *really* good mood."

"She's been in a *really* good mood for a few days now," Lark added in a girly sing-song voice.

She and Aurora fed off each other as they continued to tease. "So I take it that means things are going pretty damn great with her new *boyfriend* then?"

Lark looked at her and bugged her eyes out. "Oh, I

think things are *definitely* going pretty damn great with her new boyfriend."

"You two are ridiculous," I said with a giggle-snort.

"That we are, my shimmery little moonbeam," Aurora laughed. "Now spill. Besties deserve deets. So . . . Gimme."

God, my friends were ridiculous. And I freaking adored the hell out of them.

"I'm really happy," I said softly, looking out the window and returning someone's wave as they passed by and spotted me sitting in the booth. "Things with my dad are rough, and my sisters and I still have some mending to do, but . . . I don't really know how to explain it. I haven't had a whole lot to be happy about in recent months, but . . . he's made things better."

"Oh my God," Lark whispered, her eyes going misty. "You're in love with him."

My lips tipped up in a ridiculously giddy smile. We hadn't said it to each other yet, but that was okay. There was plenty of time. Besides, he showed me every day with the way he touched and looked at me, how he worshipped my body every single night, so I could wait. I was happy to wait.

"It's still new," I told my friends. "We aren't there yet. I'm just really happy." *And you love him like freaking crazy*, my brain screamed.

"Oh, Lark," Aurora cooed, looking just as damn glassy-eyed as the woman beside her. "Our little beansprout is all grown up." She placed her hand over her heart and sniffled. I'd have thought it was just dramatics if a tear hadn't actually fallen from her eye.

Reaching across the table, I placed my hands on theirs

and squeezed tight. "I love you guys. I know I said I hadn't had much these past months to be happy about, but I hope you know that becoming friends with you guys is one of the best things that's ever happened to me."

It was Lark's turn to sniffle. "We love you too."

"And the feeling is totally mutual," Aurora added.

Best. Friends. Ever.

I WENT through the rest of my day feeling like my head was in the clouds, and by the time I got to my dad's house, I couldn't have wiped the smile off my face if I'd wanted to, which I absolutely didn't.

Still in Stone's truck—and not the least bit bothered by it—I shifted it into park and threw the door open, so excited to finally see my dad that I put a little too much strength behind it, and it nearly slammed back on me.

More careful this time, I opened the door and shot out, all but running all the way up to the front porch, only slowing once I got my key in the lock. I needed to be calm. He didn't remember what had happened the night he hit me. If there was any mercy at all with this illness, he wouldn't even have noticed my absence, and that was what I hoped for.

I needed to be as normal as possible to keep him from asking questions.

The door creaked open, and the familiar smells of my childhood home welcomed me back like the warmest, most familiar embrace.

"Dad?" I called as I kicked my shoes off out of habit and lined them up beside the door.

"In here, pumpkin," he called back, and from the tone of his voice, I knew it was a good day. *Thank God.* I reached the living room and stutter-stepped so hard at what I saw—or more to the point *who* I saw—that I would have face-planted on the rug if I hadn't caught myself on the doorframe.

"Stone?"

My man was sitting on the sofa across from my father's recliner, one booted ankle resting on the opposite knee, and a long, thick arm extended across the back. His other hand lazily held an open beer bottle that looked to be half-drunk already against his powerful thigh. He turned to look at me over the back of the couch, smiling in a way that melted my insides. "Hey, mouse."

My eyes bugged out a little as they bounced from him to my dad and back to him again. I'd been so excited at the thought of seeing my dad that, apparently, I hadn't noticed Stone's motorcycle parked out front. "Uh . . . hi? What are you doing here?"

"Your young man came to join us for dinner," my father beamed. I had to bite back my smile at my father referring to Stone as a young man. He was a hop, skip, and a jump from forty, only a few months shy of being a full decade older than me. "Isn't that nice, sweetheart?"

I felt my lips curl up into a grin as I looked back at Stone, answering softly, "Yeah. It really is."

"Why didn't you tell me you were seein' someone, Willow

girl?" Dad asked, and when I looked back at him, I could practically see hearts in his eyes as he looked from me to Stone. He'd never said it, but I knew he worried about me, especially after his diagnosis. I could tell he was scared that his memory would go completely before I had someone else in my life to love me as wholly as he did. It seemed like this big, scary, tattooed biker showing up on his doorstep and announcing himself as my boyfriend was an answer to my father's prayers.

"Jon and I were just hanging out, talking about cars while we waited on you," Stone declared.

"Still can't believe you got a '70 Chevelle you're restoring," Dad said, his eyes lighting up like a kid on Christmas morning. With everything that had been going on recently, it had totally slipped my mind that my father was a classic car enthusiast.

"Well, your girl can vouch for it," Stone replied. "She's seen it up close and personal." The heated way he looked over at me made my belly curl in the most pleasurable way, and I knew *exactly* what he was referring to.

"It's, um . . ." I had to clear my suddenly dry throat. "It's a beauty," I told him, my cheeks catching fire.

"Well, this I gotta see," Dad said, breaking through the haze of lust fogging my head.

"You name the time, and I'll make it happen."

Snapping out of my stupor, I belatedly rounded the couch and moved to my father, leaning down to press a kiss to his cheek. "Hi, Dad," I whispered, choking down the lump that had formed in my throat.

"Hey there, pumpkin," he returned with tender affection. He clasped my hand and gave it a squeeze. "Feels like forever since I've seen my girl."

I understood the feeling more than he could possibly know. "Well, I'm here now. And I'm starving, so how about I start on dinner?"

"I'll help," Stone said, rising to his feet. He tilted his chin toward my father's perspiring, nearly empty glass of iced tea. "Need a refill?"

Dad shook his head and picked up the remote, ready to aim it at the TV to put it on whatever game for whatever sport was currently playing. "I'm good, son, but thanks."

Stone followed me into the kitchen, and as soon as we were out of sight and earshot, I spun around. "How did you —" I started, but before I could get the rest of my question out, he grabbed me by the hips and pulled me flush against him, and sealed his mouth on mine. The kiss worked to melt my knees, and by the time he pulled back, I'd have been a puddle on the ground had he not been holding onto me.

"Hi," he rasped in a low, gravelly voice dripping with want. God, I loved it when he used that tone. It meant he was close to losing control.

"Hi," I whispered back, feeling goosebumps spread across my skin and my nipples tighten into stiff peaks. "Not that I don't love that I get to see you, but I'm kind of surprised you're here. I didn't think we were really at the 'meet the parents' stage of our relationship."

He reached up to tuck a lock of hair behind my ear before dragging his fingers down my temple and cheek, across my jaw. "Didn't want to go a full night without seeing you." Okay, I *really* loved that answer. "And I figured this was as good a night as any to meet your pops. He's important to you; that means he's important to me."

I gave his solid chest a smack before faceplanting into it, my words muffled as I said, "You have to stop being so freaking perfect before you make me cry. I am *not* a pretty crier. There's no hiding it, then my dad'll ask why I've been crying, and it'll just be this whole big thing. So . . . knock it off."

His chest vibrated with silent laughter that shook my body with it. "All right, baby. I'll try not to tempt you too much with my perfection."

I looked up at him with a fierce scowl that I knew had no effect on him, mainly because I didn't mean it at all.

"Good. Then stop lazing about and help me cook."

Chapter Twenty-Seven

WILLOW

The evening ended on one of the highest notes I'd ever experienced. My dad and Stone had gotten along better than I ever could have imagined. We'd enjoyed a delicious meal full of stories and laughter, and I knew the evening had wound down to an end when Dad started nodding off in his recliner while we all watched TV together.

Stone stuck around while I got my father his meds and got him up to bed, only preparing to leave once I was ready.

Stepping into my house a short while later, I turned to thank him for all he'd done for me tonight, only to have the words dry up on my tongue as he entered my house behind me and closed the door, twisting the lock with a resounding *thwunk*.

The look in his eyes was so wildly savage that it stole the air from my lungs and made every inch of skin on my body erupt with goosebumps. "Stone," I whispered through the wad of cotton that suddenly felt wedged in my throat.

"Christ, Willow. Do you have any idea what it was like sitting next to you all fucking night, watching you smile with so much joy it lit up the entire room? Or having to hear you laugh that adorable fucking laugh of yours and not being able to do what I wanted to do to you?"

I swallowed thickly, trying to quench the desert dryness in my mouth. "What—what did you want to do to me?"

He took slow, measured steps in my direction, his eyes pinned to me like a predator tracking its prey. "I wanted to feed my cock past those sweet pink lips and watch them stretch as you took as much of me down your throat as you could. Then I wanted to fuck you so hard that you'd feel me for days."

I suddenly felt this gnawing, painful emptiness in my core, a desperation to be filled that had me clenching my thighs together.

At the sound of my needy whimper, his eyes flashed, making him look positively feral. "You want that, baby? You want me to fuck you hard?"

There was no hesitation when I answered a breathy, "Yes, I want that, Stone."

A growl rumbled up his throat, and before I could blink, he was on me, his lips crashing down on mine in a kiss raging with desperation, even as our tongues tangled together.

He fisted my hair, using it to move my head exactly where he wanted it so he could trail nipping kisses down the sensitive skin on my neck, causing my body to erupt with goosebumps.

I hummed wantonly as I dragged my fingers through his

hair, scraping my nails along his scalp. I wanted to be fucked hard by him. I wanted to feel him between my legs again for days. But more than that, I wanted to taste him the way he'd just described.

Pulling my mouth from his, I lowered to my knees and palmed the massive bulge already forming behind the rough denim.

"Fucking hell," he grunted as I popped the button on his jeans and lowered the zipper. There was no other barrier between his straining length and my face, and the realization that he'd been going commando all day long flooded my panties with a new wave of arousal.

He really did have the most beautiful cock, and just the sight of it was enough to make my mouth water. My tongue peeked out to moisten my lower lip, sliding across the tip of his erection and making him hiss.

When I looked up, he was staring down at me, his gaze wild, his pupils nearly swallowing up that rich whiskey-brown color I loved so much.

"Fuck. Look at you," he grunted. His fingers trailed through my hair, brushing it away from my face and holding it at the back of my head. "Open your mouth and stay still, baby," he ordered. "I want to watch your face while I fuck your mouth."

I'd never had anyone talk to me the way he did when it came to sex. The few men I'd been with in the past had been downright timid in comparison. Before Stone, I hadn't thought I'd like dirty talk, but he'd succeeded in changing my mind on that. With each word he spoke, I grew that much needier.

Doing as he'd commanded, I parted my lips wide so he could feed his length into my mouth on a low, raspy groan. His lips curled back from his teeth as he slid himself in and out in slow, languid thrusts. "Jesus. So goddamn hot. I could come just from watching you like this."

I loved that I could make him lose control like that, that he wanted me so badly it wouldn't take much effort to get him to explode for me. But I needed more.

He was being gentle, trying to make sure I was comfortable instead of testing my limits. And while I loved that about him, how he was always trying to take care of me, I wanted to be pushed. He was the only man I'd felt that safe with, and I wanted *more*.

To let him know, I reached around and grabbed his ass with both hands, sinking my nails into the taut flesh back there, and forced his hips forward, filling my mouth with even more of him.

"Oh *fuck me*," he snarled as I hollowed out my cheeks and sucked harder. "Does my dirty girl want it rougher?"

I looked up at him just in time to catch his lips curl into a devilish smirk and hummed in agreement.

"All right, mouse. I'll give you what you want." With that, he snapped his hips harder, causing the head of his cock to bump against the back of my throat. It was nearly too much. He was so big, so thick, but I freaking *loved* it.

Breathing through my nose to keep from gagging, I squeezed his ass tighter as he fucked my mouth like he'd promised he would. Each thrust, each grunt I ripped from his throat, turned me on so much I thought I might blackout.

He was getting close, I knew it by the way his thrusts became erratic, but instead of coming like I thought he'd do, with an animalistic growl, he grabbed me under my arms and jerked me off my knees.

"What—" I started, but he cut my question off with a bone-searing kiss as he shuffled me back toward the couch.

"You wet for me, Willow?"

"I'm always wet for you, baby."

Something in him snapped. One second we were making out, and the next, I was stripped naked, standing before him as he ripped his shirt over his head, revealing all that inked skin and defined muscles.

I'd always known he had a gorgeous body, but I could never have guessed it would have been the most beautiful thing I'd ever lay my eyes on. His skin truly was a work of art that I had taken immense pleasure in and time tracing with my tongue over the past few days. Between his muscles and his ink, I wasn't sure I'd ever grow tired of looking at or touching him.

"Stone, *please*," I heard myself beg as he kicked off his boots and pushed his jeans the rest of the way off.

Laying back on the couch, he grabbed my hips and lifted me up like I weighed next to nothing, arranging me so I was facing his feet and my knees were straddling his head. It was a position I'd never been in before, and I suddenly felt unsure. "Stone, what—?" My words died on a moan when his tongue came out and swiped across my slit from end to end. "Oh God."

"Want you like this," he grunted against my slick folds.

"So you can suck me off while I bury my face in this sweet pussy until you come screaming."

I was pretty sure I could handle that. Bracing one hand on the cushion by his hip, I wrapped the other around the base of his cock that was still standing tall and proud, the head swollen and purple, and swallowed it back down just as he speared his tongue inside me, causing us to moan simultaneously.

With each flick of his tongue against my clit, each sinful lick inside me, it was getting harder and harder to concentrate on what I was doing to him as the pressure deep in my core built.

He snapped his hips up, driving himself deeper into my mouth. I groaned around his length while writhing against his face, growing frantic with the need to come.

Each snarl he made, every groan, vibrated against my folds, driving me out of my mind. His hands slipped over my hips so he could grip my ass, using his hold to force me down harder on his face. I wasn't sure I'd ever been so wet in my entire life.

I froze for a moment when his fingers breached the crease between my cheeks; the tip of his index finger circled around that pucker. My head snapped back on a sharp gasp, his erection falling past my lips when he pressed against that tight ring of muscles. It felt unnatural, yet . . . exhilarating all at the same time.

"Breathe," he ordered from between my thighs, his voice gentle and coaxing as he applied more pressure. "Just relax and breathe. Won't do anything you don't like, baby. You don't like it, just tell me to stop and I will."

I trusted him completely, so when he went back to devouring me like I was his favorite meal while applying just a bit more pressure against my hole, slipping in to the first knuckle, I sucked in a deep breath and did my best to relax—something that was growing increasingly difficult given I was strung tighter than a guitar string.

The feel of him at both of my most intimate openings was almost too much.

"Oh God, *Stone*. I can't—" He growled against me before his teeth nipped my sensitive lips, sending a shockwave through my whole body.

"You can, and you fucking will," he demanded as he began to stroke that long finger in and out of my ass. Then, as if to prove himself right, he scraped my distended clit with his teeth and drove his finger deep, setting off an earthquake inside me that had my head snapping back and my throat working as I cried his name over and over, rubbing my pussy against his mouth as I came longer and harder than I ever had before.

Aftershocks riddled my body, draining so much of my strength that I couldn't keep myself upright. Collapsing on top of him, I licked and sucked along his shaft, trying impossibly to concentrate on him while he kept at me until I had absolutely nothing left.

"Fuck," he grunted, shifting me once again, flipping us over so that I was on my back, and he was hovering over me, his hips nestling between my thighs, pushing them open wider. "So goddamn sweet." He licked his lips, making me shiver. "I could die a happy man, hearing you scream my name like that." He notched his cock into place, murmuring, "Give me another, baby," before snapping his hips and filling me up, stretching me wide.

"God, *yes*," I cried, throwing my head back against the cushion and arching my back, dragging my nipples across the thin smattering of hair on his chest. He pulled out and slammed back in so hard the couch creaked across the floor. "Again," I panted, savoring the fullness of having Stone inside me. "Don't stop. Don't ever stop."

"Never, baby," he grunted, grabbing hold of the armrest above my head to use as leverage to fuck me even harder.

A misting of sweat dotted across his brow, a single drop running down his neck. I lifted my head, running my tongue along the column of his throat before biting down.

"Fuck me harder," I demanded.

A grunt rasped past his lips, letting me know he liked it, so I bit down again. "Christ, my dirty fucking girl. You were born for me, weren't you? Absolutely fucking *perfect* for me." A second release crashed over me, pulling me under. "That's it. Let me have it. Let me feel you drench my cock."

I did just that, raking my nails down his back and crying out over and over again until I felt absolutely boneless. My channel clenched and spasmed as he followed me over the edge, burying his face in my neck and grunting as he shot deep inside me, coating my walls.

It felt like an eternity passed before our breathing returned to normal. When he finally lifted his head so he could look down at me, what I saw in those whiskey eyes made my chest squeeze.

"Don't want to scare you or anything, mouse, but I think I'm addicted to you." A laugh-snort bubbled past my throat before I could stop it, making his lips spread into a blinding smile. "Christ, I love that laugh."

God, every day I fell more in love with this man than the day before. "I'll let you in on a little secret," I whispered as I reached up and brushed a lock of hair off his forehead. "I'm addicted to you too."

He let out a breath and lowered his forehead to rest against mine. "Thank Christ."

Chapter Twenty-Eight

WILLOW

Sitting back in my chair, I let out a breath and pressed my hand against my belly. "I think that might have been the best meal I've ever had."

Stone smiled at me from across the table. We'd been an official couple for nearly two weeks, and so far everything had been beyond my wildest imagination—and that was really saying something, considering I'd been fantasizing about him for nearly a whole year.

It took several days after that dinner where he and Stone had met for the first time for my dad to have a good enough day for me to take him out to see the Chevelle and Knucklehead at Stone's place, but when we finally did, I thought that might just go down in history as one of the best days of my life.

Truth was, I'd gone from crushing on the man to falling head over heels, but despite how good things were going, I couldn't bring myself to say those three words just yet, even though I was pretty damn certain he felt them too.

Tonight he'd surprised me when I got off work by picking me up on his bike and taking me straight to the Cattleman for dinner.

"The food was good," he agreed, his eyes taking on a devilish gleam. "But I wouldn't say it's the best. I'll be having the best later tonight when I bury my face in your pussy." A spark of electricity zoomed between my nipples and clit, making me squirm in my seat. He saw me shifting around, and his lips pulled into a big grin. "Now you're thinking about it too, aren't you?"

"No," I lied. I was totally thinking about it. In the past two weeks, we'd gone at each other every opportunity we had—and even some opportunities we'd had to create ourselves—and it was as if our desire for each other had only gotten stronger. I constantly caught myself drifting into daydreams about all our different times together. But two could play this game. "I was actually wondering if it would be possible to slide under the table and suck you off real quick before the waiter showed up with the check." That got him, and I felt a little spark of delight at the way his fingertips dug into the tablecloth. Leaning forward, I lowered my voice to a whisper and smiled as I asked, "Think we have time?"

The waiter chose that moment to return, placing the black leather billfold on the table before scurrying off at the sound of Stone's threatening growl.

My giggle turned into a snort as he pulled his credit card out of his wallet to pay. "Thank you for dinner tonight, honey. It was great."

"I have a lot of making up to do," he told me. "Figured this was as good a place to start as any."

The waiter came back to take the card and made quick work of ringing us out. As we stood and started toward the exit, I took his hand in mine, lacing our fingers together. "You don't have anything to make up for. We're good."

He let go of my hand, but only so he could swing his arm over my shoulders and pull me flush against his side. It had been like this for two whole weeks now. If I was close enough to touch, it never failed that he'd grab hold and situate me in a way that gave him maximum contact. Even in our sleep. I'd never taken Stone as the cuddling type, but I'd been very wrong. "The goal is to get you to better than good, mouse. When I achieve that, I'll be happy."

I opened my mouth to tell him he'd already succeeded when my cellphone started to ring, cutting me off.

I stopped at the curb right next to his bike and pulled it out of my purse. "Hey Elaina. What's up?"

"Are you at home?" she asked, her voice laced with panic that made the tiny hairs on my body stand on end. "No. Stone and I are leaving the Cattleman right now. What's wrong?"

I heard something through the line that sounded like a door slamming and an engine starting. "Dad's security company called me. His fire alarm was going off and they couldn't reach him on his phone. James and I are on our way there now, and the fire department has already been called."

It felt like my whole body had frozen solid. I couldn't

move. I could barely breathe. "Oh my God," I breathed into the line, my skin feeling like ice. "Oh my God."

Stone came up beside me and looped his arm around my waist, looking down at me with concern etched into his face.

"I'm not close," I started, panic clawing at my insides and tearing them to ribbons. "I'm all the way across town. If I'd been home—"

"Stop," Elaina ordered. "Don't do that to yourself. You're allowed to have a life. I'm sure everything is fine. Just get there when you can, okay? I'm getting off with you to call Crissy and let her know." My big sister used a tone I'd never heard from her before. It was a tone that said she was the oldest, and it was her job to take care of us. "It's all going to be okay, all right?"

"All—all right," I wheezed.

"See you there."

I disconnected the call and looked up at Stone, feeling my entire face drain of color. "We have to go. The fire alarm at my dad's house is going off and no one can reach him."

He hauled me up off the ground and deposited me on the back of his bike like I weighed next to nothing, and took off out of the parking lot like a shot.

I was so lost in my fear, so close to letting it swallow me whole, that I didn't remember a single aspect of the ride. It felt like an eternity dragged by, but it also felt like the blink of an eye when we pulled onto my father's street.

My heart dropped right out of my chest as we got closer.

There were lights everywhere. I saw a fire engine, an ambulance, and a couple of police cruisers.

Stone got us as close as possible, and as soon as he had the kickstand down, I was jumping off and running into the fray.

My eyes darted around frantically, but all of the faces were a blur; then Stone's hand came down on the small of my back, and he began to guide me.

"There, sweetheart. There they are."

Thanks to his steadiness, I was able to spot Elaina and Crissy. I took off at a full run—in heels—going right into my oldest sister's open arms as soon as I reached them.

"He's okay," she said into my hair. "He's going to be okay."

I pulled back, darting frantic looks at each of my sisters. "Where is he?"

"He's in the ambulance," Elaina told me, then began relaying everything that had happened. "He has a third-degree burn on his arm, and they want to check him out to make sure he didn't inhale too much smoke."

"How did this happen?" I asked, but I had a sinking feeling I already knew.

A cloud of tears welled up in Crissy's eyes as she started to explain. "Apparently the fire started in the kitchen. We think maybe he tried to cook and forgot the stove was on again, but we couldn't figure out for sure." The sadness in her eyes deepened, and her husband Phil reached out to pull her into his side as her tears fell free. "He wasn't in any frame of mind to tell anyone what happened when they got him out. It looks like there was a dishtowel close by that caught fire, and it spread from there. The kitchen is destroyed and they're worried about the structural integrity of the second floor since the fire reached the ceiling, but the rest of the house is okay."

Elaina picked up the conversation then, her husband James coming to stand behind her to place two bracing hands on her shoulders. As she started to speak I felt an arm circle my waist and Stone's heat pressing against my back, letting me know he was there. What he was offering me just then was a bit of relief in a chaotic storm of fear and sadness. I couldn't possibly express how much that meant to me in that moment.

"They're taking him in for the burns, but also so they can give him something to calm him down. He was extremely confused and agitated."

I sagged against Stone's body as I started to cry, and he didn't hesitate to hold me up.

James looked over my head at Stone and asked, "Do you guys want to ride to the hospital with us?"

He looked down at me to answer, clearly willing to do anything I needed or wanted him to do. But I knew that the most comfort I'd get until I could see my dad and talk to him was to be wrapped around my man.

"We'll meet you guys there," I told my brother-in-law.

Crissy, Elaina, and I embraced one more time before we all broke apart and headed toward the hospital, and I knew we were in for a long night.

Stone

I'D STAYED at Willow's side all night long. I held her whenever she needed it, pouring all my strength into her while we waited for word on her father. The few times she'd broken off to huddle with her sisters, I'd used as an opportunity to text those closest to her to let them know what was going down. Lark and Aurora had both asked if they should come to the hospital to be with her, but I saw the way the Thorne sisters were banding together, leaning on each other, and I felt like they had it.

She'd need her girls when she got home and didn't have her family all around her, but for now, she had the support she really needed, so I held them off.

Jensen told me to make sure I kept her ass at home the following day, but that was already something I had every intention of doing.

The doctor had come to talk to them, letting them know that Jon would be okay, and that was the first time I felt the tension in the waiting room lighten. They'd asked to see him but had been told to check back the following day. He'd been too agitated and disoriented when he arrived, so they'd given him a sedative so he could rest.

Her sisters left the hospital before us, both of them needing to get back to their kids, but we didn't leave until well after two in the morning. Before climbing on my bike, Willow had informed me that she wanted to sleep at my house, so that was where we were.

She stopped inside the door just long enough to bend

and greet Chief, who'd been waiting anxiously for us to come in, before dragging herself through the living room and past the kitchen to the master bedroom. As if sensing his girl wasn't okay, Chief followed after her, and when we finally got in bed after undressing, he curled up in a ball on the floor on her side, as though standing guard.

Reaching across the bed, I pulled her over to me, pressing her head against my chest and hooking my arm around her waist to hold her close.

"I wish there was something I could do to make this better," I said into the dark.

That was something I'd been struggling with all damn night; the feeling of abject helplessness when it came to my woman's pain. I'd have given my life in that moment to take it all away for her.

I heard a sniffle, then felt her shift against me. She stacked her hands on my chest and propped her chin on top of them so she could look up at me. Even in the dark, her clear-as-sky eyes sparkled. They were still full of sadness, but there was something else in them that had every muscle in my body tensing.

"You're doing it, baby," she said quietly. "Right now, being here for me the way you are. I couldn't have made it through tonight without you."

Christ, that was nice to hear. But I still wished I could do more. Reaching up, I tucked a long strand of hair behind her ear so I could see all of her gorgeous face as best I could in the moonlight filtering through the blinds. "I want to take away your pain. I don't want you to be sad, not even for a second. And it kills me that I'm not able to do that for you."

"Stone," she said on a barely-there breath. "I don't need you to take my pain away. When you hold me, you make everything bearable. When you make love to me, I feel like I can handle anything. You told me weeks ago that you want to make every day better than the last for me. Well, you've done it. We aren't good, honey. We're great," she said, throwing back my words from earlier that night. God, it felt like a lifetime had passed since I said that to her.

"I know this may be early, and I don't expect you to say it back, so please don't feel like you have to. I just need you to know that I love you. I loved you when you sat beside me in Big Red while I shredded her gears, but never once lost patience with me."

At the flare of my eyes, Willow giggle-snorted. "Shane told me what that truck means to you, which only proves how special it was that you let me drive her. And I love you for that too. I love you for being so incredibly loyal, and I love you for wanting to protect me from the world, even though you can't. You're the best man I've ever known, Gavin." At her use of my given name, I sucked in a breath and a wave of warmth filled my chest, spidering outward like a crack in a windshield to every part of my body. "You wish you could have done more for me tonight, but I'm telling you right now, what you *have* done has been everything to me, baby. And that's why I love you."

"Christ," I grunted, my throat feeling painfully tight.

"I don't want you to think that just because I said it, I expect you—*oh!*"

Her words died on a yelp when I whipped her over onto

her back and wedged her thighs open with my hips so they could rest between them.

"I love you," I grunted, the emotion I was feeling right then making it hard to keep my voice steady. "You're the only woman I've ever loved. The only one I ever *will* love. I thought my life was as good as it was going to get until I met you. And even while I was fighting it, you still managed to somehow make it better. When I say you're mine and I'm yours, I mean forever, mouse. There's nothing in the world strong enough to change that. *You're* my forever."

Tears welled in her eyes before slipping down her temples into that beautiful silky hair.

"You love me," she repeated in a whisper, almost like she couldn't believe it.

"With everything in me. I'll love you even more tomorrow, and the day after that, and every day going forward. Then I'll love you even more when we eventually get married and you give me our babies."

Her eyes flared wide. "You-you want to have kids?"

"If they're with you, hell yeah."

She sniffled, then smiled so brightly it nearly blinded me.

"See?" she said softly. "That right there."

My brow furrowed in confusion. "What, baby?"

"With that right there, you just made everything better."

Chapter Twenty-Nine

STONE

It had been three days since the fire, and this was the first time since Jon had been admitted to the hospital that he'd been in his right mind enough for his daughters to be able to see him. Not that it kept them from coming up to the hospital every day as soon as they woke up and sitting in that waiting room until after the sun went down just to be close to him.

I could see my woman hurting, the pain was written on her face and swimming in her eyes, and I fucking hated how helpless I felt to take that pain away. Watching her suffer was killing me, but my woman was strong. She was the strongest person I'd ever had the privilege of knowing. And even with all that pain in her eyes, she was holding her head high and giving her sisters as much support as possible. Since she was pouring all of her support into her sisters, I was doing my damnedest to give her all that I had, to be her rock.

But as I stood in the background and listened to the doctor giving them the hard truth, I could see it was weighing heavier and heavier on her with every word he said.

"I'm sorry," the doctor continued, "but I think it's time you consider placing your father somewhere where he can have permanent supervision. I know families don't like to hear these kinds of things, but there are very some good facilities right around here."

"Thank you, doctor," Elaina said, bringing the conversation to a close.

"I want to keep him for one more night to monitor those burns, but I feel confident he'll be ready to leave tomorrow. For now, you can go back two at a time and see him whenever you're ready."

He left the waiting room, and I immediately moved to Willow just as she lifted her hands to massage her temples. I pressed in behind her, wrapping my arms around her to hold her up mentally and physically. She fell against me like everything she'd just heard was too much of a strain to keep her standing on her own.

"I can't—" Crissy started but stopped to shake her head in sadness as a tear streaked down her face. "I know he can't go back to that house—not that it's even an option after the fire. I understand he can't be alone, but if we put him in a home, it would just wreck him."

"He can come live with me," Willow said without missing a beat. "It'll be hard on all of us, letting go of the family house, but it'll be even worse for him. He needs *us*, so he can come live with me."

Her sister Crissy reached out to take her hand as another tear fell. "Sweetie, you can't. You work full time."

My mouth opened, and the words fell out without a single thought. "I'll help her. We can do it together. Maybe we can alternate schedules or something so one of us is always off." Even as I said them, I didn't regret the words I'd spoken one damn bit. I meant them, down to my very center. Especially if it meant helping my woman *and* her father, who I'd come to really like.

Willow's head whipped around so fast her hair slapped me in the chest, love swimming in her watery eyes as she stared up at me. "*I love you*," she mouthed, and my arm clenched tighter around her. I didn't know how we'd do it, but we'd make it work.

"You've done enough," Elaina spoke, pulling everyone's attention to her. She looked up at her husband, and he gave her a reassuring nod before she continued, turning to look back at her youngest sister. "James and I have been talking about this since the night of the fire. We knew Dad wouldn't be able to live alone anymore, and we knew you'd jump at the first opportunity to take up the torch when it came to taking care of him. But you've already done so much. It's time I step up." Willow reached out to take her oldest sister by the hand. "I'm a stay-at-home mom with two kids in school all day. We want Dad to come live with us."

My girl sniffled and batted at her tears with her free hand. "You know we'll help in any way we can."

Elaina's face crumpled with sadness. "I know, honey. We all know."

"We're all going to help," Crissy added. "We'll all do our part."

It was an awe-inspiring thing to watch the three of them band together like that.

We went in to see him, two at a time, after that, and as Willow and I waited for our turn, I guided her over to the little loveseats under a window that faced out into the parking lot and pulled her into my lap instead of bringing her down next to me. I knew she needed the closeness, but I also needed the full contact to help me gauge her emotions better. Not to mention, I just wanted her as close as possible all the time.

She snuggled into me, resting her cheek on my chest and pressing her forehead into the side of my neck as I banded my arms around her. "How you doin', mouse?"

She let out a heavy sigh, sinking deeper against me as I trailed my fingers through her hair, relishing that honey and sunshine scent of hers. "I've had better days . . . or better weeks. It's hard for me to keep track of what day it is or how many have passed. My brain is fried."

I tightened my hold on her. "I know, baby, but it'll be okay. You're tough as hell; you got this. And I'm right here with you if you need anything. Just say the word, and I'll get it for you if I can."

She lifted her head to look up at me, those blue eyes as clear as a bright, sunny day. "I can't tell you what it means to me, you being here for me. I'm not sure I could have gotten through these past few days without you."

She was the only woman who'd ever had the power to undo me completely. "Yes, you would've," I assured her, knowing down to my bones that she would have pulled through just fine. "You don't give yourself nearly enough credit, baby." Reaching up, I traced my fingers along her jawline and down the side of her neck, loving the way she shivered against me. "Never met a person in my life as strong as you."

"You're right," she whispered, her shoulders lifting a bit. "I could have done it on my own. But I wouldn't want to. Having you here made it so much easier for me. So I guess what I'm trying to say is that I don't ever *want* to go through the hard times without you. You make everything better."

Closing my eyes, I lowered my forehead against hers and breathed in that beautiful fragrance that was all Willow. "I love you," I rasped, needing to get the words out to loosen the vise-grip on my chest.

"I love you too, Gavin," she returned.

We stayed like that until Crissy and her husband came back into the waiting room to tell us it was our turn. After Willow hugged her sister and brother-in-law goodbye, Crissy moved into me, giving my waist a tight squeeze.

"Thank you for being here for her," she whispered before pulling back. With a clap on the shoulder from Phil, the two of them took off, and Willow and I headed down the hall to Jon's hospital room.

With my arm around her shoulders, I kept her locked to my side as we pushed the door open and stepped in. Jon looked up from the hospital bed and smiled as soon as his eyes landed on her. "Hey there, pumpkin."

Willow's chest stuttered, and tears began leaking from her eyes at that first glimpse of her big, strong father lying there, a white bandage wrapped around the burns on his arm. "Oh, Dad."

On a broken sob, she launched herself at him, wrapping her arms around his shoulders and burying her face in his neck.

From my vantage point, I could see the rise and fall of her back as she cried silently and the creases in the corners of Jon's eyes as he squeezed them shut and held onto his daughter like she was his lifeline.

Even under the circumstances, I was glad as hell that Willow had a parent like Jon, that she'd grown up knowing what it meant to be loved unconditionally. I never had that with my own parents, but I knew down to my soul that the woman I'd claimed as my own, the one who had claimed me right back, would teach me how goddamn good it felt to have that, day after day for the rest of our lives.

They stayed like that for a while before Willow finally stood up with a sniffle, brushing at the dampness on her cheeks. She sat on the edge of the paper-thin mattress and took his undamaged hand in hers. "How are you feeling? Are you in any pain? Do you want me to call a nurse?"

"I'm okay, honey. It's not so bad. They've given me some nice meds to help." He studied her face and inhaled deeply as his expression creased with sadness and guilt so acute it made my own chest ache. "So it appears I gave my girls a scare. I'm so sorry—"

"Dad, stop," she ordered, lifting her hand to cut him off. "It's not your fault. We know that. We're all just so glad you're okay."

His gaze came to mine, and he gave me an appreciative grin. "Thanks for bein' there for my girl while all this was going on."

"Don't have to thank me for that, Jon," I replied as I moved to the foot of the bed and curled my fingers around the railing. Truth be told, I wasn't much of a fan of seeing him like this either. "It's just part of my job as her man."

His shoulders sunk, and I had a sense it was with relief. "Damn lucky for me she picked a good one then, huh?"

I looked to Willow just in time to catch her cheeks heating with a blush and shot her a wink. "Think I might be the lucky one in this situation."

We hung around for a while longer until we could see Jon starting to fade. The pain meds were doing their job, but they also knocked him on his ass, so when he started to snore, Willow pulled the wispy covers up to his chin and pressed a kiss to his cheek before whispering her goodbyes and joining me at the foot of the bed.

Neither of us spoke as I led her through the sterile, brightly lit corridors toward the exit.

"Where do you feel like going?" I asked when we finally reached my bike. "Your place or mine."

She looked from the bike to me. "I don't want to go home right now," she said in a sad, defeated voice. "Can we maybe just ride for a while?"

I wouldn't deny her anything she wanted if it was in my power to give her, and a ride was definitely in my power.

"Absolutely, baby."

I pointed us in the direction of my house, but instead of turning off at my lane, I just kept going, past neighboring towns and deep into the foothills, taking the old roads and well-worn trails that came with being a biker town in the middle of the mountains.

I'd have gladly kept going, but despite how much Willow loved riding, she was still too new to be able to go long stretches of time without an occasional break. I pulled off the edge of a quiet winding mountain road onto the soft shoulder, coming to a stop just behind a small copse of trees.

"Why'd you stop?" she asked once I killed the engine.

I looked back at her over my shoulder. "Figured you'd need to stretch your legs a bit. Long rides can be hard if you're not used to them."

I felt her shift around a bit behind me, her face pulling into a small wince. "Yeah, okay. You're right. Climbing off the back of the bike, she moved a couple feet away and placed her hands at the small of her back, arching deep to stretch it out.

I followed behind her, placing my hands on her shoulders to rub out the knots bunching her up that had nothing to do with the ride up here. She let out a sigh and dropped her head as I dragged my thumbs up her spine. "Thank you, honey," she murmured.

"I'm here," I told her, knowing that tension had to do with everything that had been going on the past few days. "You can talk to me whenever you want, about anything. You know that."

"I know," she whispered, turning to look up at me. Those big blue eyes of hers made my heart thud in my chest. "But I don't want to talk right now."

My dick stirred to life, swelling behind my fly. "What do you want? Just say it, and I'll give it to you."

Stepping in closer, she reached down and placed her hand on my already-throbbing erection. "I want you to make me forget," she said as she massaged my cock through my jeans. "I want you to fuck me so you're all I can think about or feel."

That request was all it took for me to snap. With a growl, I grabbed her ass in both hands and hauled her up my front, forcing her to wrap her legs around my waist as I sealed my mouth with hers in a wild, untamed kiss as I carried her back to the bike.

"That's what you want," I said as I tore her pants down her legs, never more thankful for the thin little leggings she favored on her days off than I was at that moment. "Then that's what you'll get." The sides of her thong shredded easily, and I didn't hesitate to stuff the worthless scrap of lace in my back pocket. I'd take it home and put it with the ruined pair I'd kept from our first time in my garage.

"Straddle the seat facing the back," I ordered as I undid my jeans and pulled my cock free.

She did as I told her, watching raptly as I stroked my length and seated myself on the bike, so I was facing her. Grabbing her by the backs of her knees, I pulled her legs up to rest over the tops of my thighs. "Lay back against the tank and grip the handles."

As soon as she was in position, I dragged my hands up her tiny waist, along her ribs, lifting her shirt as I went until it was up around her neck. Wrenching the cups of her bra down, I bent and sucked one of those stiff, rosy pink nipples into my mouth.

Willow gasped, arching her back so hard it lifted completely off the gas tank. "Stone, please," she begged, her knuckles turning white with how hard she was squeezing the grips. "I need more."

I flicked one turgid bud with my tongue before doing the same to the next, loving how the damp tips glistened in the sunlight. "And I'll give it to you," I promised. "But I need you to tell me how you want me to fuck you." Cupping her slit, I dragged one finger slowly through the wetness building there. "Do you want me to fuck you slow?" I teased until she was writhing against my hand. "Or do you want it hard and fast?"

Her heavy eyelids could open halfway, and her tongue peeked out to wet her bottom lip. "I want you to fuck me like you always do," she breathed. "Like only *you* can do. I want you to make me feel alive, just like I always do whenever you're inside me."

Her words ended on a sharp cry when I plunged into her with one hard, brutal thrust. I used to think that being buried in her hot, wet pussy was the closest I'd ever come to heaven. Then she told me she loved me, and I knew I was wrong. But *fuck me*, this was a close second.

"Jesus," I grunted as I fucked her hard and fast, just like she wanted. "I'll never get used to how incredible you feel."

"Mmm. Yes, baby." She circled her hips to meet mine every time I fucked into her. "God, so full. I feel so full."

I kept my feet braced on the ground so we wouldn't fall over, but concentrating on anything other than the way her sheath fit me like a glove was proving harder than I could have imagined.

"Stone," she panted, her tits rising and falling with each desperate breath. "I'm close."

"Don't hold back," I grunted, driving in and out of her heat, feeling her walls rippling around me. "Give it to me." I needed her to let go. It was taking everything I had to keep from blowing. My balls were drawing up tight, and the tingle at the base of my spine was spreading outward through my whole body.

"Oh God," she whimpered, getting impossibly tighter. "Stone, oh shit, *Stone*! I'm coming, baby!"

Just like that, she went off, clamping down around me so hard it was a wonder I could pull out, but I kept going, fucking her through her cries until I couldn't hold back for another second.

Three thrusts later, I shot inside her, coating her walls with my cum as we both climaxed, her pussy milking every drop I had inside me.

Once it left me, I fell forward, resting my forehead on her chest as we both sucked in huge gulping breaths.

"Christ, you undo me," I managed to get out once my heart stopped trying to escape my chest.

Her giggle morphed into that goddamn snort I adored. "The feeling's mutual." She finally let go of the handles and dragged her fingers through my hair. "Thank you," she whispered several seconds later. "Thank you for always being there for me."

Lifting my head so I could look into those clear sky eyes of hers, I asked, "You better now?"

Her smile lit up my entire fucking world. "Yeah. Like I said, you make everything better."

"Christ, I love you." Then I said the first thing that

popped into my mind, words I felt down into my bones. "Move in with me."

Her eyes went wide. "What?"

Lifting up, I pulled her to sitting with me and placed my hands on either side of her neck, repeating, "Move in with me."

"Stone," she started, giving her head a shake, "If this is because of my dad—"

"It's not," I replied. "It's not because of that. I'm asking you to move in with me because I want to go to sleep next to you every night and wake up beside you every morning. I want to come home from a long day at work to you in my house. I'm asking because I *want* you there, always. But if that's not enough of a reason, then think of Chief. The traitorous bastard likes you more than me anyway. He gets sad every time you leave. If not for me, then do it for him. Put him out of his misery."

She giggle-snorted again, reaching up to drag her palm across the stubble on my cheeks. "All right," she said softly. "I'll move in with you. For Chief."

I felt myself smile back as I looked at her, my whole world, my heaven. "For Chief."

"And, you know, because I love you."

"Thank God for that."

She leaned forward, placing a kiss against my smiling mouth. "Well, if we're going to do this, then you need to help me find my pants . . . you know, so you can take me home."

Like I'd told her before, whatever she wanted, I'd give it to her. And this was no exception.

Epilogue

STONE

Three months later

A WHOLE HELL of a lot had changed in the past three months.

For one thing, Sunday family dinners were drastically different than they used to be. I went from attending them once in a blue moon and only by force, to going to Scooter and Caroline's every weekend, even without my sister threatening to maim me in very permanent and painful ways.

And not only did Willow attend with me every single week, but it never failed that at least some—if not all—of her family tagged along too.

It had been two months since she moved in with me— I'd wanted it to happen a whole hell of a lot sooner, but she'd claimed she needed to pack and put her house on the market and all that, so I'd given her that time she needed, but not a single day more. I had to admit, there was something totally addictive about coming home to the same woman night after night. Especially when that woman was Willow.

Another change over the past few months was her car. Even after we got together in a very official capacity, she'd still fought me tooth and nail on that goddamn car. So I'd done what any reasonable, level-headed boyfriend would do.

I'd sold it without her knowing and drove her to a dealership on our way to dinner one night. Sneaky and underhanded? Maybe, but my woman was now in a safe, new Ford Explorer with airbags that actually *worked*, so as far as I was concerned the end justified the means. As a bonus, I got to hold it over her head, because she loved her new car so much more than that older piece of shit.

The back door opened, letting out the loud, raucous noises coming from inside, and I turned from my perch resting against the banister of the back deck as Jon came out to join me.

"Figured you'd want a fresh one," he said, extending a beer bottle my way.

I set the empty one I'd been holding down and took the one he offered. "Thanks."

Just like my little sister had done months ago, Jon came up beside me and mimicked my stance, looking out at the view past Scooter and Caroline's backyard. I let the silence linger, knowing he'd come out for a reason, but not wanting to rush him.

"You know, these Sunday dinners really are something else," he finally said. "Back when Colleen was alive, we did something like this every week with our girls and their families."

"Glad you like it, Jon. We all love having you guys here." And that was the truth.

Scoot and Jon got along great, Caroline loved having a houseful of screaming kids, and the Thorne sisters had no problem joining in with my own to give me shit just for fun. They were chaotic, but they were great.

"Colleen used to worry about Willow. She was so worried our shy little wallflower would end up alone because she was too scared to take any chances. Not a doubt in my mind she's lookin' down right now, smiling that her girl finally found the man who'd make it safe for her to break out of her shell."

He turned to look at me, and I rasped, "Means the world you think I'm that guy. All I want to do is make her happy."

He shifted to look out at the view from the backyard, and I knew whatever he was gearing up to say was going to be heavy, but I didn't feel my muscles tense or my gut churn like it would have in the past. That was all thanks to Willow. She balanced me. She fed that adrenaline rush I sometimes craved. Now everything in my life was great.

"I know you guys are still new, and I don't want you to think I'm putting any pressure on you, son. I want you to know upfront that's not my intention at all, but I don't know how many good days I have left. So if you think my girl's the one, and you see a forever with her—which I suspect you do, because you look at her the same way I used to look at my Colleen—I want you to ask for my blessing while I'm still of sound mind enough to give it to you."

"Jon—"

He stood tall and turned to look at me. "I'm not sayin' you have to ask her in a week, or a month, or hell, even a year. I'm just asking that if you think it's a possibility, ask me now. Just in case. This is a memory I want to have for as long as my mind will let me."

I smiled, and at the sight of it, some of the tension melted from his shoulders. "Jon, I love your daughter more than I've ever loved anyone in my whole life. She's it for me. She's my forever. I bought the ring three weeks ago and planned to ask you when she wasn't around, but this seems as good a time as any." The rest of the tension drifted from him, and he stood tall, shoulders square and head held high and proud. "I swear to you that I'll treat her like the most precious thing in my life, mainly because she is and always will be. I'll be good to her. I'll break my back to make her happy, and I'll give her a family as big or small as she wants. So do I have your blessing to ask your daughter to marry me?"

He pulled in a stuttered breath and looked off to the side while clearing his throat and blinking his eyes rapidly. Finally, he gathered himself enough to look back at me. "Depends on one thing."

Well I hadn't been expecting that. "What's the one thing?"

His lips spread in a shit-eating grin. "Take me out for a ride in that Chevelle of yours."

My head fell back on a bark of laughter. "That's something I can do." I held my hand out to him. "So we have a deal?"

His palm clapped against mine, and we shook. "We have a deal, son. And just so you know, I couldn't have picked a better man for my girl if I'd sent out for one in a catalog."

The door squealed open just as we broke apart, and Willow's head poked out. "Hey guys." She gave us a curious look. "What are you two talking about out here?"

I moved away from her father and pulled her to me, brushing my lips against hers when she tipped her head back to give me access. "All good things, mouse. All good things."

Truer words had never been spoken. Because I was going to make this woman mine forever in the very near future.

My mouse.

My wallflower.

The woman who changed me with one look without even knowing it, taking a man made of stone and giving him the kind of happiness he never expected.

Hell yeah, everything with us was so much better than good. And it was only going to get better.

The End.

Thank you so much for reading!
*Keep going for a sneak peek at **Ravage**.*

Enjoy an Excerpt from Ravage

You may not know this, but years ago, before Redemption was even a twinkle in my eye, I originally introduced Stone Hendrix in a totally different series.

If your curious to see how his journey started (namely, his time with Lyla and Will), check out the excerpt below.

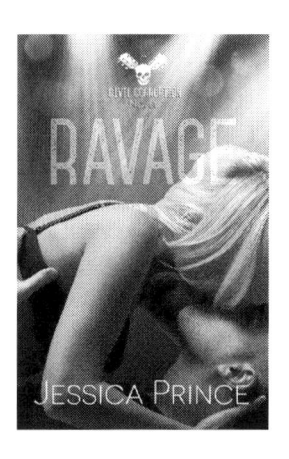

Enjoy an Excerpt from Ravage

Chapter 1

Lyla
Thirteen years old

I could still remember the very first time I laid eyes on Mason "Mace" Keller. The way my heart threatened to beat out of my chest, the goose bumps that broke out across my skin, the blood rushing to my cheeks and setting them on fire. That day, that moment, had been burned into my brain and would remain there for the rest of my life.

I'd been ten years old at the time, and everything in my little world changed the moment he stepped into it. At that age, my sense of romance was inflated thanks to the standards set by every princess movie ever made.

I firmly believed that a handsome prince would appear one day and I'd fall madly in love. I went as far as to act out elaborate wedding ceremonies with my Barbie and Ken—when I still played with dolls, of course. I wore the cheap metal ring I got out of the machine at the grocery store on my left hand like a badge of honor, even after it turned my skin green and the plastic diamond fell out of the setting. I was totally going to be Drew Barrymore in *Ever After*, just without the evil stepmother and all that jazz.

The second I laid eyes on Mace, I knew he was it for me. My one and only. My true love. My heart swelled, and I knew without a shadow of a doubt that I'd never feel for any other boy the way I felt for him.

Unfortunately, while I was quickly falling head over heels for the first time in my young life, the boy holding my heart in his hands looked at me as nothing more than his best friend's annoying little sister who had a habit of embarrassing herself on a regular basis.

For three years, I harbored those feelings, my unrequited love slowly crushing me with every girl he brought around. And there were *many*.

My brother had been part of a garage band with three friends he'd grown up with, Garrett, Declan, and Killian. When Mace moved to our town at fifteen, it hadn't taken long for his talent on the guitar to outshine my brother's mediocre musical skills. Will had been happy to step back, more interested in building cars than making music. They shuffled, and Mace found his place as lead guitarist for their band, Civil Corruption. I used to sit and watch them for hours, entranced by the way his fingers plucked at the strings of his prized Gibson with incredible speed, creating the most enchanting melodies. He cherished that guitar, given to him by his grandfather, like it was the most valuable thing he'd ever have the privilege of owning.

Word eventually got out, the guys' talent became well known, and the girls practically threw themselves at them. Of course my brother's friends were all too happy to take advantage, bringing random chicks over to show off in our garage.

The only one I'd bothered getting to know during those years was Declan's best-friend-turned-girlfriend, Tatum Valentine. She was kind and funny. It was obvious she was in love with Declan, and he was just as crazy about her. Despite the five-year age gap between us, she never made me feel like a pathetic little girl trailing behind them. True, I was only thirteen, and they were all set to graduate high school soon, but she'd quickly become a close friend, taking me under her wing and giving me a feeling of belonging in their little circle.

Will might have been the typical big brother at times, picking on me whenever he was in the mood and being a general pain in the butt, but he never made me feel unwanted. It was because of him and Tate that I became an official part of the Civil Corruption family. I grew to love each and every one of them in my own way, but it was always Mace who held the largest chunk of my heart. However, being a thirteen-year-old in love with a boy who was quickly becoming a man meant I'd already been dealt a fair share of heartache.

Still, I was a glutton for punishment. I couldn't get enough, and that day as I sat on the crate that had become known as "my seat" over the past three years, I listened to them talk about their plans for after graduation, and a little piece of me died inside.

Tate sat on the taped-up box beside me that held all our Christmas decorations and bumped my shoulder with hers. "Hey," she said, speaking loud enough to be heard over the song the guys were playing. "You've been quiet today. What's the matter?"

"Nothing," I replied with a shrug, my lie made obvious by the pouty look on my face.

"Ah, ah," she chided, giving me another bump. "You've been sitting here moping for the past hour, so don't bother lying. Tell me the truth."

I turned and looked up at her, feeling inferior as I took

her in. I adored Tate, but I couldn't help but feel self-conscious whenever she was around. With the swell of her hips and her round behind, the way her glossy, fiery hair draped over her full breasts, she was everything I wasn't. She was built like a woman while I was still in that awkward, boney phase between child and teenager.

"I can't wait until I look like you," I whined. "I can't wait to get boobs so I don't look like an ugly little boy anymore."

She let out a tinkling giggle that reminded me of wind chimes. "Is that what's got you all sour-faced today? Ly, babe, you're beautiful just how you are. You're thirteen. Give yourself some time. Don't be in such a rush to grow up."

That was easy for her to say. She was the same age as the rest of the guys, which meant that when they left in a few months, she'd be going with them. "Yeah, well you aren't the one being left behind," I grumbled, my melancholy growing worse and worse.

"Oh, I get it now," she murmured knowingly.

"You're all gonna graduate and take off, and I'll be left here alone."

Crap. I was going to cry. The last thing I wanted to do was cry in front of Tate and the guys. If Will or any of the others suspected how I felt about Mace, I'd most likely die of mortification. I might've been young, but I wasn't stupid. I knew I didn't stand a chance with him until I was older, so until then, I had to keep it a secret.

"We won't be gone forever, Ly," Tate stated sympathetically. "It's only for six months. It'll be over before you know it. And who knows, maybe by then you'll have met a boy you really like and won't even notice we're gone."

Not likely. There was no other boy but Mace. Not for me. And those six months they planned to be gone, touring up and down California, were probably going to be the most miserable months of my life. Tate would be gone. The guys would be gone. And Will would be working. Everyone was growing up and moving on. Everyone but me, that was.

"If you say so," I muttered sullenly.

"I do," she replied, trying her best to sound cheerful. "Because I'm right."

It was then that Declan called for a break, pulling Tate and me from our conversation. She might have been convinced that everything she'd just said was true, but it hadn't done anything to make me feel better.

Four months later

The music and laughter filtered up from the backyard through my bedroom window, driving the knife deeper into my chest. My brother had asked me to come down and join the party. Even Tate and Garrett had knocked on my door asking why I was locked in my room instead of downstairs with everyone else. I gave them all them all the same excuse —I had a headache and just wanted to sleep it off.

The truth was I couldn't bring myself to join the celebration. To me, there was nothing to celebrate. They were leaving. My parents had grown into a second family to all

Enjoy an Excerpt from Ravage

the guys in the band, so my mom planned a big going away party for them and all their friends to, in her words, "send them off the fame the right way". But I couldn't do it. I hated having to say goodbye to all of them, but especially to Mace.

Instead, I laid in my bed, writing in my diary and doodling random, nonsensical patterns while wishing everything could be different. I didn't hope the guys would fail on their trip. Honestly, I wanted them to succeed. I knew how hard they worked and how talented they were. I wanted them to end up rich and famous, to get everything they wanted. I just wished I was old enough to go with them.

A knock on my bedroom door startled me out of my melancholy. Lifting my head, I turned to find Mace standing in my open doorway, and my heart immediately lodged in my throat. "Uh, hi. What are you doing up here?"

"Came looking for you, Goldie."

He'd taken to calling me that about two months ago, and the nickname never failed to create a riot of flutters in my belly.

"Oh, um…." My whole body began to tremble with nervous energy as he moved into my room and took a seat on the edge of my bed. Suddenly remembering what I'd been doing before he interrupted, I slapped my journal shut and shoved it beneath my pillow.

"How come you aren't at the party, darlin'? We boring you?"

Was he joking? "No!" I cried, sitting up and folding my legs under me. "No, I just… I didn't… you aren't—"

"Relax, Ly," he said with a chuckle, bringing his hand

down to rest on my knee. The touch made my skin crackle and burn, and I couldn't drag my eyes away from those long, callused fingers until he finally pulled them away. "I was just teasin' you."

"Oh." I somehow managed a weak laugh that sounded more awkward than anything. "Well, um… you're kinda missing your party." I pointed out the window where the crowd sounded like it was beginning to swell.

"Yeah, but I wanted a chance to talk to you." In the past months, Mace had started acting like another brother to me. All the guys did, really, but it was more with him. Every time they practiced in our garage, he made an effort to take time out to visit with me. We shared our own private jokes, and he was the only one who'd given me a nickname, but there wasn't anything romantic lingering beneath the surface. It felt more like a familial bond than anything, which only made the ache in my chest hurt that much more. "I got you something, Goldie."

"A present?" I chirped excitedly, sitting up straighter.

"Always so damn greedy," he chuckled. And he was right. It wasn't the first time he'd given me a present. He had a tendency to show up to hang with Will with a gift in hand for me. Sometimes it was something as small as a candy bar he got in the vending machine at the high school and kept in his backpack for me, and sometimes it was more, like the time he brought me a little pewter picture frame with flowers etched into the design. But no matter what it was, I got excited, and I loved it more than all my Christmas and birthday presents combined. I'd never let him know, but I still had every candy bar and bag of chips he'd given me stashed in my nightstand drawer, all of them unopened.

"What is it?" I asked, my voice going high-pitched as I bounced in place. "Gimme, gimme!"

Mace's laugh grew more prominent as he reached around his back and pulled something from the waistband of his jeans. "It's nothin' big or anything," he explained, handing over a crinkled plastic shopping bag. "I just saw it at the mall the other day and thought of you."

I snatched it out of his hands and ripped the bag open. All the air whooshed from my lungs the second I reached in and pulled out the thick, gorgeous journal. The leather binding was stamped with a beautiful fleur-de-lis pattern, and a leather cord wrapped around the middle keeping it closed.

"Mace…," I breathed, looking up at him with wide eyes.

"It's not a big deal. I just noticed you're always scribblin' in a journal, so I thought you might like this one. It's pretty big, so you shouldn't have to replace it for a while."

I'd been keeping a diary since I learned to write. I'd gone through countless little spiral-bound notebooks, most of which my mom would buy in packs from the drugstore. But I'd never had one this nice. I had to bite my lip to keep the tears at bay. It was the most thoughtful gift I'd ever received, and it made me fall in love with him even more.

"This is…." I couldn't find the right words to express how much his gift meant to me. "I love it," I whispered, hugging the journal to my chest as my eyes grew misty. "This is just…." I swallowed down the lump in my throat.

"It's just… I can't even…." I let loose a sniffle just as a lone tear broke loose and slid down my cheek.

His face stretched into a gorgeous smile. "So I take it you like the present?"

"I l-love it," I answered brokenly, the floodgates on my emotions bursting open. I couldn't hold it back any longer, and the words started pouring out with barely a breath in between while tears trailed down my cheeks. "I love it so much. And it sucks that you guys are leaving. I'm so happy for you, and I want you to be super successful, but I hate that you're leaving. I'm gonna miss you. I wish I could go, and I'm just… I'll miss you guys. I'm excited for you, but I'm sad. I don't want to be sad, but I am. That's why I wasn't down at the party."

Mace pulled his bottom lip between his teeth and bit down, drawing my attention in that direction as he examined my face. "Ah, Goldie. Come here, darlin'." He pulled me into a hug—our very first hug—and the subtle smell of his cologne wrapped around me, settling like a warm, comfortable blanket. I never wanted him to let me go.

"I'll miss you too. We all will. But it's not like you'll never see us again. This is our home. Always will be. You're a part of our family, sweetheart. And that's never gonna change."

I managed to get my tears under control, pulling in a heavy sigh as I turned to press my cheek against his chest. As I held tight to the hug all I could do was hope with all my heart that he was right.

CLICK HERE TO KEEP READING

About Jessica

Born and raised around Houston, Jessica is a self proclaimed caffeine addict, connoisseur of inexpensive wine, and the worst driver in the state of Texas. In addition to being all of these things, she's first and foremost a wife and mom.

Growing up, she shared her mom and grandmother's love of reading. But where they leaned toward murder mysteries, Jessica was obsessed with all things romance.

When she's not nose deep in her next manuscript, you can usually find her with her kindle in hand.

Connect with Jessica now
Website: www.authorjessicaprince.com
Jessica's Princesses Reader Group

Newsletter
Instagram
Facebook
Twitter
authorjessicaprince@gmail.com

Printed in Great Britain
by Amazon